NO COMFORT
FOR THE
UNDERTAKER

NO COMFORT FOR THE UNDERTAKER

A Carrie Lisbon Mystery

Chris Keefer

First published by Level Best Books/Historia 2022

Copyright © 2022 by Chris Keefer

All rights reserved. No part of this publication may be reproduced, stored or transmitted in any form or by any means, electronic, mechanical, photocopying, recording, scanning, or otherwise without written permission from the publisher. It is illegal to copy this book, post it to a website, or distribute it by any other means without permission.

This novel is entirely a work of fiction. The names, characters and incidents portrayed in it are the work of the author's imagination. Any resemblance to actual persons, living or dead, events or localities is entirely coincidental.

Chris Keefer asserts the moral right to be identified as the author of this work.

Author Photo Credit: Creative Imaging Photography

First edition

ISBN: 978-1-68512-188-4

Cover art by Level Best Designs

This book was professionally typeset on Reedsy. Find out more at reedsy.com

For my boys.

Praise for No Comfort for the Undertaker

"Fast-paced but rich in historical detail and featuring a bold woman establishing herself in the male-dominated field of mortuary practices, *No Comfort for the Undertaker* is a wonderful mystery debut."—Edgar Award-winning mystery writer Gary Earl Ross, author of the *Nickel City* Mysteries with PI Gideon Rimes

"If victims of crimes could choose, they would ask to be laid out by Chris Keefer's beguiling central character, Carrie Lisbon, a spunky undertaker preparing corpses in 1900. Readers will race through the novel, admiring Carrie and her creator every step of the way."—Marlie Wasserman, author of *The Murderess Must Die*

Chapter One

"I need the undertaker," blurted the man in withered shoes as soon as Carrie Lisbon opened the front door. Beyond him, at the edge of the lawn, a splintered two-wheeled cart stood on the dusty road, behind a sway-backed nag who drooped under her reins.

Just a moment ago, when their bell jangled pleasantly on its wire, Carrie and her uncle Sav Machin looked up from their morning paper in surprise. Accustomed to early doorbells when she and her husband's mortuary services were requested back in Nanuet, Carrie had yet to learn why social etiquette would be breached in her new hometown.

"We don't usually get callers this early," Sav said. He craned his neck and leaned sideways, his elongated torso, knobby Adam's apple, and bushy hair cleared the kitchen door jamb and gave him an unobstructed view up the hallway. Like a human metronome, he swung back, settled his coffee cup on the table, and followed Carrie up the hall. She was still in her nightdress and robe.

Most of her belongings, including her trunks of clothes, were still outside. After a four-hour journey by train from Nanuet, an insufferable two hours on the bench seat of a two-horse hitch, over ridiculously rutted roads, and a harrowing, prayer-filled scramble over Hope Bridge's namesake covered bridge, she had arrived at her uncle's place last night in the dark. Exhausted and needing the outhouse in a severe way, Carrie persuaded her late husband's only living relative to leave her assemblage of travel trunks, baskets, and crates out in the yard until they could tackle the unpacking in the morning—this morning—when they were fresh.

The bewhiskered man in threadbare clothes stood in the open doorway, looking upward to meet Sav's eye. He greeted them by pinching the brim of his frayed hat.

"I saw your sign," the man said. He gestured to the placard Carrie had hauled from Nanuet, a memento she couldn't part with. Her last-minute sentimentality had *Lisbon & Shay, Undertakers* removed and packed with her scant possessions, rather than pitched into a burn pile. The carefully scripted gold letters leaned against her stacks of belongings in the front yard.

"I need to have this done, sir. Today, if possible. I—we can't let her go no longer."

"Well, I'm so sorry for your loss," Sav replied, confused. "But I'm not the undertaker. That was, uh …well, my niece and nephew. The sign is all that's left—"

"Uncle Sav," Carrie said, reacting instinctively. Clearly grieving, the stranger's drooping shoulders and exhausted face told a story she had seen countless times. "What does the young man need?"

"Please, ma'am." The unkempt caller pressed his request on to Carrie. "I need an undertaker. I saw the sign."

He gestured again to the upended advertisement that had given Carrie such pride nine years ago, when she had married Phee Lisbon, and her father had made him a full partner.

"My little girl… Suzetta. She…well, she drowned three days past. We was coming south, on the Cherry Valley Road, and we stopped to rest a spell. We thought she was nearby!" The man looked around wildly, as if reliving the desperate search. "She wasn't, you know, right. Since she was born. She had that foreign look to her and she, she didn't talk too good. We lost her—" The man stifled a sob. "She went into the water, into some creek!"

Carrie and Sav glanced at each other while the man wrestled himself under control. His mouth turned down in anger.

"I been to two undertakers! They wouldn't do nothin'! I ain't got no money to pay, and nobody wants my wagon, nor my horse. I ain't gonna bury my little girl in the woods, like a dog! I saw your sign. I thought—I can work off the cost. I can work it off!"

CHAPTER ONE

Carrie stepped around her uncle. *Nightclothes be damned. I'm decent enough.* She put a hand on the man's trembling arm. The gesture uncapped his grief. She tiptoed onto the porch in her bare feet and weaved him through the stacks of baggage to a wooden chair. He collapsed into it and slid his palms over his face.

"Rest here, Mr...?"

"Scuttle. Wyatt Scuttle."

"Mr. Scuttle. I can take care of your little girl." Carrie said, using a quiet voice, practiced and smooth, holding reassurance and comfort. She hadn't come all this way to re-enter the funeral business, but when presented with a family's grief, and from a loss of the worst kind, her natural impulse to assist simply took over. "I'm Carrie Lisbon. My father, my husband, and I were undertakers. I've just arrived from Nanuet, but I've laid out loved ones my whole life. I'll take care of your daughter. Please, show me where she is."

While Sav's eyebrows rose and his fingers crept up to tug at his wavy hair, Scuttle deflated in relief. He rose from the chair and shook Carrie's hand in a wooden clamp of gratitude. Carrie followed him to the ramshackle cart. A woman sat in the bed, facing the rear, sobbing openly, her toothless mouth quivering. She embraced a child on each side; their frightened faces were slick with tears. The children drew their legs up, so as not to touch the small lump hidden under a thin, patched blanket. Several large flies landed and busied themselves on the cloth. The warm May temperatures would not be helpful to the situation.

Carrie turned to Scuttle. "I'll take care of Suzetta," she repeated. "Please, pull your wagon into the shade and give me a few minutes to prepare. I'll be with you shortly."

She hurried back to the porch, her mind clicking through the list of things to do. Washing and dressing the little body. Ordering a casket. Which church will offer a lot in their potter's field? Where are my tinged face creams? *Wait. I haven't even had breakfast. I've just attended a dead body in my nightdress, and I don't even know if this town has an undertaker.*

Still, she didn't hesitate. This family needed to bury a child today, a non-negotiable fact, given Suzetta's state of mortification. That the Scuttles

3

landed at her doorstep as a result of her sloppy arrival was fortunate for them. They clearly occupied the itinerant class; their scant financial means revealed in their threadbare clothing and their pathetic horse and cart. But their poverty didn't mean their loss and grief were trivial. Scuttle and his wife were clearly overcome. The idea of turning them away not only hadn't occurred to her, it was too late now.

Sav, still bewildered and clutching his rampant hair, now stood with Thomas Bale. Her uncle had frequently included news of his friend and boarder in his letters, and Carrie pictured Thomas as a reliable anchor to her uncle's effervescence. When she arrived in the dark last night, she and Bale greeted each other like old friends, while Sav fluttered around like an anxious wren. Carrie turned to Bale instinctively now for support.

He gave her a frank look of concern, but no more. The calm assessment in his dark eyes contrasted with Sav's botheration. As did their physical disparity: where Sav Machin was tall and bone-thin, with the pale complexion of a perpetual scholar, Thomas Bale's heritage was African, with powerful muscles rounding out his stout frame. Where Sav's curvy lips and horse teeth dominated his wide-eyed face under a veritable prow of a nose, Bale's features were evenly appealing. Carrie stepped onto the porch to consult with her uncle and his best friend.

"That poor family. How did they find us? Isn't there an undertaker in town? It's 1900; every town should have an undertaker."

"That's not always the case," Sav said. "Lots of families still take care of their own funerals around here."

Bale waved a hand to the right. "They must have come in on the Shun Pike. North Street intersects it about a mile up the road. They haven't gotten to Worley's yet. He's our undertaker."

"Should we be involved, niece?" Sav asked. "I can get Worley. Otherwise, we need to notify the church, get a coffin, get Digger up and get him started. Thomas, do you know where we can find him at this hour?" His spindly fingers, now free of their unruly tangle, splayed and waved.

Her uncle had the nerves of a spooked cat. Naturally, Carrie thought. She had managed the sudden arrival of a family in need of funerary services a

CHAPTER ONE

thousand times, but Savoir Machin, scholar, ombudsman, and civic arbiter, had not. Carrie had never seen his slim fingers unstained by ink or graphite, his nose never unburied in a book or newspaper. Back in Nanuet, with the population of a small city, *Lisbon & Shay, Undertakers* had never had a slack season. With the need for funeral planning, preparing the dead, maintaining records and supplies, and the increasingly favorable practice of embalming, Carrie's life work had never ceased. Despite the fact that she was a new widow, still struggling with her own grief, that she arrived not eight hours before, and yes, that she was still in her night dress, this was her milieu.

"Uncle Sav," she said firmly, "the main thing is for me to get dressed right now. I'm still licensed. New York law still permits the deceased to be laid out by anyone. Let's not pass these people on again. They're at their limit. They need food, a place to sleep. A place to wash up."

"I can take care of that, Miss Carrie," Bale said. His dark eyes and confident smile were steady. The early sun cast a glow on the brown arcs of his cheeks. "I can fetch the family some breakfast, and some wash buckets. I'll have them set up in the orchard; it's just out back. There's some privacy, and it's pretty there now, with the apples in bloom. I'll take care of them."

"Thank you, Thomas." Not surprised by his thoughtfulness, having been apprised of his character, so casually and frequently in her uncle's letters, Carrie welcomed his assistance. "I'll be out in a few minutes. I need to see what I can do in the house. Uncle Sav, can you come with me?"

Carrie turned her uncle's hand to making more coffee and preparing a basket of food for the Scuttles, then hurried to her room. She flung open her trunk and tossed clothing every which way. She had intended to unpack and organize today. How plans change.

This was home now. A quiet village with a single main street, populated by grumpy teamsters, and errant people showing up with dead children in the back of their wagon. Her late husband had quipped once, "Uncle Sav lives in a little town called Hope Bridge, but I've heard him say the town motto is 'Hope the Bridge Holds!'"

Yesterday, the old driver didn't bat an eye as his listless team approached the town's namesake, a single-span, covered bridge that sagged like last year's

Christmas bunting. Carrie shot alarmed glances back and forth between the old bridge and the old man.

"Wait! We're not going over *that?* Will that thing hold?"

The driver clucked his protruding, whiskered lips and snapped the reins over the greasy humps of his horses, encouraging them to move quickly across the rickety structure.

"Hope so. Just 'til we get acrost," he concluded fatalistically. "Then, don't matter."

The horses clopped into the darkened maw; bats burst from gaps in the shingles. The wagon lurched into the frightening cave, causing the timbers to pop and creak. Holding her breath and clutching the wooden seat, Carrie thought angrily that she hadn't just sold her house and livelihood, and wrenched herself from her husband's grave, just to die in a collapse of wood, wagon, and stones only a half mile from her destination.

She had been both eager and devastated to move. It meant leaving behind the earthly remains of Ephesians Michael Lisbon, her husband of only nine short years, in a crowded church cemetery, and the familiar neighborhood she grew up in. It meant paring down a life of purpose and security to a set of trunks, and small mementos. It meant being adrift until she landed on some shore of stability. But leaving Nanuet gave her grieving soul a chance at respite.

The wagon had lurched over the final planks, and Carrie let out a breath of profound relief. By the time the wagon reached Uncle Sav's home, a narrow, two-story clapboard that mimicked his stature, the darkness was complete, and Carrie's backside and bladder were suffering considerably. She paid the mute driver his fee and a generous tip that she hoped would inspire him to curry his horses.

Her uncle had ushered her into the two-room "suite," and she closed the door and found the commode. The physical relief had been as exquisite as her safe deliverance from the dubious bridge. Thomas Bale carried in her small wardrobe trunk, which she exhaustedly gutted last night, searching for her night clothes. The rest of her things remained outside on the lawn, including her now problematic business shingle, *Lisbon & Shay, Undertakers.*

CHAPTER ONE

Carrie frowned at her room, now a shamble of yesterday's discards, an unmade bed, a brimming chamber pot, and a disemboweled travel trunk. *A matter for later,* she mused as she high-stepped into clean underwear and yanked up her stockings. She strapped her corset over her camisole and tugged it around her breasts. She had work to do. Her blue cotton blouse, as wrinkled as the old wagon driver's face, and her light gray work skirt would do. She pecked at her hair, caught the brown length in a ribbon, and wound it into a knot at the back of her neck. She had to stoop to see herself in the mirror.

She *was* going to work, she thought grimly. A family had to bury a child today. Carrie reached into the trunk for her cotton apron, a familiar length of cloth that had seen the laying out of hundreds of dead.

Another sentimental item, she thought, as she passed the strap over her head. She fingered the dark blue *L&S* emblem she had painfully sewn into each apron. Needlework confounded her. She recalled how Phee had sucked the pinprick of blood from her finger when she cursed after poking herself for the third or fourth time. That intimacy had lit a fire that left the apron, and all their other clothing, forgotten on the floor.

Lisbon & Shay had been sold last month to Messrs. Lennox and Martin. Its sale marked the finality of a life that was abruptly wrenched away last August. The house sold yesterday, and her journey north to Hope Bridge in rural Duncan County began.

She tied a bow behind her back. The apron may represent the past, but she was grateful now she had it. Dressed, and on familiar ground, Carrie returned to the kitchen.

"Uncle Sav? Where can we get a casket? And which church has a potter's field? I'll go speak to the minister myself, but I'll need you to come along and make my introduction."

"I think Bookhoudt's has, uh, a regular-sized casket in the store. Not one for a child; I'm not sure. We can ask Worley about it. Carrie, are you certain—?"

"I can make a casket for the little girl." Bale's deep voice preceded him through the screen door. He reached for the basket Sav had filled. "That's my trade, Miss Carrie. Carpentry. I have the right pine in the barn."

Carrie hesitated. An undertaker thought first of the quality of presentation. The casket, the flowers, the dressing of the deceased, and the setting of the features all required an absolute professional touch. Unable to divest herself from her life's work just yet, she asked, "What will it look like?"

Bale accepted her doubt with a nod, and replied with assurance. "It won't look slap-dash. If you have some soft material, I can tack that inside, stuffed with hay. If you have some yarrow, I can use that for the stuffing too."

Carrie arched a brow. "Have you made caskets before?"

Bale held her gaze. "Many times, Miss Carrie." He added coffee cups to the Scuttle's basket. "I got an idea of what size to make, when I delivered their wash buckets. I'll bring this to them. Then I'll get started."

"I'll find you that cloth," Carrie murmured at his retreating back, then turned to Sav. "Uncle, how good a carpenter is Thomas?"

A question concerning the citizenry of his hometown stabilized Sav's nervous fretting. "He can build anything. He's been overseeing the repairs on the bridge for years now. He used to have a shop of his own." Sav's voice trailed off.

"And?" Carrie prompted him.

"Well, it burned. Or rather, it was burned."

"Ah, I remember that now," Carrie said. She had lived in a blur of grief for the last eight months. Sometimes, memories of things other than pain and anger came back, blooming like mushrooms after a summer rain.

"Arson," Sav grimaced. "Vigilantes; last year. They burned the homes of some Negroes in the area, including Tom's house and his shop." Sav shrugged. "He lives above the carriage barn. That's his shop now. He's welcome to it. It's been a long time since the place has seen a horse or a carriage."

Carrie got back to the matter at hand. "I'm going to bring the little girl's body into the cellar. I can work on her there."

Sav's eyebrows shot up. *"Work on her?"*

Carrie put a hand over his. "The deceased has to be dressed, washed, laid out," she said evenly. "I prefer to do that where it's cool. Is there a table down there? Can you set up two lamps for me?" Carrie didn't give him time to

CHAPTER ONE

question. Best to get things moving so the momentum of the impromptu funeral could not be stopped. "Thank you, Uncle," she said, and set off for the orchard.

Wyatt Scuttle and his wife sat on the end of the cart; their two little boys sat on the ground at the base of an apple tree. Ragged trousers ended halfway down their tender shanks. Their bare feet were pulled up close again. They stopped cramming the jellied biscuits in their mouths when they saw Carrie coming, but they held onto them tightly. Scuttle stood up. His wife began a desperate protest.

"Ya can't take her! Ya can't! Wyatt! Ya hear me? Don't you let her go!"

Carrie stopped a few feet away, dropped her chin, composed herself with a deep breath, and approached. The woman turned and flung herself onto Suzetta's body, pulling the dead girl under her bosom. "Ya can't have her! *Wyatt!*"

"Mr. Scuttle," Carrie said quietly.

Scuttle went to his stricken wife. "Alma. Alma, hush now. We gotta let her go now. It's been three days, Alma. Jesus, we gotta let her go." Mrs. Scuttle moaned as her husband tugged her from the shabby cart. The tattered blanket slipped off the child's body. The cloud of bluebottle flies buzzed up and around the exposed corpse with excited vigor. Scuttle looked over at Carrie, who stepped to the wagon, prepared to take the child's body. Suddenly, Bale was at her side. "I'm here, Miss Carrie. Let me take her."

Carrie helped Bale tuck the pathetic blanket around the child. An odor of decay wafted up. Carrie pressed her lips together. *The poor woman hadn't noticed?* Bale kept his eyes lowered on his task. If he was at all nauseated by the smell, he didn't let on. Gently, Carrie raised the child's flaccid head and torso until Bale could slip his arms under and lift her. Carrie knew that a dead body acted like rope after the rigor mortis dissolved: boneless and tricky to hold. But Bale hugged the body to his chest, and his grip held. *He must have handled dead people many times as well,* Carrie observed. They walked away under apple blossoms while Mrs. Scuttle wailed.

Chapter Two

Sav had lit two lamps in the cellar. The stone walls and dirt floor kept the temperature ten or twelve degrees cooler than outside. A crude table, long unused, presided among murky shelves and an old, vinegary-smelling barrel. Carrie directed Bale to place the body on the table. She carefully set the lamps at the head and foot of the child. Bale gently pulled the blanket away.

Suzetta's hair was blonde and braided. She wore an old dress with no undergarments, and her feet were bare. Her lips were so pale, they were indiscernible from the rest of her skin. She had the small ears, thick fingers, and slanted eyes of the feeble-minded. Carrie remembered an article she had read in *The Century Magazine*, written by a British doctor describing Suzetta's condition as the "mongoloid syndrome." The faint smell of decay rose to an undeniable height.

Bale twitched his finger under his nose and held it there.

"I know. It's bad," Carrie acknowledged.

She turned back to the child's body. "Look at how they braided her hair. They cared for her. They loved her. Mr. Scuttle said they couldn't find an undertaker to lay her out. Or bury her. That's an awful predicament."

"Scuttle said they were coming south. He saw an ad for a laborer in the paper," Bale responded. "If they came through Frenchtown and Oakes Grove, there is no undertaker. Or a preacher. I know both towns have churches and a graveyard, but they use a circuit rider for their Sunday services."

"Still?" Carrie asked. The practice seemed so archaic. Another thing she'd have to get used to in this provincial place.

CHAPTER TWO

Bale shrugged. "Or maybe they didn't want the burden. It's hard times up there, Miss Carrie. Folks probably thought the family would be better off down here in Hope Bridge. Tell you the truth, I wouldn't buy his horse either." Carrie agreed with Bale's practicality.

Still holding his finger under his nose, Bale said. "I expect you're used to this? Let me get up to some fresh air, and I'll get that little casket made." Carrie watched him trot up the cellar steps and turned her attention to Suzetta.

The child was in active decay; Carrie would need to be careful about laying her out. The main problem was the stench. The cool cellar would slow the process, thereby easing the smell. No need to wash the body. Carrie shuddered with dark humor, remembering that the child had, after all, drowned. She'd add color to the lips and cheeks, pose her to look peacefully asleep, but the dress and braids stay. She would be laid out as her parents knew her.

For the next hour, Carrie ran up and down the stairs, rummaging in her room for face cream and powder, and Sav's pantry for soaps, wax, and a basin. While she worked, she heard the faint sounds of sawing and hammering from the carriage barn.

She left the child, prepared and cool, and looked back at the little mortuary scene from the top of the steps. A single lantern, its wick turned low, kept a vigilant glow for comfort, while not compromising the cellar's chill. She took her time washing up, and used a flannel cloth soaked in lemon oil from her embalming kit to eliminate any scent of death from her hands. She burrowed again into her gaping trunk for a clean blouse and tucked it into the waist of her gray workaday skirt. Her rooms included a back door, and she stepped outside onto the tiny porch and shook the travel dust from her plum jacket.

She assessed herself in the hall mirror. She got her height from her father and her dark looks from her mother. The cynicism came from years of rejection by her female peers, and from men who doubted her ability to be among them in their profession. The frown lines around her eyes came most recently from grief and worry. She grimly pinned on her mourning cap, satisfied with the way she had modified the dainty chapeau. The black lace now billowed artfully above the brim, instead of draping drearily across her face. *My grief for you is real, Phee. I will not make a maudlin show of it.*

She'd have to find her straw boater in her belongings, soon. With a resolute nod to her attire and her new station, she called up to her uncle that she was ready to accomplish their next task.

* * *

"The closest potter's field is the Methodist Church," Sav said, hustling down the stairs, his scarecrow arms and legs swinging. He grabbed his homburg, popped it over his frizzy hair, and offered his elbow. "If we are turned down, we can try the Presbyterians. They have a grand place on Liberty Street. In either case, we may have to provide a contribution of sorts. Some compensation would be proper."

They weaved past her crates and headed for the Methodist Church on Main. Carrie judged Sav's prattling as a spend-off of nerves. Her grip tightened on his arm; assurances about the deceased down cellar would come later.

"Why would we be turned down?" she asked. "All churches provide a consecrated patch of land to inter the poor."

"Yes, of course, but there can be a *lack* of space, or a *circumstance* that impedes the, er, *digging* of the grave. We only have one grave digger and we sometimes have trouble finding him."

"Do both churches employ the same man?" Back in Nanuet, each of the nine churches had their own sexton and a team of gravediggers. "Surely, there are other able-bodied men who can perform such a task?"

"Well, Digger is the preferred man. He's dug nearly every grave in Hope Bridge since I can recall."

"Where is he, that you can't find him?"

"Well," Sav hedged, "he can be under the weather at times."

Carrie guessed that, although she and Sav were related by marriage, and were each other's only remaining relatives, they didn't know each other's

CHAPTER TWO

precise sensibilities. Sav was being delicate.

"He's a drunk?" she asked bluntly.

Sav hesitated in mid-stride. Carrie smirked, watching her uncle decide by the end of his next step that his niece's sensibilities were not just indelicate, they were rather stout. "Well, in a manner of speaking, he has been known to imbibe more than an acceptable amount. He has a difficult job, of course, and no one begrudges him his solace."

Carrie scoffed. "I just replaced the eyeballs of a four-year-old child, Uncle, with wax from your kitchen pantry. I don't require solace. The man you speak of has to dig holes in the ground. Neat holes. Within a short period of time. If he's too drunk to dig a proper grave, why doesn't the church get someone who can?"

Sav laughed nervously. "We shall appeal to the Reverend Borden. We'll find Digger before long."

"Perhaps Mr. Scuttle might do the job. Often, hard work eases grief." Carrie knew the itinerant man could perform a more than passable task for his daughter. Perhaps, he could find work in Hope Bridge as another "Digger."

"We can ask."

"Thank you, Uncle. I look forward to making the Reverend's acquaintance. Is that the church?"

The white clapboard façade of the Methodist Church was crowned with a bell that hung in a vault open on four sides, and atop that, a sharp copper spire that gleamed with a rich patina. Narrow windows were modestly stained with panels of colored glass, unlike the ornate scenes of Nanuet churches. A series of uniform stone slabs led to the annex in the back, where Sav rapped on the door. He bounced on the balls of his feet as they waited. Carrie spotted a shade of her late husband in Sav's pleasant face. He was Phee's father's cousin, and that side of the family carried an exuberant trait.

"Mrs. Peters is usually about when the Reverend is in," he prattled. "She attends to the accounts and records. She lives on East Meadow Street and keeps a lovely garden. She and her sister are spinsters. They're devoted to each other."

"Perhaps, she can spare some blooms for Suzetta's wake?"

"Oh! I wouldn't ask—"

The annex door opened a few inches, and a gray-haired woman barred the space with her body. When she laid eyes on Sav, her glare eased. Then, she darted a look at Carrie, with her hand still fondly tucked into Sav's elbow, and the suspicious look resumed.

"Mr. Machin. What a lovely surprise." Mrs. Peters opened the door and stepped aside. When Sav introduced Carrie, Mrs. Peters looked as though she'd sniffed a glass of bad milk. She offered Carrie her fingertips.

"Yes, the Reverend is in," Mrs. Peters responded warmly to Sav's inquiry. "Is there a message I can take to him as an introduction?"

Carrie followed behind Sav, who had deftly taken up Mrs. Peters' elbow and led her through the annex to the sanctuary. The woman's backbone softened visibly while Sav murmured his need to discuss a 'matter of mourning.' The older woman turned coyly, and swished through another doorway, promising to get the Reverend 'in a trice.' When she exited, Sav turned to Carrie with a devilish grin.

The Reverend Borden wore a full-length cassock and collar over pressed trousers and shined shoes. His hair was pomaded and, Carrie observed critically, too long. Not quite a man of middle age, his short stature, clean-shaven jowls, and thickening belly gave Carrie the impression of a chubby youth. His eloquent voice filled the hallway with practiced importance as he ushered them to a pair of overstuffed chairs in his office. Borden was solicitous to Carrie, but after hearing of her widowed status, eyed her dubiously for an instant, taking in the plum jacket, white cotton blouse, and gray skirt, distinctly un-mournful colors. The scrutiny was not lost on Carrie; Borden's was not the first disapproving glance she'd encountered, since she quit mourning attire after less than a year.

"I understand your request for a plot in our pauper's cemetery, then. Is that correct, Mr. Machin?"

"A small plot, yes. The child has been laid out, and my tenant, Mr. Bale, is preparing a casket today."

"Laid out by whom?"

CHAPTER TWO

"I dressed and prepared the child, Reverend," Carrie said.

The Reverend turned to her with an indulgent smile. "So thoughtful of you, Mrs. Lisbon. And so soon after your arrival. I hope you weren't too distressed to be tasked with such an endeavor?"

"Not at all, Reverend Borden. That's my field of expertise. The family was quite tormented by the child's death and their subsequent treatment, as they recalled, by less than Christian proprietors who, we were told, refused to manage the burial, simply due to the family's destitution." Carrie wasn't devout, but felt the addition of the religious reference would spur the Reverend's pity. Instead, the Reverend Borden stiffened.

Sav patted Carrie's hand, an odd patronizing gesture. He used a long leg to step on Carrie's foot out of the Reverend's sight.

"Of course, the child's parents could have been overwrought and unable to express their needs," Sav said, smoothing over her faux pas. "Sometimes, the less fortunate aren't able to articulate the necessary requests to those in positions of authority."

Reverend Borden had taken on a calculating look, but accepted Sav's explanation. "Of course. That is often the case. The indigent should be cared for in death, as they are our responsibility in life." His voice rose and fell as though he were sermonizing. "It is also our responsibility to provide for those who perform tasks which comfort those in grief. I believe it is customary for Mr. Louis to be compensated for the preparation of the ground. Is that a measure you'll be willing to provide, Mr. Machin? Or is that expected to fall on the church?"

Carrie wanted to blurt a comment about the cost of a bottle as compensation for Digger Louis, but in deference to her uncle, kept her remarks in check. She'd be gracious, regardless of the drunken gravedigger's predilections. She could donate to the church poor fund once Suzetta was interred; the sale of her home and *Lisbon & Shay* had provided her with substantial funds.

Sav continued the diplomatic line of inquiry. "I'll take responsibility for Mr. Louis's services, of course, Reverend. Is Mr. Louis available today?".

"Today? I'm afraid Mr. Louis is engaged otherwise."

"Oh? I hadn't heard of anyone else passing," said Sav. "Did I miss something?"

The Reverend met Sav's eyes alone. "Not at all. Mr. Louis has been indisposed of late."

Carrie asserted quietly. "Reverend, the child is three days dead. I cannot stress the importance of having her interred by sundown today. Her parents have been distraught by her death, and her condition is likely to cause them substantially more discomfort, if she is allowed to linger."

"Mrs. Lisbon, you are most kind to want to spare those unfortunate parents any more despair. But I need to stress the importance of practices here. Mr. Machin and I can discuss the next opportunity for the child's internment, if you'd care to wait with Mrs. Peters in the annex?" The Reverend offered Carrie a doting smile. "She prepares a wonderful bergamot tea."

Carrie smiled back. "I'm sorry to decline your offer of tea, Reverend, as well as your suggestion of 'the next opportunity.' Our position here is urgent. And I'm sure you understand the expedience of internment after such an extended period of time? May I propose an alternate grave digger? The child's father is a capable man, and willing to work. What better way to honor his child than to prepare the ground for her funeral?"

Borden's smile deepened, a more patronizing gesture than the one Sav just used to cover her gaff. "While I understand your concerns for the deceased and the family, our customs in Hope Bridge, as well as in our church, Mrs. Lisbon, are long standing. We will make every effort to locate Mr. Louis so that he can perform the duties in the pauper's cemetery as soon as possible. If the family is unable to wait, they can make other arrangements, I presume?"

Carrie hesitated deliberately before responding, knowing the Reverend would see in her pause that she recognized his threat. Poor folk had to take what hand-outs were offered. Or settle for even lesser accommodations. She recalled Wyatt Scuttle's anguish, rejecting a woodland burial for his daughter. She was dangerously close to losing the cemetery plot for poor Suzetta, but was unwilling to be bested by this pious Napoleon. She pulled out her last card.

CHAPTER TWO

"I do appreciate your sentiments, Reverend Borden, and your adherence to custom. You have been most generous with your offer of a plot for an innocent child. However, there is no legal statute that prohibits persons other than the *customary* individual from preparing a grave. I'd like you to consider Mr. Scuttle, the child's father, to simply begin the work while Mr. Louis is sought. I'm sure Mr. Louis, with his *infirmity*, will certainly appreciate the assistance. I believe Mr. Scuttle does not need to be compensated, while Mr. Louis, with a light duty, can be amply rewarded."

Borden considered Carrie for a moment; his expression guarded. Carrie drew a checkbook from her reticule, uncapped her late husband's stylographic pen, and leaned forward onto the Reverend's desk. She paused before writing, aware the appearance of immediate compensation would likely push the man over the finish line.

"What is customary for Mr. Louis?" she asked.

Chapter Three

Mrs. Peters proved as uncharitable as her employer.

"My garden flowers are reserved for the church, Mr. Machin." She addressed her response to Sav, even though it had been Carrie who posed the question. "Whitsunday is this Sunday. And there's the picnic after. I won't have enough to decorate the sanctuary if I provide for a pauper's funeral. I'll remind you that Mr. Worley is accustomed to having a reliable supply from myself and Florence. I would not want to jeopardize my account with Mr. Worley, I'm sure you realize."

"Yes, quite right, Mrs. Peters. Do forgive me, and please, give my best to Miss Florence." Sav tipped his hat to the spinster and steered a fuming Carrie away.

"What the *hell,* Uncle!" Carrie stomped out every word. Her use of this particularly satisfying profanity had become frequent and heartfelt since Phee died. She applied it liberally to situations ranging from a lost button to social disputes. Sav heard her cursing plenty of times; she wouldn't hold back the unabashed use of it now. "This is a *church!* I thought they'd be compassionate and understanding. That stingy woman wouldn't part with a few measly tulips for a child? And, I had to pay off that little bas—"

"Carrie," Sav appealed. "Mrs. Peters considers herself the guardian of the Methodist church. She and her sister have provided altar flowers and funeral arrangements for every wake held in Hope Bridge since time began. Those arrangements are her egg money. The Reverend Borden is half-brother to Arthur Worley, the undertaker. We don't know which undertakers rejected the Scuttles, but no sense in characterizing the Reverend's family as 'un-

CHAPTER THREE

Christian.' Digger Louis is the Reverend's wife's brother, and although he drinks himself stupid night after night, he's never going to be dismissed for it. We achieved our objective here. Please, let's get on with it as best we can. I'm sure the Scuttles will accept whatever is provided for them."

"Why don't they deserve flowers and a proper viewing? Because they can't pay for it?"

Sav stopped Carrie on the sidewalk and put his long-fingered hands on her shoulders. "Niece, I can see you are dedicated to this family's dignity, but you barely avoided slighting several prominent members of our town. The Scuttles are grateful for all you've done for them. The child can do without flowers. Digger will continue to dig. The Reverend and Mrs. Peters' affections will remain intact, and by nightfall, I won't have a dead child under my roof."

"And that's how things are done here?"

Sav sighed and took up Carrie's hand, tucking it into his elbow and walking slowly. "It's how things are done everywhere, niece. Please don't look for a fight. Let it be for now."

"I'm not looking for a fight, uncle. I just refuse to lose one." Carrie said, and considered Sav's advice in silence. He was right: there were bigger fish to fry today. She had to remember that he keenly felt the presence of a body in his cellar, there were distraught strangers in his orchard, and that her presence in his life had to be a strain until she learned the lay of the land, both geographically and socially. He had covered for her in the Reverend's office and took Stingy Peters' parsimony on the chin. Carrie patted her dear uncle's hand.

"You're right, uncle. Thank you for your diplomacy. I'll see to it that Suzetta and her family are accommodated as quickly as possible, with whatever we have to offer."

Bale produced a simple pine box, with sanded corners and a precisely tacked liner. It smelled overwhelmingly of cut pine, yarrow, and fresh hay. Making do with apple blossoms, the only abundant flower immediately at hand, Carrie had wired together several short branches that sprayed across the open width of the casket and draped down the sides. *Nothing in the*

19

manual of mourning arrangements about apple blossoms, she thought, but the gay sparkle of yellow stamens bursting from pink petals declared innocence and exuberance, a fitting tribute to the little girl.

The sun had slid into the western half of the sky when Carrie lugged her crates aside, searching for the box containing her Star View camera. The oak-legged tripod already splayed in the parlor; she just needed to find the camera among her dishes and books, her mother's rocking chair, and her desk. She fervently hoped the camera and the glass plates had not been damaged in the carriage ride.

Suzetta had been placed in her casket and carried up to the parlor. She lay cozied in her blanket, all but one hand, which Carrie had posed in a fist beneath the chin, mimicking a natural sleeping position. Face paint on the lips and cheeks blushed away the pall of death. The resulting picture was serene.

The Scuttles arrived when all was ready. The hesitant family looked washed, but not better dressed. Their poverty ran deep; the clothes on their backs represented all they had in the world. The two small boys clung to Mrs. Scuttle's dress, as if to a lifeline. Mr. Scuttle edged into the parlor first, then beckoned his wife forward.

"Alma, see her? She's at rest, she's peaceful. Ain't gotta worry about her, now. Don't be scairt." He took his wife gently by the elbow and led her into the room; the children towed behind. They gathered tentatively around Suzetta, touching her gently, fingering the casket, dabbing their noses with their clothes. Carrie gave them their space, torn between the desire to offer a kerchief and the good grace to not appear condescending. She stopped Sav's clock on the mantle as a symbol of respect. She wasn't sure if Mrs. Scuttle considered such rituals to be proper, but the ticking of the thing could be annoying among the bereaved sniffles and solemn contemplation. Sav clasped Scuttle's hand and offered warm condolences. His confidence was restored once he saw Mrs. Scuttle refrain from hysterics.

Carrie supervised the procession of men pall-bearing Suzetta's little box, feet first, out the front door. No one noticed the forgotten stacks of travel cases, trunks, and boxes that stood like headstones in the front yard. The

CHAPTER THREE

Scuttle's mare plodded toward the pauper's lot with Suzetta's casket, its only cargo, in the creaky, swaying contrivance. The Scuttles trailed behind.

Reverend Borden spent all of five minutes on the committal service, put a silent, fatherly palm on Wyatt Scuttle's shoulder as he passed, then hastened away. Carrie watched him retreat into the church's annex and glimpsed Mrs. Peters' sour face shutting the door. She manned one end of a rope that lowered Suzetta's casket into the hole. Digger Louis never showed up.

The two boys had been tasked with carrying the bundles of apple blossoms from the parlor to the gravesite. They dropped the flowers onto the top of their sister's casket. Bale said he'd stay behind to fill in the grave and set a bundle aside to adorn the fresh dirt. Mrs. Scuttle stumbled on the way back, but Sav's neighbor, Mrs. Woodruff, who delivered meals all over town, came through with a sturdy basket full of bread and a pot of stew with lamb and carrots. While Sav and Carrie hosted the repass meal, the sun set on Carrie Lisbon's first day in Hope Bridge.

Chapter Four

Within three days of her arrival, a funeral for an elderly benefactress of the proposed Hope Bridge Library, a tepid church service, and the Whitsunday picnic constituted Carrie's debut.

On Monday, another early morning jangle at the door interrupted their breakfast conversation. Carrie insisted on making the morning meal. She could handle eggs and toast, but the rest of her kitchen skills had never developed. Ever since the day Carrie had arrived at Melinda Haskell's eleventh birthday party bearing a plate of ginger crackles, and Melinda had recoiled, sneering, 'No one wants cookies from the undertaker's daughter!' Carrie had no inclination to pursue any culinary accomplishments other than the basics.

A slender young woman in a housemaid's apron stood on the porch. Sparkling blue eyes and a halo of auburn hair complimented the woman's cinnamon freckles.

"Good morning. Are you Mrs. Lisbon?" A strong lilt gave away the woman's heritage.

"Yes, I am. Good morning."

"I'm Mr. Arthur Worley's housemaid, mum." She pronounced the name 'Wahr-ley.' "Mr. Worley sent me to ask if you could come as soon as you are able."

Sav wandered up the hall and spoke from above Carrie's shoulder. "Good morning, Marta. How are you?"

"I'm well, Mr. Machin, thank you." Marta bobbed her head as Bale crowded

CHAPTER FOUR

in with Sav and Carrie.

"How are you today, Miss Marta?" he asked with genuine warmth. Marta's attempt at formality relaxed as he returned Bale's greeting. "Well and fine, Mr. Bale. And you?"

"What does Mr. Worley want of me?" Carrie interrupted, annoyed by the shift from the professional summons to social pleasantries. She had just been personally requested by a peer, and she was thrilled that Mr. Worley might want to discuss their mutual professions. These pleasantries could take all day.

"He needs your help, Mrs. Lisbon." Marta shifted her attention from Bale to Carrie. "With a body."

In the sobering pause that followed Marta's announcement, Carrie said cheerfully, "Excellent. I'll just get my things." When she hurriedly returned from her bedroom, pinning on her hat, she interrupted the trio still lounging and chatting in the open doorway.

"I've only met Mr. Worley in passing, uncle. At the Briggs funeral this past Saturday. I've forgotten if you introduced me as an undertaker."

"Yes, Mrs. Ester Briggs. A champion of the library," Sav inserted his social tidbits whenever he could. "I'm sure I included your professional acumen as part of your introduction, niece. I'm so pleased Mr. Worley took note."

"Nah," Bale said, shaking his head. "Mrs. Peters put that bugaboo all over town. How you paid for the little girl's funeral and how you're an undertaker."

Carrie suspected the gossip when she was cornered at the Whitsunday picnic with a gaggle of women who peppered her with comments about her wealth, her status, and her profession.

"Nanuet?" they'd asked. "Is that in Connecticut? I understand there are a frightful number of poor in Connecticut. Did you deal with them often?"

"You're a widow?" Another glanced up and down. "Plum is an unusual color for half-mourning."

"Your Christian charity with that family was admirable. A similar contribution to the Ladies Temperance Society would be most appreciated."

Instead of trying to set her record straight, or attempt to educate at this juncture in her new residence, Carrie relied upon her tried and true methods of nodding politely, refuting graciously, and excusing herself. She'd reserve her challenging retorts until she got her bearings; knew how to navigate her new neighbors.

Now, she pressed toward the door, eager to get on with this opportunity, and invited Marta to lead the way.

Bale escorted them to the Worley residence. He and the Irish maid chatted cordially as they walked, the easy banter of working-class folk. Carrie listened with only half an ear. Hope Bridge was tiny compared to Nanuet; Worley's Funeral Parlor was only a few minutes' walk from North Street. She tried to remember the parlor and the viewing room, but had to admit, the funeral of Ester Briggs had been too overlaid with the specter of Phee's agonizing funeral service for her to take much notice. She had, however, observed the flowers more closely.

Floral tributes had crowded the casket. Sav had pointed out the calling cards accompanying each arrangement to Carrie, muttering a string of incomprehensible social connections that Carrie gave up trying to follow. Loops of carnations from the proposed library committee meant, according to *The Ladies Guide to the Language of Flowers,* "I'll never forget you." An orb of deep crimson roses ("mourning for you") came from Ester Briggs' children. Urns of lilies ("rebirth") and palm fronds ("heavenly victory") were a tribute from the Christian Ladies Aid Society. Stingy Peters supplemented her tulips ("what's on hand?") with thick bundles of mint to hide the paucity of flowers she'd included in her arrangement. Carrie realized happily that the selection of flowers meant a greenhouse did business within a day's journey. She couldn't cook, but she excelled at flowers.

Bale delivered the women to a wide, two-story clapboard with a modestly arched portico. Marta led them around to the back door, a slight Carrie excused as the maid's habit of entering the home herself through the rear.

Marta showed Carrie to a small room furnished with a slender wardrobe, a spindle-backed chair, and a dainty table and lamp. A narrow brass bedframe supported a thin, striped mattress, covered in oilcloth. The bed's current occupant lay under a white sheet.

CHAPTER FOUR

Arthur Worley joined Carrie and Marta in the tiny room. As tall as Sav, the undertaker wore a dark suit and a bland expression. He clasped his hands loosely at his belt and made subtle gestures as she spoke.

"I appreciate your coming, Mrs. Lisbon," he said. "It has come to my attention that you have some experience in the mortuary profession. I'm afraid Mrs. Worley is not up to this particular task. She knew the deceased and simply cannot bring herself to prepare young Ophelia's remains. She had been such a lively young lady. They are often harder to lay out than children."

Carrie felt another insult. *Some experience in the mortuary profession?* She'd grown up in it. As for *his* wife, squeamishness and avoidance had no place in the funerary business. Hadn't she laid out Ester Briggs just a few days ago? She must possess a sense of responsibility, of obligation to her husband's business, no matter what her personal proclivities. What was different? Pushing aside the ire that pairs with insult, Carrie drew down the sheet and bent to peer at the dead woman's features.

"This is Ophelia Morgan," Worley continued. "She was thrown from a carriage last night and was killed in the fall. A broken neck, I'm afraid. Our county coroner has authorized me to make the decision regarding her manner of death."

Carrie nodded, vaguely aware of how different an official cause of death was declared here, as opposed to a city like Nanuet. But her focus was on the dead girl.

Carrie remembered Ophelia Morgan from the Whitsunday picnic yesterday. She was one of the few people who made an impression amid her uncle's incessant murmur of familial extractions, but not because she was 'such a lively young lady' as Worley described.

The picnic had been a beautiful affair, on the lawn of one of Hope Bridge's finer homes, with idly blowing tablecloths and a feast of delicacies. Most townsfolk had been polite, but Carrie's enjoyment had been dimmed by the reception she'd gotten from others. The good Reverend Borden studiously ignored her. Younger women inspected her, assessing a threat to their prospects. One had given her such a malevolent stare, she looked around to make sure the evil eye had been directed at her. Men lingered over their moist handshakes, and one leered openly, sweeping her from head to toe with an ugly expression.

She understood the skepticism, even the appraisal. She was a new species. A tall, slender widow, with apparently independent means, available to marry again. Her worth included comfortable finances, which were now well-known, thanks to Stingy Peters, and sexual experience. Men sought those assets in a wife. But the animosity? She couldn't understand antagonism toward her at this early stage.

She remembered Ophelia from the picnic because she had been the opposite of lively. She'd been downcast and timid as she followed—no *crept*—in her husband's shadow. Ophelia's husband was the man who leered at Carrie.

"This is Germond's wife? The sister-in-law of Sheriff Morgan?" Carrie said, pleased to remember a small bit of her uncle's blathering genealogy. She recalled Germond's ogling with distaste. "Her husband must be distraught," she said drily.

"Yes," Worley concurred. "Germond brought her here late last night. He said they had been out in their carriage, and they hit a rut. Ophelia was unseated and fell out."

"Ruts are certainly plentiful," Carrie murmured. "But you'd have to be going awfully fast to be thrown from a carriage. How bad *are* the roads around here?"

Worley didn't respond. Carrie resumed her study of the dead girl.

Ophelia had been pretty, with an elegant neck, a small nose, and lovely arched brows. Her face retained the unblemished quality of youth; her thick chestnut hair was still shiny. But dirt embedded a deep and bloodless scratch on her cheek. Her brown eyes were half open, as was her mouth. Carrie pulled the sheet back further to reveal the torso and frowned. Ophelia wore no jacket, and the long sleeves of her blouse twisted around her upper arms. Her shirt spread open at the throat, revealing dark bruising on her neck. Her corset had slid down below her breasts, a vulgar disclosure. Her skirt was scuffed and torn.

CHAPTER FOUR

"Was she brought to you like this, Mr. Worley?"

"Yes. After the accident, Mr. Morgan lay her in the trunk bed of the carriage and drove directly here."

"Was Mr. Morgan injured?"

"I don't believe so."

"Are we to embalm her?"

"I would imagine so, yes. But I have not made formal arrangements. Mr. Morgan is seeking the assistance of his brother before he tells Ophelia's family."

"Mm. I'm sure that's wise," Carrie agreed.

"If you would please, make her presentable to the family for the initial viewing. There are supplies—glue and ladies' garments and bedclothing—in the cabinet." Worley gestured to a bell pull. "Please ring the bell if there is anything else you need. Marta will be at your disposal. She'll collect Mrs. Morgan's funeral attire later. Now," he concluded, "shall I leave you to your work, Mrs. Lisbon?"

"Yes, Mr. Worley." Carrie straightened and looked the tall man in the eye. She would match his polish with her own professional courtesy. "And thank you for requesting my services today. There is something I need. Can you send Marta to my house to request my camera? Mr. Bale or my uncle will be able to bring it over. The equipment is heavy."

"You take mortuary photographs, Mrs. Lisbon?" Worley looked interested. "We may have use for such a service."

"Yes, I do. Once we get Mrs. Morgan into your parlor, I'll be able to take a picture."

"I'll send Marta before she collects the clothing." Worley scrutinized her for a moment and left.

Carrie washed her hands and dried her fingers as she circled Ophelia's body, intent on where to begin. She peered more closely at the bruises on Ophelia's neck and noted abrasions that would need to be covered with creams and powder. She picked up one of Ophelia's limp hands; the fingers were slim, clean, and cold. Carrie moved Ophelia's head from side to side. She paused, and repeated turning the head, bending more closely to pick up a sound she had become familiar with over the years. She heard nothing and decided the absence of crunching, broken neck bones could be attributed to the onset of the body's rigidity.

She centered a cotton strip under Ophelia's jaw, pulled it tight, and knotted it at the top of her head. She hoped she wasn't too late with the procedure and that the jaw would stiffen shut. As she removed Ophelia's garments, Carrie felt another twinge of incongruity; there was something irregular about her clothing. Odd, the woman hadn't worn a jacket to go for a ride, especially at night. And no gloves. The hat was absent as well, but it may have gotten torn off and left behind. It stood to reason that a distraught husband would not have stopped to fetch his wife's hat if she had just died on the roadside. Several skirt buttons were popped and missing; the petticoat beneath smudged with dirt. Her shoes were partly buttoned, no doubt having been wrenched around, like her skirt, by the impact of her fall.

The woman's body smelled of a man's cologne, a scent that carried too much sweetness. It was the same scent Carrie found objectionable when Germond Morgan leaned in close for his uncouth perusal of her at yesterday's picnic.

The bloomers wouldn't come off without a struggle, and as Carrie bent nearer to gain leverage, she caught the familiar whiff of masculine residue. For an embarrassed moment, she thought, the couple had engaged in a passionate interlude before going on their fateful wagon ride. But when the long stockings slid off Ophelia's slender legs, revealing bruised thighs, Carrie stopped short.

She would have bet a nickel on what she would find under the rest of Ophelia's garments. She and a housekeeper had once laid out the body of a maid at the home of one of Nanuet's wealthier patrons. A suicide, the girl had thrown herself off the lavish parapets; *her* neck made a considerable crunching noise. When disrobed, the body revealed the same bruising on the inner thighs. Carrie had watched the housekeeper gasp and turn away with a hand to her mouth. Weeks later, the same woman beckoned to Carrie at the grocers, and in a quiet whisper, gossiped that the patron's son had been sent to Europe to "further his education," and the other women who worked at the house were relieved.

Grimly, Carrie removed Ophelia's underclothes. As she suspected, Ophelia's upper arms showed the bruises that came from struggling in an unwanted grip. She was scratched across one breast. In Carrie's experience, the injuries, in conjunction with the husband's issue, meant the interlude had not been a pleasurable intimacy shared between a husband and wife, but an affair of violence, suffered by the woman. *My God,* she shuddered, *how could he put her in a carriage and take her for a ride after what he did?* Carrie remembered Ophelia's cowed demeanor in the presence of her oafish husband and condemned the man as a brute.

She sat down heavily in the slender chair and looked up at the ceiling to quell the tears filling her eyes. Worley's pleasant viewing room now seemed cold and ugly. This poor girl. Raped by her husband, whom she most likely married with the highest of hopes and the brightest of future dreams, then killed in a wagon accident caused by lousy, rutted roads.

Carrie stared at the dead girl's eyes, her dirty hair, and her injuries. The bruises around Ophelia's throat contrasted starkly with the pallid skin. They stood out like sore thumbs.

Thumbs.

Carrie's eyes narrowed. She stood, reached out, and placed her own hands on the girl's neck. Her fingers matched the thick bruises at the hairline. Her thumbs overlapped across the soft dimple at the base of Ophelia's throat, and there, above the dead woman's windpipe, was the missing crunch of broken bones.

Chapter Five

Ophelia's mother, Mrs. Rowena Grant, and her sisters, Ada and Sylvannia, startled Carrie, bursting into the viewing room in anguish and horror. They sobbed and screeched curses at the absent Germond. Ada, the older sister, tall and black-haired, and Mrs. Grant, a matron whose former beauty had silvered over the years, yanked Ophelia upwards, hugging the stiff body fiercely, and displacing the carefully arranged nightdress and ruffled bedclothes Carrie had fussed over. Ophelia's hand fell off the bed and the middle sister, Sylvannia, pressing a kerchief to her shocked face, picked up the lifeless fingers with her own delicate hand. Carrie recognized her as the girl who threw the unaccountably hostile look at her yesterday. Now her blank stare dimmed in comparison to the wild mourning antics of her mother and sister. Worley finally led the women to his office and, a short while later, exited, looking only slightly discomposed after the wailing and the comforting, and the arrangements had been concluded. The family had emphatically agreed to the use of "petrifying solutions" on the poor girl "so that she may remain in youth and beauty forever." Several women, presumably from the community, came to take the stumbling and fainting trio back to their home.

"We shall have some lunch, Mrs. Lisbon," Worley announced. "If you'd be so kind as to assist with the embalming after that?"

Marta supplied them with a thick vegetable stew, buttered slices of crusty bread, and cold milk. She and Carrie ate in the kitchen after she delivered a tray upstairs to Mrs. Worley's parlor. The mortician ate with his wife.

"She seems poorly today," Marta said evasively about the squeamish Mrs.

CHAPTER FIVE

Worley.

Carrie considered the older couple's breach of etiquette. Mrs. Worley hadn't thanked her for her services after the hullabaloo of the Grants' visit. In addition, Worley relegated her to eat in the kitchen with the hired help. Her insecurities flared. *Is yet another woman threatened by my presence?* she asked herself. *First, Stingy Peters turns sour because I arrive on my uncle's arm. Now the wife of the undertaker must think I'm here to usurp her role. Good lord, if I'm a new species in town, I must present as a hostile one!*

Shrugging away her turmoil, she complimented Marta for the excellent bread and dug into her meal, thinking ahead to the delicate work she and Worley were to perform after lunch.

* * *

Marta helped transfer Ophelia down to the preparation room on a canvas litter. She was forthright about the task, holding as much regard for the dignity of the human remains as the undertakers. When they had finished placing Ophelia on the embalming table, and before she went back upstairs, Marta had crossed herself in that reverential way the Irish did when they felt a compunction for holy strength.

Carrie observed the mortician's work room, impressed with the polished handrail that descended the cellar stairs and the number of lamps that lit up the space. Worley's preparation chamber was lavish compared to the cobwebbed cellar where she had prepared Suzetta Scuttle. The lawn fell away from the stone foundation below Worley's house, allowing for a pair of multi-paned coffin doors and a well-proportioned double-hung window. The amount of light in the cellar equaled that of an upstairs room. A body could be delivered, prepared, placed in its casket, and removed with ease and discretion. The open window created a draft for fumes to exit, clearing the air of both the toxicity and the clinging scents of the embalming procedure.

More lamps waited tidily on painted shelves. Jars of face paint, pomade, powders, and whisker lacquer sparkled on a polished table. Shears, brushes, a shaving kit, hair ribbons and string lined up neatly, as did a layette of needles and thread near an ironing board and a hair curling wand. Shining enamel basins hung within easy reach; a ceramic dish cradled a fat bar of soap.

"You have some fine embalming equipment, Mr. Worley," Carrie remarked as she and Worley tied on bibbed aprons. A caned Passmore table bearing Ophelia took center stage. Rubber tubing coiled on iron hooks above an enamel sink, which had been cleverly sunk into the floor. Shallow ribs in the bottom shunted fluids into a drain hole, while a brass water spigot above could be turned on to douse the blood away. Carrie guessed the arterial syringes were stored in the polished wooden case on a nearby shelf.

"I studied under Dr. Albert McMillen, who trained under Dr. Holmes, himself." Worley's reverence for the champion of modern embalming techniques made his voice richer. As he adjusted the bow on his apron, he lamented. "We have little use of such extravagance here, however. And your husband? Was he knowledgeable in the subject?"

Carrie noted the term 'knowledgeable' as opposed to 'trained.' Knowing *about* a procedure was much less important than knowing *how* to do it. Worley's question crossed into condescension.

"We were both trained in several procedures." She smiled at him. "As was my father. We prefer Dr. Auguste Renouard's methods, of course." She paused to let her response sink in. She suspected Worley, being an older man, would have been using Professor Crane's methods, since Crane's school pre-dated Renouard's. There often existed a heated competition among embalmers, whose preferences in the medical and aesthetic results of their work meant increased business for their establishments. *Lisbon & Shay* prided themselves on such outcomes.

"But I agree, there may be less need for such extra measures here. Shall we begin?" she asked, pressing on briskly before Worley could counter the challenge.

They fell into step. Worley's movements were careful and steady; his conversation monosyllabic. Carrie smiled indulgently when she saw the name "Crane" stamped on the syringe's brass barrel. Outdated tools, but still quite serviceable.

CHAPTER FIVE

Carrie positioned herself at the head of the body, maneuvering Ophelia's slender arm so Worley could raise the brachial artery. She saw again the bruising from the husband's treatment, but discarded her intention to bring up her observation of Ophelia's broken neck. Right now, she was better served demonstrating her competence rather than her suspicions. Instead, she turned on the water faucet a moment before the draining blood emptied into the sink, thinning it as it trickled away.

When Worley thumbed a brass valve closed with his bony fingers, she took the dripping tube and needle from him before he could ask, expertly tucking a shallow enamel basin under the equipment. She wanted her willingness to wash and care for his tools, and her anticipation of his needs to clearly demonstrate her expertise.

Carrie rinsed the equipment while Worley probed the woman's belly with a long steel needle. Carrie noted he kept the cotton sheets discreetly folded above and below Ophelia's belly, allowing only a wide strip of abdominal skin to be exposed. Carrie offered to stitch the incisions. Worley simply nodded. They stood still for a moment, satisfied with their results: Ophelia's skin retained its white pallor, not the yellowish hue of the dead.

Carrie left the Passmore table flat; easier to dress a body in the prone position. When Ophelia went into her casket, Carrie would have time to apply the face paint. She deposited the remaining tools into the sink and rinsed them under the spigot. She lathered her hands with Worley's lemon-scented soap and poured out a measure of distilled alcohol into a cloth. She used that to further disinfect her hands and forearms. Worley stood beside her in silence and did the same. They glanced around the cellar to ensure the room's orderliness before Worley dismissed her with a nod and exited the preparation chamber. He stood outside in the afternoon sun with his back to her. Carrie thriftily turned down the lamps and went back upstairs to the kitchen.

Chapter Six

Sav man-handled the bulky, oak-legged tripod down Worley's cellar stairs. He had arrived with the photography equipment and happily volunteered to assist with the mortuary shot, stating his long-standing intrigue with photography and his desire to learn. "So, if this is the current subject," he grinned, "I suppose I'll have to start here!"

"Uncle, who owns a telephone in town?" Carrie asked, ignoring his enthusiasm. The streets of Nanuet were excessively crisscrossed with overhead 'phone wires, but Carrie had seen only one in Hope Bridge.

"Oh, several families. The Worleys have one. And the post office. The Chester, of course. The Clevingers have two: one at their store, and another upstairs in their residence. Oh! The Valley Star Hotel on the other end of town. The Peters sisters have one. Um, the Grants. The Clarkes. I remember Ophelia and Germond receiving one as a wedding gift. And the Marshalls. They just got a new one a few weeks past. They call it an 'oil can.' It's rather clever looking—"

"Uncle, can you start setting up the camera while I make a call?" Carrie interrupted. She still felt alarmed about the bones in Ophelia's neck. She had to let Worley know about the girl's injuries, and if a phone call to a colleague in Nanuet would bolster her evidence, so much the better. She bustled by Sav's surprised expression, mounted the cellar stairs, and called back over her shoulder. "She's not going anywhere. The camera is self-explanatory."

She found her way to the kitchen and found Marta sitting on a stool, looking out the back door at the late-day sun. Marta wore an intense expression of fear, and startled when Carrie came in.

CHAPTER SIX

"I'm so sorry to alarm you, Marta," Carrie said. "I need your telephone. Can you show me where it is?"

"Yes, of course, Mrs. Lisbon. It's in the hallway." Marta rubbed her face and straightened her apron as she stood.

"Are you well, Marta? I don't mean to trouble you again today. You've done a great deal for me already."

"No trouble, Mrs. Lisbon."

"Did you know Miss Ophelia?"

"I knew her. I'm sorry she's dead. What a dreadful accident." Marta, pronouncing the word *'ox-ident',* led the way through Worley's tasteful home. "Here's the telephone. Can I call up the operator for you?"

"No, that's kind. I know how to use it. Thank you, Marta."

Carrie sensed the girl's preoccupation, but pressed on to the matter at hand. Delighted by another one of Worley's modern conveniences, she tapped the handset cradle, and a woman's voice asked for her desired connection.

"Please connect me with Nanuet. *The Nanuet Daily.* Mr. Bill Bemis. The number is NAN-4887. She heard the crackle of hundreds of miles of wire in the earpiece. A click generated a sharp response from the operator.

"Glynnis? This is a call from Mr. Worley's house. You get off the line right now." Someone huffed, and the phone clicked again. Carrie offered her thanks for the operator's protection of her privacy.

"Not at all, ma'am. Glynnis Marshall is a nosy busybody." Carrie chuckled at the assessment. This was a pleasant surprise. No operator in Nanuet guarded a caller's privacy. There were too many calls. Operators connected the parties, and moved on to the next request, or not. They might linger, listening in. The sharing of phone lines, with hundreds of conversations was tantamount to open discussion at a community dinner table.

"Bemis." The voice on the other end barked out the word.

"Bill? It's Carrie Lisbon."

"Eh? Carrie? Speak up!"

"Hello, Bill! I'm calling from Hope Bridge!"

"Well, you made it!" A hissing sound overwhelmed his next words. "—awful?"

"What? No! It's fine. I'm busy. I need your help! Can you hear me?"

"Yes. Help. What."

"I need some files. On the Freed murders. Can you—"

Bill Bemis cut her off. This time, his voice cleared the static. "You called the *Nanuet Daily* to ask me for files? I thought you'd be calling to tell me you'd changed your mind and accepted my marriage proposal! I'm crushed."

Carrie laughed. Bill Bemis could lift her mood with his carroty hair, his infestation of red freckles, and his quick humor, no matter what her circumstances had been. He had been asking her to marry him, since the first day they'd met, even as Phee good-naturedly looked on. Bill Bemis was a scarce consort. He viewed Carrie as a person in possession of intelligence and skill, not a ghoul to be shunned and ridiculed.

"Not today, I'm sorry," Carrie's reply had been their playful exchange for several years. "I want some information about the Freed murders," she shouted.

"No need to shout. I hear you loud and clear. Maybe not for long, though. They're big files; can you narrow it down?" Static spurt through the line again. Carrie cursed under her breath. "I want the details of the strangulations. The pictures? The doctor's reports?"

"Christ, you –" A squall of electricity swept over the line. Bemis's voice sounded much farther away when she heard him again. "—post tomorrow."

Carrie was shouting, holding one finger in the opposite ear. "Yes! Put it in the post tomorrow. Thank you, Bill. Tell—"

"Mrs. Lisbon?" Arthur Worley stood at her side. She hadn't heard his arrival with the static and her shouting.

"Oh! You startled me, Mr. Worley. Good-bye, Bill!"

"And you're using my telephone."

"Yes. I had some questions about Ophelia. I have a friend in Nanuet that could help. It was most important."

"I don't see how Miss Ophelia's preparation needs the assistance of a long-distance phone call to an associate in Nanuet, when I'm available to you…right here." A heavy-lidded stare punctuated Worley's admonishment.

Flustered, and feeling chastised, Carrie hung up the earpiece. "It really

CHAPTER SIX

was important. I don't think you could have answered this question for me. We consulted on a series of murd—"

"I assure you, Mrs. Lisbon, that I'm able to answer whatever questions you may have regarding any deceased in my home. I consider your telephone call a lark, as do many who discover its novelty and suddenly feel the need to 'have something important' to say to someone on the other end of the line. I'm assuming you'll resume your attendance of Miss Ophelia now?"

"Yes, of course." Carrie frowned as Worley turned his back on her, yet again, and drifted into another room. She wanted to tell him about Ophelia's broken neck—not the broken neck supposedly caused by the fall from a wagon—but the broken neck and throttle marks that clearly indicated an alarmingly different cause of death. But Worley's schoolmaster scolding had her fuming as she marched back down the cellar stairs.

Sav grinned up at her from his bony perch on the middle risers. His long fingers draped over his knees; his homburg dangled loosely. He smiled up at her.

"Ol' Worley gave you a tongue lashing for using his 'phone? He's awfully proprietary about that contraption."

"I'm reminded of Oscar's favorite phrase," Carrie groused as she squeezed by her uncle. Sav kept a macaw, an enormous, leather-faced bird with a shocking combination of azure and yellow plumage. The parrot had stopped nibbling on a coconut shell when Carrie entered the upstairs room the morning after her arrival, and rhythmically lurched toward her along a maze of polished sticks and thick ropes.

"Tom adds pieces to the roost regularly," Sav said, looking fondly at his bird, "so Oscar doesn't get bored." Oscar made his own introduction, squirting guano onto the newspapers below his perch. His white eye gleamed with petulance. He croaked, "Frrrruck you!" Carrie burst out laughing. Sav joined her nervously.

"That's why he can't ever be in public."

The swearing parrot provided the cursing Carrie could not. She puffed out a determined breath and positioned the camera over Ophelia's body. "A matter for later. Now, if you could hold a lamp over her head and throat, I'll tell you where I want the light."

"Why are we taking a picture of Ophelia down here? Shouldn't we wait until she's upstairs in the parlor?"

"I want to get a picture of those strangulation marks on her neck." Carrie busied herself with the camera's wooden box and leather bellows while Sav's jaw hit the floor.

"Strangulation? Carrie, what's going on?"

Carrie lowered her voice, whispering quickly. "I don't think Ophelia died from falling off a wagon, Uncle. I think she was strangled. See? These marks look like the ones I saw on a murder victim in Nanuet. I phoned my friend, Bill Bemis, just now. You remember him? He reported on the cases. He's sending me some of the details, specifically, photographs and autopsy reports demonstrating what strangulation looks like. Here, quickly! We have to get this done, before Mr. Worley grows suspicious of us."

"Why would Worley be suspicious of us? Haven't you told him?" Sav asked with a shrill voice. His eyes widened, and both his hair and nostrils flared as Carrie handed him a lamp.

"No, I haven't. I was going to, but he just scolded me like I was a child. And I wanted to talk to Bill and get some pictures to confirm my theory first."

"Theory? Carrie, Arthur Worley is our undertaker. You'll have to get Doc Wells to confirm a theory. Oh, my God. This is Germond's wife. Del Morgan's sister-in-law. Del's the sheriff. What are we doing?"

"Uncle, hold the lamp up."

Carrie maneuvered Ophelia's head and neck into an arched position. She got behind the camera's thick lens and squinted at the resultant image. She returned, moved the body, had Sav hold the flame higher, returned to the lens and repeated the process. "Hold it right there!" she said. The camera's shutter clicked, and Ophelia's body slowly flattened out again.

"Excellent. I think I've got it!" Carrie breathed with excitement and, ignoring her uncle's shocked expression, asked, "Could you be a dear and bring the camera and tripod up into the parlor? I just have to finish laying out Ophelia."

Sav clattered up the stairs with the heavy box, trailing the long tripod legs

CHAPTER SIX

in his haste.

"I'll be back home before supper," Carrie called up after him.

Chapter Seven

Bookhoudt's Dry Goods, one of two general stores on Main, delivered a burnished chestnut casket just before dusk. Ophelia was stretchered back up the stairs in the same manner she had descended. Without speaking, Worley and Carrie arranged her final pose. Marta lit two globed lamps on elegant brass columns, drew the curtains in the parlor, and took delivery of Mrs. Peters' flowers. Carrie craftily rearranged the insufficient blooms when Worley wasn't looking. She set up the camera, but the light had faded; she assured Worley that the photo would be taken in better conditions tomorrow.

Worley eyed Carrie's finished product critically. Ophelia's damaged cheek was smoothed over with thickened face cream and blushed with powder. Carrie had combed and curled her hair and tinted her lips a slight rose color. Worley bent in close to examine the thin line of glue Carrie had used to seal the girl's eyes before applying the minutest brush of lamp-black paste to her eyelashes. He straightened without a word and nodded once.

As she left Worley's home and stepped into the dark blue evening, she looked back at the drawn parlor curtains and the golden glow of the lamps behind them. Unlike most people who admitted to getting the creeps when seeing the undertaker's parlor thus lighted, Carrie took pride in the scene. Inside, a person had been laid out with dignity and care. Their family would see them in beautiful repose. Their grief would be lessened because their loved one appeared whole again, and peaceful. The service at the church and the ensuing trip to the cemetery was another affair. Carrie had little to do with the religious aspects of the internment. The finality of the graveside ritual was truly crushing, as she could personally attest, but she knew her preparation of the deceased would not cause more agony for a grieving family.

She walked down the wooden plank sidewalks, hearing only her footsteps. The mild spring days still gave way to a damp chill that required a fire to assuage. She hadn't thought to bring her jacket with her when she left in high anticipation this morning. The orbs of archaic gas lamps measured the distance up Main, until they ended at the junction with North Street. Nanuet had done away with gas lamps years ago, in favor of the more efficient electric lights. Hope Bridge's lights were throwbacks by comparison.

She looked briefly at the homes she passed. She overheard pieces of conversations from within each; they seemed to flash by like cars on a train. But she was the one rushing.

Her head swam with alarm and indecision. She discovered wounds on a dead woman's body that spoke of violence done to her, not those sustained in an accident. Carrie knew what a violated body looked like. She knew what a strangled neck looked like. She knew what broken bones felt like. Her jitters were not about the presence of these things, but the course of action she must take.

If she were in Nanuet, she would have told her father and her husband what she had found. They would have called a policeman with their concerns. The police would have looked into *Lisbon & Shay's* suspicions; they'd have found evidence to pursue; they'd have restored law and order. In Hope Bridge, however, Sav had proudly described the county's law enforcement strategy on their walk home from the Whitsunday picnic.

"Delphius Morgan is the sheriff of our county. Newly appointed since Nate Edwards stepped down last year. He travels all over, so he's not positioned here all the time. He deputizes, of course, when it's necessary."

"We had twenty-three policemen in Nanuet," Carrie said. Like the traveling preachers, and the shared services of a few undertakers, Hope Bridge's law enforcement fell short of her expectations. "If there was a complaint to be made, or someone died suspiciously, you could always find an officer to see to it. I've seen no policemen here, so, to whom do you make a complaint?"

"Do you have a complaint, niece?" Sav asked.

"Well, no. Not at the moment. But in case I do, what happens?"

"We have a grievance day once each month. Sheriff Morgan is here every third Tuesday at Clevinger's. He has a room in the back. He'll take a statement and investigate. Something urgent is wired to Duncan, of course, for his immediate attention. There was that time when the Proctor's boy…."

On the darkening street, Carrie considered her position. Did Hope Bridge lack the violent crimes of a small city like Nanuet, as well as the populace, law enforcement, and telephones? Did the newly appointed sheriff have any idea how to investigate a crime like Ophelia's abuse and murder? Should she offer her expertise to the sheriff? She might be able to help, as she had some prior experience.

Carrie and Phee had been married for three years when *Lisbon & Shay* served as the undertakers for a Nanuet woman who had been strangled by an unknown assailant. Carrie knew how the woman died before she worked on the body, and she fulfilled her morbid curiosity by examining the woman's wounds as she laid her out. Scratches, perpendicular to bruises, showed where the woman had tried to tear away the hands that held her windpipe. The grisly feel of crushed bones sounded like fragile twigs crackling underfoot. One of Nanuet's physicians examined the body, and Carrie had stood by while the doctor dictated the extent of the wounds and reiterated the cause of death. The woman's family deserved to remember her in a peaceful state, and Carrie, hoping to mitigate the horror of the victim's demise, had taken special pains with the hair and face paint. She encountered Bill Bemis for the first time at the funeral.

He attended with a scratch pad, a tip from the police, and a reporter's pugnacity. He wrote without looking down. He took the indignant rebuffs to his pointed questions without batting an eye, turning to other mourners in relentless pursuit of quotes. He badgered Carrie for answers, his questions about the deceased coming in rapid fire, until she raised a hand, indicating her ongoing discretionary role with directing the funeral. Bill Bemis paused and asked one more.

"Will you marry me?"

CHAPTER SEVEN

Carrie didn't break stride. "Not today, I'm sorry," she said, barely containing the mirth that shouldn't be shown in a parlor with an active funeral taking place.

Bill Bemis pestered her again when a second woman died in a similar manner nearly a year later. This time, she and Phee sat with him at a tearoom on Dorsett Street, and they compared notes about strangulation. This time he asked Phee his perennial question. "Can I marry her?" Phee had thrown back his head in laughter; his humor had always been ready to bubble over. "Not in this lifetime, friend!"

When a third woman was throttled a year later, Bill Bemis came to them again, this time with photos from the police that showed the familiar bruises and the accompanying scratches that gave Carrie the chills. Another terrified woman had fought for her life. How many agonizing moments had passed before she lost the battle?

Bill Bemis interviewed families, dogged policemen, and gained access to the jailed husbands who stood, dumbfoundedly, accused. He plotted the women's movements; he established no relationships between them, no coincidence of addresses. He bought himself a telephone and kept it at his desk, guarding it like a dog over a bone. Eventually, he amassed anecdotal and physical evidence.

He discovered all the victims had hired out repairs to their homes prior to their murders. But not until another woman's body was found, strangled like the others, did Bemis' efforts garner serious attention. By that time, Nanuet citizens were clamoring at the doors of the police station, phoning and petitioning daily, pointing fingers, demanding safety.

Lambert Freed, a vagrant who came to Nanuet for occasional work, was identified, arrested, and convicted of the crimes. Bemis wrote daily about the search, the capture, the confession, the trial, and the eventual execution, selling papers by the hundreds. His phone rang off the hook. His salary increased. He spent many evenings with Carrie and Phee, discussing the cases. Carrie longed for Phee and Bill's steady presence again as she hurried home; longed for the surety of police officers and night watchmen who knew what to do.

In Hope Bridge, the only law enforcement was a month away, and it appeared he became involved only if someone complained. But this was different. This was the Sheriff's sister-in-law. Surely, he would hear her concerns.

Another jolt of doubt coursed through her. Was she right about Ophelia's death? Would the gruesome details of the Freed murder victims be consistent with what she found on Ophelia? What if she brought her concerns and her evidence to the sheriff, and he refused to investigate his own brother?

What would Worley say? Nearing her house, she halted suddenly. She hadn't even told him. But how could Worley be unaware of the strangulation marks? Hadn't he seen them when Ophelia was brought in? Carrie knew he had sharp eyes. Even though it continued to rankle, his scrutiny of her work was testament to that. Worley was, effectively, her employer. She had accepted his formally written check just before she left this evening. She must inform him, and most appropriately, before she spoke to this Sheriff Morgan.

But beyond Worley's chastisement, beyond her distress at the evidence of murder, and aside from the quandary of how to approach the sheriff, Carrie felt a deeper sense of anxiety, one that had been with her since she heard about the mob that set fire to the homes of Thomas Bale and his friends last year.

There was a *lawlessness* here; the idea that no one was in charge if things got out of hand. A threat of malicious riders coming out of the dark, of unchecked, heartless violence, an emptiness where there should be a protector. She felt vulnerable without Phee, without her father, without the twenty-three reliable policemen, and the sheer population of Nanuet.

Her feet pattered on chiseled flagstones. Where had the boardwalk ended? Hope Bridge didn't even have consistent walkways. Her thoughts jumped and scattered. *This is no time to lose your head,* she chided herself, purposefully slowing and drawing a resolute breath.

This is a time to make notes, to write down in a logical sequence the things that needed to be dealt with. She would talk things over with the two men she did have at her disposal. Uncle Sav and Thomas Bale would be able to

CHAPTER SEVEN

help her sort through the turmoil.

Later, she could be weak, with her covers over her head, clutching Phee's picture, and muffling her heartbreak with her pillow.

Chapter Eight

Carrie arrived at the Worley residence in the morning, prepared to explain her discovery to Arthur Worley. She made a list of Ophelia's wounds, the disheveled clothing, and of the specific bones that had been broken, indicating the true cause of death. Sav's counsel, when she explained her misgivings to him last night, had been to proceed with Worley as planned. Sav was sure Sheriff Morgan would be present for his sister-in-law's wake this afternoon. He would accompany her when she met with him afterward.

In his office, Worley sat behind his desk, one neatly clad forearm resting on the surface while he regarded Carrie without blinking. Her list lay between them. She insisted Worley listen to her entire presentation before he said a word.

"So, I believe," she concluded, "that while Ophelia met an untimely end, it may not have been the result of a carriage accident on rutted roads. I believe Germond abused his wife, then choked her. Perhaps his actions were not intended, but his brutality is undeniable. It's all over her body. I'm sure of what I saw." She stilled her fingers, which had been waging a sweaty battle in her lap.

Worley's expression didn't change. The lack of response and the coldness of his demeanor left Carrie squirming like a schoolgirl.

"Mr. Worley?" she pressed on. "I believe Ophelia was not killed by accident. I believe she was murdered."

Worley unfolded himself and got up from his chair. "I understand what you have said, Mrs. Lisbon." He picked up a thin book from his desk, a book

CHAPTER EIGHT

Carrie recognized immediately, and in that instant, knew the tack Worley was about to take.

"I reviewed the *Association of American Funeral Directors Index* last evening. There were several women noted in the directory. There is no Carrie Lisbon listed. Have you misrepresented yourself in any way, Mrs. Lisbon?"

Carrie drew a great breath through her nose. She stood and straightened her spine. *This hasn't happened in a long time.* Wordlessly she stepped close to Worley and put her hand out for the book. She thumbed through it decisively and, in a tight voice, explained herself.

"My mother's maiden name was Sophia Mae Carlin. My Christian name is Carlin Sophia. You'll find my registration under my original surname: Carlin S. Shay. Or, you could just ask to see my certificate!"

She shoved the book back at Worley, the page that bore her name flapping toward the officious man. Mortuary services were now a recognized profession, and she and her husband had always been pleased to be part of its standardization. It didn't hurt to have access to the names of other registrants, new admissions, and colleges that offered coursework for their certifications. The book served as a proud admission to her profession.

Worley inclined his head and closed the book. "My apologies, Mrs. Lisbon. I need to maintain integrity for my clients as well as for my profession. I'm sure you understand."

Worley had moved silently and now stood straight as a ruler behind his desk. "And while I understand what you've just described, Mrs. Lisbon, I am unable to discern if you come to this grievous accusation as a result of a widow's distress or as the product of an overactive imagination. I now regret my request for your assistance, and I am disinclined to permit your attendance at any future preparations, as this seems an ill-suited commission for a woman in your situation."

Her jaw dropped. Anger flamed upward; anger that she had banked into coals these last few weeks. Anger about Phee's death that still smoldered. Worley's insults fanned that spark like a blacksmith's bellows. She jumped to her feet.

"Mr. Worley. You're not speaking to a novice. I made myself quite clear about Ophelia's wounds and her physical state. You could, at the very least, consider what I found! You could, at the very least, consider another look at her body. You can see for yourself that her death is unnatural." She leaned toward Worley, pointing a finger, breaching the wall of propriety. "Instead, you malign my professional standing. You insult my intelligence *and* my personal grief. You astound *me* with *your* ignorance!" She stabbed her finger at the man, who responded with a satisfying expression of surprise. She railed on.

"And don't attempt to pass me off as incompetent! I have just as many years in this business as you! Come to think of it, you could never have covered the abrasions on Ophelia's face as well as I did. Take your own damn mortuary pictures! You're disinclined to ask for my services again? I wouldn't think of accepting! Good day to you!"

Carrie spun and hurled herself out of the office, barely avoiding a collision with Marta and an elderly woman who eavesdropped just outside the door. "Good day to you, Mrs. Worley," she fumed, sweeping by the pallid woman. She flew to the parlor, where the light was just perfect for a photograph, snatched the camera off its tripod, cranked it back into its case, and hauled both cumbersome pieces out the front door.

She met her uncle outside, where his raised eyebrows and twitching fingers indicated he overheard her shouting. He took the tripod from Carrie and hurried after her.

"Overactive imagination," she muttered as she stomped off her anger. "I can't believe that pompous bastard! Of all the insensitive, stupid...."

The force of her tirade hustled her along Main Street. She would have outpaced Sav but for his long strides. He gazed off at the sky, keeping the heavy tripod out of the way of passersby, to whom he tipped his hat and waved a dismissive hand in response to their looks of inquiry. He followed Carrie all the way back to the house, where she finally set the camera down on the front porch, and turned to him, sweaty and breathless.

"Damn it, Uncle!" Carrie felt the prick of tears in her eyes and scowled anew in order to keep them dammed up. "How can he be so obtuse? I expected a professional colleague here. I'm so insulted!"

CHAPTER EIGHT

"Worley's a dry one..." Sav offered. But Carrie mashed his words under her continued rant.

"I worked for years. *Years!* I've prepared as many bodies as he has! I've kept the books, I've kept the ledgers, I've led the funerals. That pompous... skinny...*wretched...ass!*"

Sav opened the front door and ushered her in. "I'll get the equipment in a moment, Carrie. Let's get a cool drink and think about this."

Cold water, and a colder cloth swabbed over her face and neck, calmed her. "What should I do now?" she asked.

"You still have your observations. Sheriff Morgan will still need to hear about it. That much hasn't changed. You developed your photograph last night. Did it turn out all right? Can you see the, uh...?" Sav made a circular motion with his hand.

Earlier in the week, Carrie and Bale had cleaned up Sav's cellar and furnished the space with new shelving and a slender developing table. Carrie joked the new trestle could handle the process of developing photographic images, or a body if necessary. Sav looked up sharply from his coffee and paper, alarmed at this potential, while Carrie and Bale had a good laugh.

"Yes, the strangulation bruises are visible in the picture," Carrie said.

"So," Sav said and ticked off points on his elegant fingers. "You have experience with this sort of injury, from your work in Nanuet. Ophelia's clothing was incomplete for an evening ride. You have photographs of the injuries. You think Germond dressed her, as evidenced by her twisted clothing. But his mistake was forgetting that no proper lady would go for a ride without her jacket."

"Or her gloves and hat."

"There may be more, I'm afraid," Sav said as another long finger went up. "I believe it's been known, *sotto voce,* that Germond was rough with Ophelia."

"Lord, what an understatement. He was brutal with her." Carrie's anger rose, and she purposefully checked it. Now was not the time for emotion; a professional always kept that in check. She and Sav had to analyze their knowledge, evaluate their concerns and form their plans. "Wait. There are witnesses to his abuse? People knew about it?"

"Well, yes and no," Save hedged. "There were rumors. I felt Ophelia wasn't happy in her marriage—no—I take that back. I knew she wasn't... well, 'taken care of,' so to speak. I didn't think Germond treated her the way a man ought to treat his wife."

Carrie narrowed her eyes. "To say the least, given what we know now! Did you know, uncle?"

"I witnessed him strike her, about a year ago."

"Oh, no! Did you say anything?"

"I spoke to Sheriff Morgan, as an aside. I didn't make a formal complaint. The complainant would do so, not the witness. Having imparted the information, I felt Del Morgan would intervene, at least as an older brother."

"Good lord. The sheriff knew?" Her hopes of an investigation fell.

"He knew about Germond striking Ophelia, at least. I can't say that he knew the extent of things."

"What about her family? Marta said they live on...what street?"

"Piccolo Street. We haven't strolled up there yet. The Grants own a corner lot; it's lovely."

"I have no doubt. But, surely, they'd be concerned about Ophelia's happiness and her well-being. Did they know?"

"I can't say for sure, niece. I don't run in their circle. I know *of* them. We have a passing acquaintance, but I'm not privy to their intrigues. It may be that a young bride and her mother or her sisters talk about these things as...well, as a new marriage progresses?"

Carrie agreed that was certainly true, although she lacked that benefit. Her mother was gone by the time she was three; there were no siblings. The best she had were elderly aunts on her father's side, whose chastity avoided any discussion about bedchamber activity. Having been ousted from most girlish circles as a result of her father's vocation and her association with it, Carrie also lacked teatime contemporaries who might have offered whispers of commiseration, advice, or tantalizing references to their own sexual escapades.

"What about Marta?" Sav asked. "She seemed to have some knowledge of Ophelia."

CHAPTER EIGHT

Carrie thought for a moment, thinking about her encounter with Worley's housemaid. "She said she knew Ophelia and was sorry she was dead, of course. Wait, there was something else. When I walked into the kitchen yesterday, I saw Marta before she saw me. She had a profound look on her face. It struck me as…I don't know…unusual, not as if she were grieving, but as if she were worried about another problem entirely."

Carrie plumbed the depths of her memory while Sav waited. She looked up at him, pointing a finger. "She looked frightened. Scared to death, not grieving. I'm sure of it."

Sav stood, looking pensive. "I believe Germond Morgan may have had designs on Marta. He has the demeanor of a cad, I'm afraid. Marta may have seen him for what he was and rejected him. Germond was not kind to Marta after that."

"You're right about him, Uncle. He leered at me at the church picnic. It was most uncomfortable. Ophelia was right there next to him."

Sav's face reddened, but Carrie couldn't tell if embarrassment or anger about Germond Morgan's behavior colored his cheeks.

"I'm not looking forward to seeing him again." Carrie sighed. "I had plans to attend Ophelia's wake this afternoon, but I'm afraid I've burned that bridge."

"Nonsense. I intend to go, and you'll be my guest," Sav said, recovering his buoyant demeanor. "Worley didn't tell you to never set foot on his property, now, did he? And I haven't seen your best work!" Sav suppressed a mock shiver, as he grinned mischievously. Then he sobered. "We have to meet with Sheriff Morgan quite soon, too, I'm afraid. If there is to be an inquiry, Ophelia can't be buried until he's seen her."

Chapter Nine

A long line of callers attending the wake of Ophelia Grant Morgan kept the door of the funeral parlor open for hours. Sav, at Carrie's side, maintained a quiet monologue, murmuring a who's-who list as they made their way inside. Women dressed in black veils, muffled sobs with lace kerchiefs; their men stood in a solemn row, accepting condolences. Several elders sat in fussy, velvet chairs wearing the same black, the same grief.

Ophelia lay in a bed of plumped white silk, her hands posed one over the other, her cheekbones dusted with blush. A high, lacy collar concealed her death wounds. Wreaths of flowers surrounded her casket; carnations ("I'll never forget you") sprayed upward from baskets draped with ivy ("wedded love"). A picture from her finishing school graduation nestled in an elegant spray of white chrysanthemums ("truth") and palm leaves ("victory").

She was not to be interred until the following day, when her grave was complete and the family was able to recover from the trials of the wake. Carrie thought unkindly about Digger Louis and wondered if all the burials in Hope Bridge were scheduled according to his sobriety.

Germond Morgan stood near his wife's casket, his shoulders back, his head lowered, wearing an expression of bereavement blended with guilt. He took the hands that were offered him and bent to receive matronly pecks of condolence. Carrie noticed his formal clothes were fashionable; a libertine *would* fancy himself up with the latest styles. The same cologne that suffused Ophelia's clothing the day Carrie prepared her wafted from Germond's direction.

CHAPTER NINE

Next to the grieving husband stood an equally tall man with a stern expression. He stood tensely, wearing a dark vest and coat, white shirt and collar. His hair was short, the color of dry pebbles. When he shook hands, the edge of a silvery badge emerged from behind his coat. The hazel-gray eyes scanned the room, taking in the sympathies of well-wishers, but avoiding the younger brother beside him.

The Sheriff of Duncan County kept his face neutral, but Carrie thought he masked anger. An aversion between the two men, evidenced by their purposeful distance apart, told a story: *he isn't fond of his brother.* With this observation, Carrie thought, hopeful again, she might rely on the sheriff's neutrality regarding an investigation.

A ghost of a smile crossed his face as Sheriff Morgan bent to accept the hand of an elderly woman. Carrie felt a blow to her gut. Phee's cheek dimpled like that. *Damn it,* she thought, *I will not fasten my husband's face on any man!* She looked away from Morgan and continued observing the people in the room.

Ophelia's family stood on the other side of the casket. Animosity crackled in the air between her people and Germond. Kerchiefs fluttered across the faces of the women hiding their tears, but not their darting looks of hatred. Accustomed to the wailing of the bereaved, Carrie noted an angry edge to the cries of grief. *Did they know? Did they not try to help her?*

As the line moved closer, Carrie was repulsed by the idea of meeting Germond and touching him with any expression of condolence. She had seen the evidence of his abusive conduct on his poor wife's body; she had been subjected to his lecherous perusal. She smelled his cologne over the heavy scent of flowers, crowded bodies, and perfume. When Worley stepped close and asked her for a quiet word, she stepped out of the line, grateful to be spared the encounter.

"The sheriff has asked about the facts of Miss Ophelia's death, Mrs. Lisbon," Worley said without the slightest inflection. "I gave him my accounting of the event." Worley looked off across the crowded room, seeking to postpone, even for a moment, a distasteful task. "He'd like to have a word with you, since your impressions about Ophelia's death are at odds with mine."

Carrie suppressed a smile. She worked hard to keep the triumph from her whispered response. "I'd be more than happy to oblige, Mr. Worley. We'll use your office, right after the wake."

Worley worked equally hard to minimize the contempt on his face. He nodded curtly and turned to receive another mourner. A plump woman with tight curls and an overflowing bow on her chest reached for Carrie's hand instead.

"Oh, she looks lovely!" the woman said, clutching Carrie with gloved hands and pulling her close. "I'm Ina Barnstable. I write the Hope Bridge correspondence column for the *Duncan Herald*," she whispered quickly. "You're Mrs. Lisbon? I plan to write a thorough and exact account of your preparations! You did wonders for her. Everyone will want your services!"

Carrie didn't know what to say. Beside her, Worley stiffened. Mrs. Barnstable let go of Carrie's hand and nearly slapped herself with theatrical anguish. "Oh! The poor, poor thing!" she said, just loud enough to be overheard.

Chapter Ten

Sheriff Delphius Morgan paced slowly in Worley's office. He frowned intermittently. Carrie sat in one of the leather chairs next to the cold fireplace. Sav stood beside her, and demonstrated none of the usual twitching that often accompanied his discomfort. *Indeed,* Carrie observed, *it's like he's attending a lecture in an academic arena.* Arthur Worley presided over the inquiry from behind his desk, his bony elbows upright, bloodless fingers intertwined below his chin. He studied Carrie intently, as if a slight misstep on her part would give him license to pounce on her, like a mantis on prey. Evening shadows dusted the corners of the room.

"That's correct, Mr. Morgan." Carrie answered the sheriff's question in a clear voice. "Mr. Worley asked me to assist with Miss Ophelia's laying out. I came over right away."

Morgan turned to Hope Bridge's undertaker. "Why didn't Mrs. Worley do it?"

The undertaker cleared his throat. "Mrs. Worley was not up to the task, Sheriff. She's been in a delicate condition for some time now."

Morgan turned back to Carrie, apparently satisfied, but she remembered Worley told her that his wife couldn't bring herself to work on Ophelia, having been so fond of the 'lively' girl. *He lied to me!* The Reverend Borden hadn't been honest with her regarding the check she wrote to cover Suzetta's grave. Now Worley was being disingenuous with her as well. Carrie banked the discrepancy for later, focusing on Sheriff Morgan's questions.

"And you have experience laying out the dead, Mrs. Lisbon?" Morgan asked. "As a profession? Is that right?"

"Yes. My father, my husband, and I were partners for many years at our funeral home in Nanuet. I'm a certified member of the Association of American Funeral Directors, the Women's Licensed Embalmers Association, and a graduate of the Renouard School for Embalmers." Carrie resisted the urge to lean around the sheriff to glare at Worley with her declaration. She knew he heard. He'd get the point.

Morgan held a sheaf of papers. Carrie's notes. She had left them behind when she stormed out of Worley's office the other day. "Mr. Worley told me that you had some misgivings about Ophelia."

At this, Carrie did swing about to stare hard at Worley. Why hadn't Worley mentioned to *her* that he took her concerns seriously enough to let the sheriff know? Recovering from her surprise, Carrie launched into an explanation of the bruising on Ophelia's body, the residue on her undergarments, and the throttle marks on her neck. The men averted their eyes at different intervals. She blushed over the descriptions, but delivered her report with practiced professionalism.

"How do you know the marks on her neck were from someone's hands?" Morgan asked.

"I prepared the body of a woman in Nanuet with similar injuries, a few years ago. She was the victim of a deranged man who killed several women by strangulation. I remember the injuries clearly, and I saw photographs of his other victims. I've taken the liberty of sending for them so that I can support my premise if need be. I'm sure my photographs will show the same strangulation bruises on Ophelia's neck. I believe her broken neck is a result of being choked, not from a fall."

Morgan frowned again. "You took photographs of her wounds?"

"I did, yes. I have also learned that Germond was unkind to Ophelia," she offered.

The Sheriff looked at her with an expression just shy of iciness. Carrie returned the stare with as much neutrality as she could muster. *We've reached the tipping point.*

"Learned, or heard, Mrs. Lisbon?" he asked, enunciating clearly.

"Well, 'heard' would be the more accurate word."

CHAPTER TEN

"Heard from whom?"

"My uncle."

Morgan turned to Sav. "And where did you get your information, Mr. Machin?"

"I'm a frequent attendee of civic and social organizations, as you know," Sav spoke grandly. "The Temperance Society; the Christian Men's League; The Society of Scholars, The Hope Bridge Library Committee, The Methodist Cemetery Care Association." He tapped his shark fin of a nose. "The Cyrano Club, to name a few. There is invariably a period of refreshment *après fete*, which includes a great deal of chit-chat over the coffee and cakes." Sav shrugged. "People catch up on the news of others."

"You're repeating fucking gossip, is that what you're saying?" Morgan said harshly. His words hit Carrie hard. *Damn, he's chosen to protect his brother.*

Sav glanced at Carrie, then back at Morgan. "Gossip is defined as idle talk, or rumor, Delphius. Your crass insinuation, for which I insist you beg the pardon of my niece, who is here as a courtesy to you, sir, would categorize the activity as something banal. On the contrary, it's how information is passed."

Carrie reached up and covered Sav's hand, which had found its way to her shoulder. *Independence be damned,* she thought. Right now, she was glad he stood by her side.

Morgan relaxed slightly; blew out a long breath.

"My apologies, then, Mrs. Lisbon. What did you hear, Machin?"

"There seemed to be a sympathetic undercurrent when Ophelia was mentioned. When I asked about her, or engaged in a conversation with others about her health and her nuptial bliss, people averted their eyes. Comments like 'Germond can be rough' or 'she tries to make the best of it' come to my recollection. Robert Harrington, the apothecary? He said Sylvannia is always purchasing laudanum for her sister."

Morgan frowned. "That doesn't sound like rumors of abuse to me. That sounds like Ophelia wasn't happy in her marriage. Germond is a man. Men are rough. It sounds like you're jumping to conclusions."

Sav met the Sheriff's imposing stare for a moment before continuing.

"Those comments, in addition to the concerned attitudes of the speakers, are what brought me to my conclusions, Delphius. I have also made a personal observation that leads me to believe Germond treated his wife with a great deal less than respect."

"This is what you told me about last year?"

"It is." Sav's sad expression turned to Carrie and Worley as he recalled his observation for them.

"I happened by their home one evening this past winter. Their curtains were open; it was dusk. I heard Germond shouting as I passed by, and I looked up reflexively. It wasn't a deliberate infiltration of their privacy. As I said, it's a reflex to look at the cause of a commotion. I saw Germond backhand Ophelia so hard she fell down."

In silence, Morgan looked at the floor, drew another breath, then looked directly at Carrie. The dimples appeared briefly, but accompanied a grimace this time.

Carrie asked gently, "May I continue?"

At Morgan's nod, she reported her experience with the young housemaid in Nanuet, and the similarity of Ophelia's wounds. "I also believe Ophelia was dressed *after* her death. Her clothing was put on wrong. It was twisted; it would not have been comfortable; she would have rearranged her sleeves if she were alive. In addition, she wasn't wearing a jacket or gloves for the carriage ride. It's unusual for a woman to go out without either, especially at night."

"Ophelia fell out of a wagon. I would think her clothing got twisted," Morgan said.

"But the absence of a hat? Or gloves? Ophelia wouldn't take a ride at night without them. Mr. Worley said the garments were not with her when she was brought to him."

"Her hat may have been knocked off. Her things left in the carriage."

"Of course. But if she wore gloves, why were *they* taken off? Her hands weren't dirty, indicating she may have worn them...." Carrie trailed off as her mind's eye saw something else. She continued.

"Her hands weren't dirty, Mr. Morgan. If she were alive when she was

CHAPTER TEN

thrown from the carriage, she'd have tried to break her fall by putting out her hands. Like this." Carrie thrust her own hands forward to illustrate. "And if she weren't wearing gloves, her hands would have been deeply scratched, dirty and bloody. I didn't see that injury. Her hands were pristine.

"There is something else, now that I think of it. The scratch on her cheek was embedded with dirt. But there was no blood in that wound, and there was no bruising. Even a short time before death, a wound like that would have bled and developed a significant bruise."

Morgan remained silent, then he nodded and said, "Tell me what you think happened to Ophelia."

Carrie reached again for her uncle's hand. "I think Germond habitually abused his wife, and on Sunday night, he abused her again. I think he choked her until she died, then fabricated the accident as a way to cover his crime."

Sheriff Morgan didn't respond. Carrie filled the silence. "You need to see Ophelia's body."

Chapter Eleven

Behind the heavy curtains, in the formal parlor, with several lamps re-lit, Carrie gently unfastened the buttons that kept Ophelia's high collar in place and pulled open the dead girl's blouse. Morgan bent over the corpse and squinted. Worley, holding a lamp over the body, leaned in from the other side. To Carrie's eye, the bruises on the neck had faded, but retained enough shape to validate a pattern of fingers.

"See those abrasions? She scratched herself, trying to pull away the hands that were choking her." Carrie mimicked clawing at her own throat.

"May I move her head so you can get a better look?" she asked helpfully. Both men turned their faces away from Ophelia and stared down the length of the casket at Carrie.

Determined not to be intimidated, she said, "I can show you the broken bones at the base of her throat."

Morgan turned to the undertaker. "Worley?"

"Will you please demonstrate the process by which you discovered the fatal injuries, Mrs. Lisbon?" Worley asked.

"Of course. Give me your hands, Sheriff. I'll guide you to the broken bones." Carrie stepped up to Morgan, but her enthusiasm was not shared.

"I'm not inclined to become so intimate with the poor girl, Mrs. Lisbon. Just show me what you did."

"Certainly, but it's my opinion that you may not hear or feel what I can, unless you're touching her, Sheriff. Bend closer. I'll show you."

Morgan glanced again at Worley, perhaps in appeal, but did as Carrie asked. He winced as she placed her stiff arms into the casket and strapped

CHAPTER ELEVEN

her hands around Ophelia's neck.

"See how my fingers match the bruises?" she asked over her shoulder at the big man. He stood close. The pleasant scent of tobacco welled from the warmth of his body.

"And now, do you hear that minute grating sound? Those are the delicate bones in her neck that—"

"That will do, Mrs. Lisbon," Morgan said, straightening up and backing away. "I concede to the presence of strangulation marks, but I cannot discern the broken bones."

"That's why I insist you feel—"

"I will not, Mrs. Lisbon. I believe that Ophelia died of a broken neck, but your demonstration does *not* conclude that her neck was *not* broken from the fall."

"But strangulation causes neck bones to be broken at the base of the throat. In the *front*. That's where *her* bones are broken!"

"Thank you for your demonstration, Mrs. Lisbon." Morgan turned away, jerking down on his vest, and addressed Worley. "I will ask that you repair Ophelia's appearance for the last viewing tomorrow morning. We're scheduled for ten o'clock, at the church, Mr. Worley? We'll be taking her to the cemetery directly afterward?"

"That's correct, Mr. Morgan."

"I thank you, then. I'll see myself out." Morgan tipped his hat to Carrie as he left the room. Carrie did not respond to the courtesy. *Snubbed. By another professional.* She turned to help Worley reestablish Ophelia's appearance.

Worley held the lamp overhead while Carrie touched up the face powder and fussed over the repositioning of the flowers around the bier. He said not a word, but motioned for her to exit into the hallway before him, a universal courtesy, certainly, but a sign of respect all the same. Worley and Sav nodded to each other as Carrie left on her uncle's arm.

Carrie walked in silence. Sav attempted to cheer her up. "Let's see what Mrs. Woodruff brought us for dinner, shall we? A hot stew and biscuits will be the perfect restorative."

He tugged her gently in the direction of home. A slight breeze swept the night air around their faces. He tried again when she didn't respond. "I'm sure Delphius will consider what you had to say, niece. He's not an antipathetic man."

"But, uncle! If he'd just *tried* to listen to me! Why won't he investigate the way he should? Why won't people listen to me?"

"Carrie, you're a professional mortician who handles the deceased for a living. That's not a common job for a woman, nor is handling the dead a regular occurrence for most people. You asked Delphius to put his hands on his sister-in-law's body. He most likely has never touched her, even politely, when she was alive."

"I wanted the *sheriff* to examine the body of a woman who was *murdered*. I wanted him to feel the evidence."

"And you asked him to put his hands on the throat of a woman he may have cared for."

"I understand his reluctance to touch Ophelia, but good lord, we were all standing there. He had nothing to be cowardly about."

"He may be quite shaken by Ophelia's death," her uncle went on. "Perhaps he has some remorse—shame—about his delinquency in stopping Germond's abuse." Sav went on quietly. "Perhaps your enthusiasm for your work blinded you from the humanity of others?"

Carrie tightened her lips at her uncle's suggestion. She *had* been enthusiastic. Why? She had been hoping for an ally. For an affirmation of her professional opinion. She missed the equality she had enjoyed in Nanuet with her father and her husband. She scoffed to hide the hurt.

"Or, he's disregarding evidence in order to exonerate his brother!"

"I can't think that's true about Delphius. He's been an exemplary lawman for a first-timer. Hope Bridge supported his appointment after Sheriff Edwards stepped down last year, and he stands a good chance of being elected this fall. I belong to the Duncan County Sheriff's Auxiliary—"

"But has his brother ever been accused of murdering his sister-in-law?" Carrie interrupted rudely. "Has there ever been a murder for him to consider? Maybe all he's had to do around here is serve a jury summons, or round up some missing chickens!" Carrie complained with a petulance she

CHAPTER ELEVEN

immediately regretted.

"Carrie, please don't fret like this. That's not a fair assumption."

"Is it fair that my findings are dismissed out of hand by two men who represent your town's most prominent vocations? Is it fair that poor Ophelia's murderer may go unpunished because of nepotism?"

"It's *your* town, now, too," Sav corrected. "And the process is in its preliminary stages. You presented your misgivings to the Sheriff, and he heard your complaint. We have to trust in the machinations of the law."

Carrie wanted to scoff again, but her uncle's reminder of her newcomer status in Hope Bridge smothered her response. She let the sound of Sav's measured steps quell her indignation as they left the globes of gas lamps on Main and walked into the darkness of North Street.

***

A long and somber cortege of mourners, weeping and shuffling, trailed the funeral carriage as the procession wound its way to the Grant family plot in the Presbyterian cemetery the following afternoon. Sav and Carrie stood in the shade of an enormous chestnut tree whose dying upper branches poked through a pannier of still vibrant foliage. Sav murmured yet another list of townsfolk who gathered at the grave.

The Reverend Borden attended, looking interested and important next to the Presbyterian minister, a salt-and-pepper-haired man with robust cheeks, who presided over the committal service.

The Grants wore finery that not even their black clothing could hide. Diamond stick pins winked from silk cravats. Veils draped from tiny headpieces sparkling with jet beads. Yards of gauzy crinoline bounced over at least one outdated bustle. One woman wore several rings on the outside of her gloves.

Germond and Delphius Morgan stood apart from the Grants. Again, Carrie noticed Sheriff Morgan stood several feet from his brother. Sav identified Katrina Morgan, the sheriff's wife, standing beside him. A stout woman, she stood just short of her husband's shoulder. Her funeral attire consisted of a plain black skirt and blouse, a black shawl, and hat.

Ina Barnstable, with a black parasol and beaded reticule, snuffled loudly into a kerchief, but her eyes darted around, taking in the details of the scene. Carrie stifled a canny smile. *She's trying to out-mourn the mourners with that mawkish display.*

A disheveled man leaned on his shovel in the shade at the far end of the cemetery. Even from a distance, Carrie could see the grave Digger Louis had opened for Ophelia failed at precision.

She tightened her grip on Sav's arm as the symbolic clods of earth thumped onto the casket; the hollow sounds like cannon fire against her core. The same thuds had echoed up from Phee's grave not even a year ago. Sav patted her hand in sympathy. Tears spilled onto her cheeks.

Stiffened velvet scraped over the ground as the family left the graveside and retreated to their respective carriages. Ina Barnstable fervently jotted notes onto a tiny writing pad. Digger Louis shuffled from the shadows, dragging his shovel. Sav pointed to the individual Grant carriages as they were driven by; his identification of the occupants droning in Carrie's ears.

"That's Gideon Grant, Ophelia's brother and his wife Orpha, and Orpha's father who's got a palsy from his service in the war...."

A lightweight barouche, driven by a liveried man handling a pair of chestnut mares, carried the three Grant women. Carrie remembered them all from Worley's viewing room. Grief spared them no mercy again today.

"That's Mrs. Rowena Grant," Sav said. "Ophelia is buried next to her father. He passed away two years ago. He served in the One Thirty-Fourth."

"And that's Ada, the eldest sister." Sav referred to a young woman who had brushed back her veil, revealing dark hair and a face set in anger. "She's a lovely girl, but a bit unbalanced, I'm afraid. She's had to be sent away to recover her nerves a few times."

"That's Sylvannia Grant Clarke, Rowena's second eldest daughter," Sav resumed, gesturing to the young woman on the far side of the carriage seat. Her features were so unremarkable, Carrie had the impression of empty clothing held up by a shadow. She remembered Sylvannia holding Ophelia's hand, while her mother and older sister threw themselves on Ophelia's dead

CHAPTER ELEVEN

body. Sylvannia was the woman who had looked at her so malevolently at the picnic.

"I always thought there was some rivalry between them," Sav continued. "Sylvannia's husband is Peter Clarke. He travels extensively. I'm sure he'd be here if he could. He's a thin, meager man. Sylvannia is known as a recluse, but she was devoted to her baby sister. She spent a lot of time helping Ophelia remodel that heap of a house Germond bought."

"And buying her laudanum," Carrie murmured. Sylvannia must have known about Ophelia's abuse and could do nothing for her little sister but provide the means to blur the pain.

Chapter Twelve

Carrie explored Hope Bridge the following day. Sav declined to accompany her, opting instead to take lunch with the village mayor, who was fond of reflecting on his glory days over a tipple of cherry cordial at the Chester Inn. Sav would accommodate the man's habits, listen to his accolades, and obtain his signature on the library charter application.

The scents of Hope Bridge were fresh, and agreeable. Grass, lilacs, warm earth and horse dung were pleasant. Nanuet's streets may have been smooth, but they smelled of gas fumes, household garbage, and sometimes sewage. Birds were a new joy as well. Orioles scolded from the dangling limbs of elms, swallows careened overhead, and fat bluebirds crooned from their perches on hollowed limbs. She hadn't heard birdsong like this in her former hometown; it had simply been too noisy.

The Grant's home, at the corner of Piccolo and Sharpe, commanded a corner lot high above the village. Two floors, an attic, and a steep roof gave them an extraordinary view. Even at ground level, Carrie could see the treetops on Main, and the wide sweep of Duncan Creek to the south. The Grants expressed their wealth in the usual fashion, not that she resented them for it.

A black crepe wreath on the front door struck a chord. Her memories shot back to Phee's funeral, and she tamped down her sharp feelings. She had torn a similar wreath from her front door in Nanuet, and threw it into the street in a fit of rage. A scandalous act for one in deep mourning, one that surely set the tongues of experienced mourners wagging. But nothing had mattered to her at that time. The pit of darkness she fell into had no

CHAPTER TWELVE

room for social conventions. Only guilt, agony, and rage.

Why had she left him? Why had she gotten on the train to Port Jervis? Why was her need to visit her complaining old auntie and her smelly little dog more important than Phee's offhand complaint of queasiness that morning? This torturous path of reflection was well worn.

Her tall, handsome husband had handed her up the steps. She blew kisses to him from the window, not recognizing his squint of discomfort. He waved her out of the station and stood with his hands in his pockets, tall and strong among the crowd, and she had settled into her seat, looking forward to a day's vacation, and she never saw him alive again.

Phee Lisbon died from appendicitis the next day. Carrie had rushed back to find her husband still warm, in their home, with two doctors present and surgery begun, but dead all the same. They told her she should be grateful she had not been present to witness his final stages. After three or four months, she supposed they were right.

Sav had arrived two days afterward and remained there, receiving visitors in her stead, making meals, and caring for her. In a few weeks, the pit that swallowed her lightened, but everything became irritating: children's laughter, sunlight, the smell of food, putting clothes on. There was a time when she wanted to smash Phee's things on the sidewalk, throw his watch against a wall, tear his clothes, and stomp on them. Once, she gave into the rage and tore one of his shirts before burying her face, sobbing, into his fading scent.

She agreed to reside with the aging auntie for the winter. She received the stiff, black outfits that came packaged in brown paper from the clothier uptown, who specialized in ladies' mourning wear, and her lips had curled in resentment and disgust. She regarded her new attire angrily in the mirror while her twice-widowed auntie looked on from behind. "This is how a proper widow *should* look," she coached.

She quit the black after a few months. A shameful act as well, but nothing, including the social disgrace of discarding her widow's weeds, could be worse than the agony of her loss. Sometimes the bitterness of losing Phee was so visceral, she wanted to vomit.

There came a day when she realized she had adopted a mantra, her first conscious thought each morning. *Just get up. Just get that far. Then we'll see.* In March, she saw the first red-winged blackbird of spring, and fled back to Nanuet, rushing through the house to the back yard, and found the white tulips Phee had given her on their first anniversary, poking through the dirt. After a while, she got off her knees, wiped her tears, and wrote her regrets to her aunt. Sav cheerfully agreed with her plan to sell everything, move upstate and start anew. He was eager to share his beloved home and village with her, his "intellectual equal."

Carrie saw the shingled roof of the covered bridge on the east end of town. Morbidly compelled by the decrepit structure, she approached from the west. A horse and wagon entered from the opposite end. The bridge trembled. She held her breath for this driver, much the same way she held her breath on her own death-defying trip over it.

The horses clopped rhythmically; harnesses jangled, and the driver touched his hat as he passed. She decided if the wagon made it over, she could chance it holding her weight. Enveloped in the hot, dusty interior, she ran her fingers over the rough-sawn timbers. Spots of light, reflected off the water below, flashed on the rafters. Barn swallows and phoebes chattered from their nests. Aged, fly-specked posters of last year's county fair, a livestock sale and all variety of patent medicines were plastered to the boards. She hooted with relief when she stepped off the threshold on the other side.

A collection of mismatched houses that straggled along the main road for a mile or more on the east side of the Duncan made up the secondary village of East Hope. Clotheslines and chickens fluttered in backyards. An inn with a wide porch and tall columns stood next to a five-stall carriage barn; beyond that the clanging of a hammer on iron rang from a smithy. Carrie turned and strolled a dirt road that paralleled the Duncan Creek, listening to the chuckling sound of water over rocks. She came upon the blackened outline of a burnt dwelling. The remains of a chimney, soot-stained and half fallen, stood alone over the ruins. Skeletons of last year's weeds crowded close to the remainder of the fieldstone foundation. The Scuttle's old nag

CHAPTER TWELVE

dozed in the shade of a half-burnt elm, where a dingy tarp tented over a rope, sheltered the family's meager possessions. The two young boys skidded to a stop in front of her. This must be Bale's old house.

The morning after Suzetta's funeral, Bale had convinced Scuttle to have his family stay on Bale's burnt-out property in East Hope, on the condition of cleaning it up. Carrie had offered Scuttle the print she'd made of Suzetta the night before. Scuttle politely declined the simple composition of the child in her casket, with a spray of the apple blossoms across her blanket.

"If I could have a pitcher of my little girl, it wouldn't be that one," he said.

"Hello, there," Carrie smiled at the two boys. "I'm Mrs. Lisbon. You stayed at my orchard a few days ago."

They stared at her until their mother barked a summons, then dashed to her side and hid behind her skirt. Alma Scuttle stood with Sheriff Delphius Morgan.

He's rather imposing, Carrie thought, taking in his wide shoulders and long legs. His gray coat and vest were a little threadbare, but clean. His hat shaded serious eyes. He didn't have the badge pinned to his vest.

"Hello, Mrs. Scuttle," Carrie said. "How are you getting on? Hello, Mr. Morgan."

"We're well enough." The woman's speech harbored no softness.

"And Mr. Scuttle? Has he found work?"

Alma frowned harder. "He's mucking out a barn today. Fella up that way—" she jerked her chin in a vague direction "—pays him a boy's wage."

"Well, it's nearly summer. I'm sure there will be plenty to do in a week or so."

"Excuse me, Mrs. Lisbon," Morgan said quietly. "I have to ask Mrs. Scuttle about the death of her daughter. I'm glad you've arrived. It's difficult for her to talk about it."

"Undoubtedly, Mr. Morgan. Mrs. Scuttle, may I stay with you while Mr. Morgan asks his questions?" Carrie said, recognizing Morgan's hint for assistance.

"I didn't wanna come here," Alma protested. "I told Wyatt, no good would come from a town what's got a sinful reputation."

"What reputation?" Morgan asked.

"The fellas we meet on the road; them that pass the news about work. They said there are women of ill repute here. We don't need that kind of smut with the children."

Carrie and Morgan glanced at each other. Morgan said, "Mrs. Scuttle, I'm sure there's no—"

"But we come here anyway!" Alma's anger turned ragged with grief. "Wyatt was sure about work! If we'd stayed over in Remus, we wouldn't have lost Suzetta!"

"Oh, Mrs. Scuttle. I'm so sorry for your loss. Truly I am," Carrie stretched her hands toward the woman, but Alma backed away. She turned, waving Carrie and Morgan off with a grimace. She and the boys ran to where the horse stood and wedged themselves behind the animal, their faces and their sorrow hidden behind their only valuable possession. Carrie turned to Morgan.

"Perhaps another time might be better for Mrs. Scuttle, Sheriff."

Morgan nodded; his eyes, a touch kinder now, considered the grieving family for a moment more. He gestured toward the edge of the property, and he and Carrie walked away from the ruins.

"Thank you for your kindness with that family, Mrs. Lisbon," he said. "I'm sure I have enough to complete my inquiry. No one can falsify that kind of grief. It looks like they'll settle at Tom Bale's place for a while. I can talk to Scuttle in a few days, if need be."

They reached the intersection. The bridge to their left and East Hope on the right. Carrie stopped, uncertain about her role now that Alma Scuttle was no longer the object of their attention. Morgan had been curt the last time they'd met. He had lost a loved one a few days after the Scuttles lost Suzetta. He attended his sister-in-law's funeral yesterday. Was he grieving, or investigating? If she stepped closer, would she smell his warm scent again? And where had that sentiment come from? His brother was an ogling brute, and handsome or not, this man was an imposing doubter. She raised her chin.

"I appreciate your sentiments, Mr. Morgan. I don't enjoy seeing a woman

CHAPTER TWELVE

in distress. I need to get back to town. Is there anything else I can offer to help your inquiries?"

Morgan's hazel-gray eyes leveled on her, considering. "No, not at the moment, Mrs. Lisbon. Good day." He turned and walked toward the inn and carriage house.

Carrie stepped back onto the bridge. This time, her thoughts kept her from worrying about its imminent collapse. Rejection wasn't a new experience. But it still hurt. Intuitively, she knew a grieving family sometimes spurned the kindness of others. Hadn't she? She had no choice but to let the Scuttles grieve as only they knew how. Wasn't she still grieving?

Morgan's rejection stung as well. She wanted to bore into that monolith and make him accept her evidence, her conclusions, and agree with her about Ophelia's death. She'd never had to prove herself to her father or her husband. Nanuet was far away now. Her importance in Hope Bridge was slim, but she'd moved here to begin anew, to establish herself as a professional. *And damn it, I'm right about Ophelia!*

She felt her resolve return as she walked back over the bridge. Morgan might be imposing; Worley might be condescending, but her competence was not to be denied.

She emerged from the bridge into harsh sunlight, and mounted the steps to Bookhoudt's Dry Goods. She pulled open the door and collided with Marta, who was juggling paper-wrapped bundles.

"Oops! Hello, Marta. How are you today?"

"I'm well, Mrs. Lisbon. And you?" Marta gave the street a quick survey in both directions.

"Just fine, thank you. Are you in a hurry?"

"I need to get these packages home to Mrs. Worley." Marta pronounced the word "pah-kages." Carrie's smile deepened. She enjoyed the young woman's Irish accent.

"She's ordered them special, and she's a bit edgy about getting them. The chemist is usually stocked with her preferred tonic, but he's been cleaned out," Marta continued.

"Chemist?"

Marta laughed. "You call him a druggist." Her accent made the word "droo-gist."

"Oh! I'll remember that," said Carrie. "How about if I walk with you? I wanted to speak with you about a small matter, if you'll allow."

Marta's expression relaxed. A tenseness that Carrie hadn't noticed until the young woman let down her shoulders slipped away.

"Certainly. But, I can't tarry," Marta said and shifted the bundles under her arms so that she could link elbows with Carrie. Carrie recognized the pungent whiff of herbs from the packages.

"By all means, I won't keep you. May I help you with your things?"

"No, I'll manage. What can I do for you, Mrs. Lisbon?"

"I'm in need of a confederate. Another woman who'll take my arm and incline her head with mine. There are so many intricacies to this town, and I don't know the ins and outs. Can I ask you about the people here?"

"Certainly, Mrs. Lisbon," Marta said. "I'm happy to help."

"Please, call me Carrie."

Marta snuggled her arm in closely. "Of course, um, Carrie. That would be fine."

"I've been across the bridge just now, and I believe I saw the remnants of Thomas's house. It was burned down last year?"

"Yes, ma'am. That was his place. He's so stubborn, he won't leave town, and he won't clean up the pile either. I think he wants people to remember what happened. He's a real pisser, that one. Oh! Excuse me!"

Carrie laughed. "I've heard that one before, Marta. And poor Ophelia, too. That's a tragedy, now, isn't it?" Although her words were meant as a segue into the questions she wanted to ask about Mr. and Mrs. Worley, Carrie was surprised at Marta's immediate stiffening.

"Have I upset you? Marta, what's the matter?"

"Mrs. Lis…Carrie. I…well, I might as well tell you, since you'll need to know the lay of the land, as you said. I'm actually so glad you can accompany me home."

"Why? What is it, Marta?"

"Well, I don't want to speak ill of the bereaved…."

CHAPTER TWELVE

Carrie pressed Marta's arm with her own. Clearly, Marta had behaved nervously when she came out of the store. She had hedged just now about something regarding Ophelia, and something more: she seemed genuinely frightened. "Please, go ahead," she encouraged.

"I don't want to bump into Germond Morgan. I saw him this past Sunday, around dinnertime. He did the same thing he'd done before. I almost dropped my basket, he startled me so. He hasn't done that in a long time."

"Done what?"

"Well, uh…loomed over me, in that awful way. With a look on his face, like he wanted to undress me. He made suggestions, too."

"Suggestions?"

"Jesus and Mary! You want me to say it?"

"I'm sorry, Marta," Carrie said, then rescinded her apology. "Yes. Yes, I do want you to say it."

Marta swore again, composed herself, and looked away. "He said, if I…lay with him…he'd make me scream his name."

Carrie put her hand over Marta's. Another woman might have dismissed Marta's comments as crass, or glossed them over with nervous tut-tutting, but Carrie had grown up with nothing but men to guide her. She had a long-standing practice with, and an appreciation for, the direct and no-holds-barred expressions of men.

"What a shit he is, Marta. I'm so sorry about that. Good lord. He's disgusting."

"I wish I could tell you that I wasn't scared. But, God, I was so scared," Marta's lovely lilt thickened. "I know what he does. He's tried it with me before. I don't know why. I'm not pretty. I just mind my own business. I never made eyes at him. Ever. I hate him. I always try never to look at him. I cross the street when he comes by."

"I understand, Marta. I do. Germond isn't a pleasant man."

"Remember when you saw me, on Monday? In the kitchen? You asked about me. I couldn't help myself. I kept thinking that he killed Ophelia. He killed her! And now, he's going to come after me." Marta shuddered with the effort of suppressing her emotions. Carrie kept silent. Marta recovered with a deep breath and continued.

"A few years back, before he married Ophelia, Germond tried to, well… have his way with me. He was always standing around when I ran errands for the Worleys. Always behind some tree, watching me. Always hanging on a post when I got to the store, or when I come out. He looked me up and down, all the time. Made me feel naked."

"Did you tell anyone? Have Mrs. Worley accompany you? Or a friend?"

"What kind of housemaid would I be if I needed the missus to go with me to run errands? My brothers have families. They work; no one is around. Besides, he's the sheriff's brother," she added bitterly. "What would happen if I complained?"

Carrie saw the point. Aggressive men accosting women were commonplace. She remembered witnessing the saucy retort of a woman in Nanuet who had turned to a whistling man and said, "You'd be much more likable, if not for that hole in your face!" The man stopped immediately, several passersby had snickered, and the woman had tossed her head and walked on. Carrie had secretly applauded her; grateful the fearless woman had cleared the way for Carrie to go by.

"Then, Germond got worse," Marta said quietly with her head bowed. "He'd get close and touch me, across my breasts; he'd brush up against my thigh. I'm not thick, Carrie. I know what he was doing. I'd just keep going, only faster.

"Then one day, he grabbed me and pulled me into the alley behind the chemist's shop. I tried to scream, but he put his hand over my face. I bit him and put a knee in his…well, his…."

"I get it," Carrie concluded for her. "Did you complain then?"

"No, I figured he got the message." Marta cringed with shame. "The next thing I know, Germond went around telling everyone that I was nothing but an Irish whore, and that he couldn't keep me off him. The bastard! I had to beg for my job with the Worleys. Beg! I still can't look them in the face sometimes. I think they may believe some of it. I know a lot of folks looked at me differently after that. And now his wife is dead. He'll start up again."

"My uncle Sav said Germond was not kind to you. I see what he meant."

CHAPTER TWELVE

"Your uncle never believed the stories. He still holds the door for me. He's the only gentleman left in town, I'm sure! Well, him and Thomas."

"I'm glad that uncle Sav has Thomas living with him now. He's such a decent and caring man to me."

"Oh, he is!" Marta gushed. "To most of us. What they did to him and the others last year was just horrible."

"Marta, will you tell the Sheriff about Germond's behavior now? I'll go with you. I think this needs to be told. Germond may have killed Ophelia and harassed you right afterward. There can be no doubt he's a rake. His poor wife took the brunt of his cruelty."

"I just want him to leave me alone. I just want him to go away and leave me alone."

"I think if you say something, he'll go away. He might even get hanged."

Marta stopped and swung around to regard Carrie with wide eyes.

"Well, bollocks!" Marta said, expressing the same comfort with masculine vocabulary. "I don't know. That's awful too!"

"I don't think so," Carrie said bluntly, resuming their progress. "You didn't see what I saw."

Chapter Thirteen

Carrie checked the post office, anxious about the Freed file that should have arrived by now. No summons from Morgan didn't help her thwarted feelings, either. After another fruitless visit, Carrie pulled shut the post office door in a pique, jangling the bell with more force than necessary. She clenched a fist and stepped onto the deserted boardwalk, heading back toward home. Storm clouds boiled up in the west. Dust blew restlessly straight down Main Street's empty corridor. The unusual afternoon heat drove people into the coolness of their homes and shady yards.

Suddenly Germond Morgan stood in her way.

"Afternoon, Mrs. Lisbon," he drawled, eyeing her bosom.

"Mr. Morgan. Good afternoon," Carrie said, and felt her lips tighten with distaste. While Germond regarded her with a nasty leer, she offered a frail commiseration. "I don't believe I've expressed my condolences to you."

"No, you didn't," Germond leaned over her. His heavy cologne wafted up through his sweat-stained shirt and paisley tie. He had taken off the black band from the brim of his rakish hat; his perfunctory three days of mourning complete. His teeth stank of rot, and the Sen-Sen tablets he ate to try to cover it. He said languidly. "Any way you can make that up to me?"

Fear and revulsion squirmed in her chest so strongly, Carrie put a hand to her neckline. She sidestepped around him. "No. If you'll excuse me, Mr. Morgan. Good day."

"I can wait," Germond drawled after her and smacked his lips. Carrie threw a glare over her shoulder and caught him watching her buttocks.

CHAPTER THIRTEEN

With burning cheeks, she couldn't think of a single rebuttal. On the other hand, responding to his suggestive taunts would only enflame him more. In addition, she felt like Marta must have felt: pursued, threatened, and shamed.

She saw Bale striding down Main Street, carrying his heavy toolbox, heading toward her. She hailed him anxiously and, glancing back, saw Germond turning away. His face had sobered in that instant. *So,* Carrie thought, *he's only a wolf when women are alone.* He doesn't have the courage to play the leering rake when real gentlemen are nearby. Thomas Bale was both a gentleman and a friend of her family. She had come to know him as a stalwart since she'd arrived. She would be able to count on his protection.

I need protection? When she left Nanuet, she had dearly wanted to be independent and savvy, accepted, and in a position to prosper in her own pursuits. But in this town, she had been marginalized by Worley, a man of her own profession, by countless biddies who postured like a coop of hens over a new bird, by the sheriff who not only rejected her expertise, but seemed appalled by it. Now, she was threatened by the town lecher. She had to rely on the social standing and craftiness of her uncle on more than one occasion, and now, she'd practically squealed for Thomas Bale's aid.

Bale, watching Germond's retreating form, approached Carrie with an easy gait. "Any troubles, Miss Carrie?" His alert eyes matched the concern in his voice. Carrie's heart slowed.

"No, I'm fine. Germond Morgan said something unpleasant to me just now."

Bale's jaw tightened considerably as he offered his elbow. "Please, let me escort you home." Carrie took his arm. They had gone only a few steps when someone called to her.

Delphius Morgan and his brother Germond stood on the stoop of Clevinger's Grocery. The sheriff beckoned Carrie with a stern face and a flick of his hand. She hesitated. "What does he want?" she whispered to Bale.

"Whatever it is, I'm not leaving you alone," he spoke quietly.

"Oh, thank you, Thomas," she said swiftly. "Yes, please come with me."

They retraced their steps and stopped before the county sheriff. Morgan stood on the top step, only a foot higher, but his position caused Carrie and Bale to have to look up to him. Morgan wore his silver badge. Where Delphius Morgan had been squeamish over Ophelia's body last Tuesday, he was hard-eyed and dauntless now. His younger brother stood behind him; his leering expression gone.

"Mrs. Lisbon," Morgan said. "I need you to come with me, please. I need the information you provided to me at Worley's the other day. I'd like to complete my inquiry."

"Exactly now, Sheriff? I was just on my way home."

"Exactly now, ma'am. We can use my office inside."

Carrie balked. She thoroughly agreed with her uncle's advice: to 'let the machinations of the law take their course.' A sheriff's summons was the law. But she had had a scare with Germond not five minutes ago, and despite Thomas Bale's presence, she still had the jitters from the intense combination of anger, fear, and humiliation. Even more so, Sheriff Morgan hadn't taken her report of the cause of Ophelia's death seriously, and now he stood side by side with his brutish brother. She wasn't certain of his integrity at all. Would he align with his brother or be objective? She stammered, torn between obeyance and self-preservation.

"Well, I suppose…um, Mr. Bale, can you tell my uncle—"

"I ain't leaving your side, Miss Carrie."

Germond's snicker was silenced by his brother's glance. Bale spoke directly to the sheriff. "I ain't leaving her side."

Morgan remained impassive. Carrie found her voice. "I insist Mr. Bale accompany me, sheriff. I am allowed to have an advocate with me. Isn't that correct? Anyone I choose?"

"Done. Let's go." Morgan turned and headed into the store.

Carrie clutched her small purse. Bale offered his elbow to her, making a show of respect for the small crowd of onlookers who had been immobilized by the spectacle. Bale grabbed a young boy by the arm and whispered fiercely into his ear. The boy took off running. He and Carrie followed the Morgan brothers down a short hallway to a spare room that served as the sheriff's

CHAPTER THIRTEEN

Hope Bridge office.

Germond swaggered in first. Carrie looked back wide-eyed at Bale, who positioned himself near the door. Sheriff Morgan glared at him. Bale returned his own warning look.

The room was spare: two wooden ladder-backed chairs and an old school master's desk comprised the only furniture. An American flag hung from a short staff mounted near the single window. Carrie wished it could be opened, as Germond's scent quickly filled the room. Delphius Morgan hooked his hip onto the edge of the desk and beckoned Carrie to sit. She did not.

"Mr. Morgan has accosted me shamefully in the street, just now. He made suggestive statements to me and impertinent noises. I'll not lower myself until he's seated. Only then will he be less of a threat to me."

"Did you threaten Mrs. Lisbon, Gerry?" Sheriff Morgan asked.

Germond scoffed as he seated himself with a dismissive flourish. "We bid each other good day." He wagged his head back and forth in mockery. "And she offered her condolences. Where's the threat in that?"

"You deliberately blocked my way, Mr. Morgan! Your proximity was not only irregular, it was distressing. A gentleman meets a lady's eyes, sir, when addressing such a person. You took a tour of my body while you made smacking noises! You were not, by any stretch, exchanging pleasantries!"

"Thank you, Mrs. Lisbon—" Delphius Morgan cut in.

"Do *not* interrupt me, with all due respect, Sheriff!" Carrie felt the impetuous heat of anger and the recent days' worth of frustration flowing up and out. "This man has exhibited a rudeness to me on two separate occasions. And while that's not a criminal offense, it certainly illustrates a consistency of poor character. I have it from another acquaintance that his conduct is not restricted to singular events, either. He's been ...*hounding* women! And directly *after* his poor wife's death! And since I have your attention, and the floor, I will make my formal complaint!"

After a brief silence, Sheriff Morgan held up a hand. His voice was steady, but his eyes snapped angrily. "I hear your complaint. Mrs. Lisbon. We will write it up formally in a short while." He turned to his brother. Carrie's hands trembled in rage.

"Gerry, I had a look at Ophelia's body over to Worleys after the wake. Worley was there. He confirms what Mrs. Lisbon found. Ophelia was choked to death, Germond. She had bruises on her body that looked like someone beat the hell out of her, violated her, and choked her to death. What do you have to say?"

"What the hell, Del? What are you doing, looking at my wife like that? That isn't decent!"

"I'm the fucking sheriff, Gerry," Morgan said, his face rigid. "I look at what I need to look at. Is Mrs. Lisbon right? Did you hurt Ophelia? I know you like to make yourself out to be some kind of Lothario, but Christ, did you force her?"

"I ain't saying shit with a nigger in the same room."

Morgan left the desk and advanced on Germond.

"She says he stays," he growled. "I say he stays. Now, *you* say something, Germond. Tell me what you did to Ophelia. Is Mrs. Lisbon right?"

Germond wouldn't meet his brother's eyes. His lips pressed together. His breath whistled out of his nose. Carrie held her breath.

"I didn't kill her, Del. I swear to Christ, I didn't kill her."

"You mistreated that poor girl." Morgan's face screwed into a bitter expression. He raised his hands and slammed them down in the air. "Son of a bitch, boy! She was so *little*! Why the hell would you need to beat her?"

"I'm sorry! I'm sorry! I…I just kept losing my head! She said she loved me, Del, but when it came to…you know…came to her duties, well, she was…you know, not willing! I'm her husband, right? She should be willing."

Carrie uttered a noise of disgust.

"I didn't kill her!" Germond protested again.

"She didn't fall from the carriage and die, either," Morgan said. Germond locked eyes with his older brother, then gave in.

"I found her," he muttered. "At the bottom of the steps. When I came home."

"After your harassment of Marta?" Carrie cut harshly. Germond shot an evil glance at her.

CHAPTER THIRTEEN

Del Morgan's looks grew more threatening, but his body went still. "You mean to tell me you went after another woman? On the day Ophelia died? *After you abused her?* You went looking for another woman?"

"No! I didn't go looking for her! Marta was just there. At Bookhoudt's. I just, you know, bumped into her."

"And tried to grope her!" Carrie said. "She told me what happened. She said she was afraid you'd be coming after her. And you did! You're a disgusting man!"

Germond glared at her. Carrie held a cold hand to her stomach to try to slow her breathing. She looked back at Bale. He nodded to her slowly, but his expression had hardened.

Sheriff Morgan rubbed his big hand across his forehead, his eyes closed. "What happened, Germond?"

The younger Morgan bowed his head, offering a semblance of remorse. "I had dinner at the Chester. You can ask the boys. I was there. Then, I went home. It was dark. I came in the house, and she was just laying there at the bottom of the stairs. She was cold. I could see she wasn't alive. I thought, my God, they're gonna think I killed her." He looked up at his brother.

"I got rough with her, sometimes, you know? But I'm her husband. She's supposed to do what I want. I didn't want people to think I killed her. I swear, Del, I swear. She was at the bottom of the stairs when I came home. She musta tripped or something. I swear. I didn't kill her."

"Did you choke her?" Sheriff Morgan asked.

"What? No! I didn't. I...I made her, you know...do what she was supposed to do. But I didn't choke her."

Carrie trembled all over now. Overwhelmed with pity for Ophelia, tears swarmed her eyes. Germond's confession was abhorrent. She wanted to hit him.

The elder Morgan shook his head. "You tell me that you violated your own wife, Gerry. That you beat her and made her submit to you. That you harassed another woman for the same favors. On the same fucking day. But, you swear to God, you didn't kill her. What the hell am I supposed to believe from a man like you?"

Abruptly, the door burst open and slammed against the wall. Sav Machin strode in, his flaring hair scraped the top of the door frame, and his long arm spanned the width of the opening. He was at Carrie's side in two strides.

"Delphius! You can't interview Carrie without me. I insist this stop at once!"

"In a minute, Machin," Morgan barked back.

"Now, Sheriff! You can't have her in here without me!" Sav insisted. In the short hallway between the office and the mercantile, an eager crowd leaned in.

Delphius Morgan didn't move. "Shut it," he said quietly. Bale reached over and closed the door. Sav put an arm around Carrie's trembling shoulders. Morgan turned back to his brother.

"Del, I'm sorry," Germond resumed his plea. "It wasn't like that. It wasn't so bad. I swear I didn't kill her. I found her!"

"What then?" Morgan said in a voice devoid of expression.

Germond cast about the room. "I put her shoes on, and I carried her out to the carriage. I hitched the mare and drove out to Shun Pike, then up to Sloane Hollow. That road is so bad."

He looked down at the floor. Maybe something like shame finally quieted his voice. Carrie's icy fingers had crept up to cover her mouth and nose; her eyes were wide with horror.

"I...threw her over the side, so I could make it look like she fell out. Then I loaded her back up and went right to Worley's."

Carrie's breath roared under her cupped fingers. Presently, Delphius Morgan said quietly to his little brother, "Get out of my sight Germond. Go to your house and stay there until I come for you. Get the fuck out of my sight."

Germond rose and shuffled out in his dandy clothes, trailing his overripe cologne. Carrie shrank away from him as he passed, as though he were the Grim Reaper himself.

Chapter Fourteen

They downed sherry and refilled their glasses. Carrie sat by the fire with a shawl around her shoulders. The rainstorm that had threatened all day broke over Hope Bridge, and her shock, compounded with the chill of wet weather, embedded ice in her bones. Bale added more wood to the fire and topped off their glasses.

"I got the Stewart boy to run and get Sav before we went in. My God, what a thing!" He shook his head in disbelief.

"You were singularly brave, Carrie," Sav said, toasting her. "The sheriff is a decent man, and a just servant. He'll not let Germond go unpunished. For his treatment of poor Ophelia, and for you."

Carrie tightened her shawl and pulled her feet up and under herself. After the interview, Sav had wrapped a protective arm tightly around her shoulders, and Bale had pushed through the crowd ahead of them. They escorted her from the sheriff's small office, through the staring, whispering cluster of spectators, and all the way home. Independence be damned, she had conceded, with the two men on each side of her. She wasn't in any condition to assert herself that afternoon.

"I'm so appalled, Uncle. What a horrible thing to do. What a horrible man."

"Do you believe him?" Bale asked them both.

Carrie looked into the fire, considering. "I found signs of abuse on Ophelia that I've seen before. I've prepared the bodies of women who met similar fates." She looked sadly at her uncle and his friend. "Injuries from that kind of assault are not easily mistaken.

"Germond confessed to abusing Ophelia, and I can confirm his actions from the evidence I found. I can also swear she was strangled. I *knew* the cause of Ophelia's death was falsified, and Germond just admitted to that." Carrie shuddered, remembering Germond's description of heaving the girl's body out of a wagon. "He swears he didn't kill her, but he's such an awful man, I can't believe he *didn't* choke her during his assault. What do you think, uncle?"

"If I were on the jury, and I may be, I'd have him hanged," Sav said quietly. "There is no reason to consider him innocent of her death. He should hang for his interference with her body alone."

While they thought about that, Carrie held out her glass, and Bale refilled it.

"He said he put on her shoes, didn't he?" Carrie asked. "He said he found her at the bottom of the stairs and decided people would think he killed her, so he put shoes on her and put her in the wagon."

Sav and Bale nodded in agreement. They waited for more.

"Why *only her shoes?* Was she already dressed? Germond didn't say 'I put clothes on her' or 'I got her dressed.' He said he only put on her shoes."

Bale shrugged. Sav waited.

"She was completely dressed when I saw her. She wore a shift, a corset, a blouse, bloomers, stockings, and a skirt. Corsets are uncomfortable. Women need help tying them up. And Ophelia's corset laced up in the front, not the back. I can't imagine her having the strength to pull it tight."

"Maybe she didn't lace it up tightly," Sav said. "Didn't you say it was askew? If it was loose, it…" he waved his hands about, "…lost its place when she was thrown from the wagon."

"But her sleeves were twisted too," Carrie pointed out. "Long sleeves fit snugly. They're an annoyance when they're twisted. And she hadn't washed herself. She was severely bruised. She must have been in pain. I can't imagine her putting on all those clothes after being so badly hurt." While Carrie finished dispensing this information, both men in the room looked down and away.

Carrie recognized the effect of her unadulterated report. "My apologies,

CHAPTER FOURTEEN

Uncle. Thomas. I'm puzzled, that's all. I'm sorry I made it awkward. I've abandoned my humanity in favor of—how did you say it, Uncle? My enthusiasm."

Sav toasted Carrie with raised eyebrows and an anxious show of teeth. "My intellectual equal. Come what may." He tossed back his sherry and continued with the puzzle. "Her clothes could have become twisted as a result of her fall, right?"

"Absolutely."

"And Germond's attempt to hide her death would explain the absence of hat and jacket and gloves?"

"Yes, that's true too."

"What else are you concerned with? Germond seems to be simply lying about the actual killing of Ophelia."

"I don't think Germond dressed her. He said he only put on her shoes, meaning she was completely dressed when he found her. If that's the case, then either she dressed herself or someone else did."

"That's a stretch, Carrie. It's simply that Germond is lying about choking her. He violated her, he choked her, he dressed her—sloppily—and threw her out of the carriage."

"But he accosted Marta that afternoon, as well. When did he have time to do all that? Dressing a deceased person actually takes a lot of time. And two people." Carrie put her glass on the table and stood, her enthusiasm revived. "Let me show you. Take off your coat, uncle."

Sav pulled off his lightweight jacket and handed it over. Carrie had him sit back down. "When a live person is assisted with clothing—here, put out your arm—" She bunched up the coat sleeve and invited Sav to insert his hand. He held his arm stiffly, turning it to maintain the sleeve's comfortable fit as Carrie slid it up his arm. "They involuntarily offer cooperation. Like so.

"But a dead person's arms and legs just push away from this force. Undertakers need one person to pull the garment from one end, and another person to pull the limbs from the other. All the clothing needs endless straightening, as well. Ophelia's garments were twisted. It looked like the efforts of an inexperienced mortician." She smiled at the impression her expertise had garnered and asked another question.

"Would Germond have taken all that time and effort to dress his wife? If I had just strangled her and needed to get rid of the body, I'd just pull a shift over her head and be done with it."

Sav and Bale regarded her in shock.

"And another thing," she went on. "Marta said she was at Bookhoudt's around dinnertime. Germond and Ophelia were at the picnic. The picnic lasted until three o'clock. Would Germond have had time to assault his wife, kill her, dress her and, what? Leave her at the bottom of the stairs while he had a nice dinner and accosted Marta?"

Sav raised his glass to her again. "You've just laid out a plausible scenario, niece. If you were a prosecutor, you'd have a conviction."

"I don't know if he lied about anything," Bale said cautiously. "He's nothing but stupid. It would be just like him to think a fall from a wagon was a better accident than a fall down the stairs. Germond broke pretty quick under his brother's questions. He's afraid of his brother. I think he told the truth. He found her, dead and dressed, at the bottom of the stairs. But, I think you're right, too, Miss Carrie. Germond would have said he dressed her, not just put on her shoes."

"If we believe Germond, he's only guilty of assaulting her and desecrating her body," Carrie said. "That leaves her strangulation unaccounted for and all the clothing unexplained."

Sav disagreed. "No. Germond killed her, dressed her, and tried to hide it with the accident."

"Why didn't he hide her body?" Carrie asked. "Why go through the charade?"

"He stands to gain an inheritance, I'd imagine," Sav said. "I believe he courted Ophelia and wed her for the family fortunes. If she simply disappeared, Germond would have had to wait years for her to be declared dead before he inherited. And, of course, there'd be a search; he'd be suspected of doing away with her until the end of his days."

Carrie frowned sadly. "She was a golden goose."

CHAPTER FOURTEEN

In the speculative quiet, while the rain tapped angrily at their windows, Bale refilled their glasses.

Chapter Fifteen

The storm rained heavily that night, then turned violent the next day. Sav ensconced himself upstairs with his library and pipe. Carrie found countless tasks to complete, specifically the final organizing of her suite and belongings. Bale returned from errands, rain sheeting off his oilcloth cape, with Bill Bemis's package held dry and secure under his arm. Glue smeared the seals, and an irreverent drawing of a tiny heart adorned Carrie's name.

With lifted spirits, Carrie found scissors in her newly ordered secretary and carefully snipped open the mailing paper. She and Bale sorted stiff photographs and well-thumbed documents from the bundle. They browsed through the pile at the kitchen table well into the night.

"Miss Carrie, I'm amazed at your fortitude. You're looking at dead people and reading detailed descriptions of how they died. Aren't you the least bit unsettled?"

"Oh, absolutely, Thomas. For certain, these are not for the faint of heart. You're looking at them too. What do you find so fascinating?"

"I don't know if fascinating is the right word. I'm impressed with your man's reports. How he linked the similarities of each woman's death to the other. And the undertakers' reports. How they listed the injuries, and the stuff they used to embalm, and the clothes the bodies were dressed in."

"It's remarkable, isn't it? Doctors keep a day book. We morticians keep a ledger of those we prepare and the methods we use."

"And here," Bale said, holding Carrie's photograph of Ophelia's neck near one from Bill Bemis's package. "Those wounds are exactly the same."

CHAPTER FIFTEEN

Carrie nodded and said with conviction, "Yes, they are."

Bale said, "Ol' Worley told Del Morgan what you suspected about Ophelia. Art Worley is a cranky man, but he'll do you a good turn."

"I suppose," Carrie said and looked aside, still feeling that rejection. "It would have been better if he had spoken to me about my discovery, like a colleague. He told Sheriff Morgan about my concerns at Ophelia's wake. Then, he validated my findings after the interview. Both times, I was excluded."

"But both times, he agreed with your assessments."

"True. I should go and have a chat with him about that. I suppose he has done me a good turn, even if he didn't count me in on it. By the way, do you know if Mrs. Worley is well?"

"I haven't seen her about town in a while, come to think of it. Why?"

"Mr. Worley told me she couldn't bring herself to prepare Ophelia's body, but then he told the sheriff that she had been poorly and wasn't up to it."

Bale shrugged. "I think Miss Marta would know more about Mrs. Worley than I. She's kept house for them for about three years now."

Carrie let it go. Since they were on the subject of town intrigue, Carrie asked about the arson. "Thomas, what happened last year? With the arson? Who burned your shop and your house?"

Bale put down the photograph and looked off. "I was raised in the Bridge. My family moved around some, but I came back in ninety-one. I hired on with Emmett Cross. Got a little house across the creek, and I set up my shop. The bridge always needs repairs. Plenty of work.

"Other Negro families were finding work around here, too. Plenty of opportunities. The cities are just so dirty, so full of disease. I'd stake some of those folks, not financing them, as such, just giving them a place to stay. I had some cabins up in Sloane Hollow on my family's land. It's hardscrabble up there, but not so bad. That's not the worst hardship.

"The problem is getting around without the *vexation!*" He shook his head angrily. "Since Wilmington, some white folks have rekindled their hate. There're some young men around here who think they're something tough, spitting at a black man, or dumping a Negro woman's trading, while she's trying to hustle up her children."

Mention of the Wilmington Massacre in North Carolina jarred Carrie. Headlines blared with the news two years ago and set the nation on edge. The ugly business, which by many accounts left hundreds of dead, had tainted the relationship between blacks and whites in Nanuet for months. She hadn't realized its ramifications continued.

The downpour drummed on the roof. Bale's voice quieted. "Anyway, last year, a bunch of young fellas wrangled up their courage. Germond Morgan, Phillip Wallace, Eustace Clevinger, Alden Louis. It wasn't enough to kick a black child in the behind or refuse to sell to a black man. But Germond ridiculed Miss Bethy Hays. She was with child, Miss Carrie, heavy with child. He let loose with some foul suggestions. She just fell down in the street and cried. I shouldn't have, but I slugged him in his foul mouth for that."

"Germond was one of the vigilantes?"

"He was. Someday that boy will learn some manners."

"I recognize the other names. Is Alden Louis the son of Mr. Louis, the gravedigger?"

Bale nodded. "And the nephew of the good Reverend Borden. Eustace Clevinger is a brat who stands to inherit his papa's store someday. Old man Clevinger ought to make him work harder for that.

"Those families that lived up in the Hollow," Bale resumed, "they just wanted to make their way, like everyone else. They didn't do anyone any harm. Anyway, I shouldn't have hit Germond. I took Miss Bethy home, but...." He shrugged sadly. "I wish they had just come after me."

The regret in his voice was heavy; Carrie dreaded the end of the tale.

"We heard them coming. They came all liquored up and egged each other on. I recognized their horses and their clothes. Idiots didn't even change their clothes. They just tied handkerchiefs over their faces, pretending to be outlaws from the wild west. *Idiots.*

"They set fire to all the cabins and ran down two men. Miss Bethy lost that poor baby the next day. She hid in the woods. Nothing we could do. Everyone lit out after that. I don't blame them. I was so mad, I walked with

CHAPTER FIFTEEN

them for half a day."

Bale paused, reflecting on the memory; then, he turned to Carrie and smiled, his eyes crafty.

"But then I turned around. I came back to let them see me carrying my toolbox every damn day. To let them know that I was gonna stay, and I was gonna keep their sin right out there in front of them. Every day. Cause Miss Bethy has to live every day, with the memory of birthing that poor baby on the ground in the woods. I am not gonna let them forget it."

Carrie's hand crept over Bale's, and she squeezed tight.

"Anyway, when I got back," he said, "my house was gone. Seems they left the colored cabins and came back and set my place on fire."

"I'm so sorry, Thomas," Carrie said, taking hold of his hand with both of hers. "Why was there no complaint?"

Bale shook his head, a resigned expression reflecting the injustice.

"A colored man doesn't get too far with his complaints, Miss Carrie. There's always a Judgment Day, though, isn't there?"

"I believe so, Thomas. But I sometimes have a hard time waiting for God to get to it."

Bale laughed. "Me too."

Chapter Sixteen

"I have no desire to join the Temperance Society, Uncle. I'd rather join your Society of Scholars," Carrie muttered as she and Sav walked under their shared umbrella to the Methodist Church Hall Friday evening. The rain had let up, but the trees dripped continuously. The muggy evening was filled with a damp mist and mosquitoes.

She lowered her voice as they neared, keeping her complaint from the other arrivals. "Why do I have to go, anyway? Will Stingy Peters be here?"

Sav fought to keep a grin off his face. "Yes, Mrs. Peters will attend. She's a true supporter. And you have to go because the Society of Scholars is currently restricted from accepting women as members, as written in its by-laws. I know! Something to remedy, but a matter for later, as you're wont to say. Besides, you haven't met all of Hope Bridge's residents, and I'd like that effort to continue."

"As long as I don't have to pledge anything! My goodness. The place is packed."

The din of Temperance supporters sprang out of the building when the doors opened to admit the newest member of Hope Bridge and her uncle. Mrs. Ina Barnstable spied them and hustled over. Powder snowed from her blouse.

"Mrs. Lisbon!" she cooed. "How good of you to join us!" A delicately balanced tea cup swept backward as the heavy woman bent forward to buss Carrie's cheek. Uncle Sav was separated and surrounded by Stingy Peters and an equally sour look-alike, her sister.

Ina Barnstable slid a moist hand inside Carrie's elbow and tugged. "Mrs.

CHAPTER SIXTEEN

Lisbon, you must tell me how you learned the art of dressing the deceased!" She steered Carrie to the outskirts of the room. "I'm just consumed with desire for your secrets. I have never seen such skill with face powder. Ophelia looked angelic!"

"You're too kind, Mrs. Barnstable. My expertise is not unusual. I—"

"Oh, just a *hint*, dear lady! The society column is one of the most anticipated features in the *Duncan Herald*. Tell me: La Blanche face powder with a brush of beet cream rouge?"

"You know your make-up, Mrs. Barnstable," Carrie smiled. "I use LaDoves Rubyline. From the Sears catalog." She and her uncle were devotees of the mail-order outfit that sold everything from garter clips to freight wagons. Sav had waxed poetic about the ease of commerce one evening while admiring his newest Sears acquisition, a double-barreled shotgun, that Bale had renounced as silly, since Sav hunted genealogies, not game.

Mrs. Barnstable squealed with relish. "And you have a selection of lipsticks and eyelash brushes?"

"Like a New York City burlesque," Carrie whispered theatrically. Mrs. Barnstable's chubby fingertips pressed against her lips, containing the excitement that lit up her face. "You simply *must* do me when I go, heaven forbid. I'll speak with Mr. Worley about my arrangements directly." She excused herself, dropped her teacup on the nearest table, and dug into her reticule for her notepad and pencil.

A new woman filled the brief vacuum left by Mrs. Barnstable. She, too, inquired about Carrie's preparation of Ophelia, her interest, of course, being the skill Carrie used to ease the family's suffering. Someone else slid a teacup and saucer into her hand. Another matron took up the next free space, then a well-dressed man, then another chatty matron. The faces appeared and disappeared while Carrie murmured her gratitude and mumbled her way through introductions and inquiries, while throwing Sav a desperate glance now and again. She caught bits of gossip from nearby.

"...poor Ada! She never misses a meeting! The whole family is in a dreadful state of mourning!"

"I was told that Rowena is throwing fits!"

"Sylvannia's been unable to reach her husband, poor thing. Where is he now?"

"I dearly hope they don't take comfort in drink!"

Carrie remembered drinking more than half a bottle of brandy one night before she made her decision to sell out and move up to Hope Bridge. Falling asleep for once without dreaming of Phee had its merits. The next day she threw the bottle away, knowing if she didn't, she'd be in the gutter within a week.

"Ah, Mrs. Lisbon. What a shocking introduction to our town you've had! We aren't prone to this type of thing, I assure you."

The Reverend Borden spoke from behind, and Carrie turned from the chatting women to greet the chubby pastor. His face was sweaty and expectant. Carrie smiled and held his damp hand firmly. "I can't agree more, Reverend. Yes, it was a shocking event. Prior to that, the only act of harm that I've been able to discern was a breach in confidentiality."

Borden's countenance lost some of its luster, but his smile didn't waver. He patted her hand and moved on. Carri sipped her tea to disguise her distaste and her small triumph. She wondered if her jab at the Reverend would be answered, or if the man would concede the touché and call it even.

Borden mounted a stage that ran the length of the room and raised his hands in a gesture of supplication that quieted the hall. He began the Hope Bridge Temperance Society meeting with a prayer of thanks and remembrance, mentioning Ophelia specifically. Carrie simmered while she waited for the prayer to end. The man hadn't waxed so poetically over poor little Suzetta.

The crowd sang a rousing version of "Bringing in the Sheaves" as an opener. Reverend Bordon spoke eloquently of the sins of indulgence and the dire consequences thereof, as manifested in the diseases of the mind and body. "Alcohol is to be reviled! Reviled as one reviles the acts of Satan!" The crowd clapped and banged walking sticks on the wooden floor. Carrie sat next to Sav, who, having slipped from the bonds of the Peters sisters, had chosen seats in the last row that allowed for his height to not impede anyone behind him, and also positioned them cleverly next to the door.

CHAPTER SIXTEEN

More hymns interspersed the witnessing of maudlin depravity due to alcoholism and several plates passed so that devotees could contribute to the Widows and Orphans of Alcohol Relief Fund. Carrie leaned toward her uncle to express her doubts. "Not if the Reverend is in charge of the pile," she murmured from the side of her mouth. Sav's eyes sparkled, and his Adam's apple jerked up and down, but his rigid posture gave nothing away.

Carrie found her way to the church backhouse, excusing herself as soon as the last notes of "We Shall Overcome" faded away. The night air was still oppressive, hinting at more rain to come. Spring peepers filled the darkness with a strident chorus, another intense sound absent from Nanuet. A small lamp lit up a circle around the wooden shed, indicating no occupancy. Lamplight from within meant the one-holer was being used. Carrie pulled the door shut and enjoyed a few moments of peace.

Halfway back to the church hall, she heard a single, quiet word from the shadows on the other side of the cemetery. Thomas Bale's rich voice. Carrie peered through a thin mist that hovered around the gravestones. Where the hill of the cemetery sloped down to the banks of the West Hope creek, Bale stood, fuzzy in the fog, with his arms outstretched. A woman with a crown of auburn hair hurried into them.

Thomas and Marta blended together, then slipped quickly through the trees along the creek bed, blending like ghosts into the mist. Carrie stood transfixed, fighting a cascade of colliding thoughts.

Her immediate response flew to shock. A dalliance between a black man and a white woman was simply not done. Society did not approve. Guilty individuals were punished. If discovered, an Irish Catholic like Marta would lose her job and her tenuous social standing. The Worleys already had a thin opinion of her since Germond Morgan had spread his lies. What would they do if they knew she was intimate with a black man?

And Bale? *My goodness, what will they do to Thomas?* A black man's ardor for a white woman was taboo. And breaking taboos often spurred bad people into awful actions. He had told her the story of how simple hatred had resulted in violence, arson, and a miscarriage. A lynch mob would feel *justified* if this were known.

Curiosity came next. How did she not notice their affection? No, wait: there were signs. Last Monday, she had been impatient and eager to respond to Worley's summons. She had overlooked Bale's warm greeting and the way he'd squeezed next to Sav, in order to get closer to Marta. And Marta had lauded Thomas earlier this week. What had Carrie said? *Thomas seems like a decent man,* and Marta had gushed "Oh, he is!"

There it was then. An illicit affair. And she the witness. The couple's embrace suddenly crushed her with loneliness. How they must love each other! How they must not be able to wait to feel each other's body pressed warm and close. How Marta must love to feel Thomas's strength embracing her. How he must love to feel the softness of her skin! How painful must be their separation. There was nothing sweet in the sorrow of parting. Shakespeare was wrong. Phee's departure, for Carrie, felt like an evisceration.

She suddenly ached for her husband. Ached in the places only he had satisfied. They had been innocent on their wedding day, but after the first tentative experiences, had learned to trust each other enough to go boldly into that aspect of marriage. Over the years, their discoveries left them breathless, laughing, feeling sordid and mischievous. She had only vivid dreams of those encounters now.

Let them be happy, she decided. Let them have what everyone else gets a chance to have. Let them love each other so fiercely, they forge bonds that can never be broken. You never know how long it will last. May as well be swallowed by the joy, before the horror of death slices one of you away.

She rubbed her hands down her cheeks and straightened herself. In the mere week that she'd been in Hope Bridge, she had found allies in these two people. She had come to admire Thomas's noble handling of the Scuttles. He fed them and made their pitiful condition tolerable at a time when they were most vulnerable. He dealt with Suzetta's decomposing body and her burial with solemnity and respect. He shared meals with her, and he lived as an equal in Sav's house. And had he not been a fierce protector just the other day when that awful Germond Morgan had accosted her? Thomas Bale was a good man.

CHAPTER SIXTEEN

Marta had just as easily found a secure place in Carrie's new world. Marta was only a few years younger, but she seemed so capable and sensible. Unlike other women, she didn't recoil over Carrie's vocation. She had assisted with Ophelia, frankly, like an apprentice. Marta confided a vulnerability to Carrie, trusting her as an ally. They had been candidly honest with each other, cursing easily in each other's company.

Carrie hurried back to the gaslit church hall. Sav stood by a table filled with plates of cookies and a cluster of jugs. The Peters sisters were not far away, their severely styled heads inclined toward each other, their speculative gazes locked on the tall scholar.

Sav presented Carrie with a glass of rhubarb shrub. She drank it down rather quickly.

"Another, niece?"

"Oh, yes, uncle. Keep it coming."

Sav's brows raised as he poured more. The crowd thinned, but the Peters sisters circled them. "I expect the Reverend Borden's message met well with you?" Sav asked.

"I'm inclined toward moderation, uncle. A weakness for drink is like a weakness for gambling. A good moderate path makes these pleasures, not vices."

"I meant his bit about the moral responsibility we all share for the comfort and care of those less fortunate, who are left without resources as a result of alcoholic depravity." Her uncle's explanation rose and fell in a slight mockery of Borden's incantation.

"I suppose he meant to remind our township to continue to provide Mr. Louis with, what was the term? 'Customary compensation?'" Carrie smiled up at him.

At the mention of Digger Louis's name, the lurking women's eyes bounced away like water on a hot griddle. Carrie downed another glass of shrub and fanned her face.

"If it's agreeable, uncle, would you mind if we took our leave?"

"Not at all, niece. My ambition of introducing you to our populace has been met. My next venture will be to alter the by-laws of the Society of

Scholars, so you can imbibe shrub without lecture!"

Chapter Seventeen

"It's like magic," Sav said intently, hovering over the developing solution, waiting for the nebulous gray on the paper to materialize into a sharp image. They had set up the Star View in the parlor and took a photograph of Sav, posed by the fireplace mantle with Oscar on his arm. The cellar, with a brown rag of burlap tacked over the small window, served as the dimmest place in the house to print the image. Rain drummed on the glass insistently, as if pestering for admittance.

Carrie lifted the heavy paper from a tray and carefully laid it down in another. "There's an outfit in Rochester touting a new camera that doesn't require processing at home. I hope it's offered in the Sears catalog. I'd like to give that a try."

"But this process is extraordinary! It's all chemicals and light. Who'd *not* want to develop their own pictures?" Sav's delightful speculation was interrupted by hurried footsteps in the kitchen overhead. A second later, Bale called their names.

"Down here, Thomas," Sav called back. "Don't bring a light. We're developing pictures!"

Bale cracked open the cellar door and peered through the gap. "I have some news, Sav, Miss Carrie."

Carrie held a wide wooden tweezer. Sav had his hands under a towel. Their pause was expectant; their eyes wide in the dim light.

"Germond Morgan was found dead at his place this morning. Somebody shot him."

Sav and Carrie stared at Bale for another moment, then exchanged looks with each other.

"Huh," Carrie said.

* * *

Rain slashed down in torrents. The clamor of heavy drops on tin, shingles, and slate rose to deafening proportions. Horses, trussed up in dripping carriage lines, trudged through the mud on Main Street as water sluiced off their noses. Teamsters shouted, cursed, and whistled their way through the suddenly crowded street.

Hope Bridge townsfolk crammed under the dripping eaves of Clevinger's porch. Carrie, Sav, and Bale crowded in with those fortunate to get a spot inside. The buzz of collective speculation stilled when Sheriff Morgan opened the door to the spare room Clevinger provided for his office. Next to him stood another man with a spade-shaped beard and a silver badge pinned to his vest.

Morgan's eyes swept the crowd and landed on the tallest man in the room. He paused, too, at Thomas Bale's dark face and at Carrie's. His eyes narrowed.

"Germond Morgan has been found dead in his home," he announced. "That much you know. He was shot. You know that too. Mr. Lamont is now my deputy. He and I are going to conduct interviews with all parties, starting now. You come when you're summoned. And stay off your telephones. I don't want anyone listening in on my conversations. If I have to confiscate your 'phones, I will. I know who's got one, so stay off. Clevinger, I'm using yours."

Someone called out, "Our condolences, Sheriff." Delphius Morgan paused, his face stony. He nodded once, then he and Lamont retreated.

It took some overt pushing to get out of the store after the announcement. Tongues wagged immediately, and speculation ran riot. Carrie heard the Grants name muttered more than once as she shuffled close behind Sav's thin form. She was relieved to be out of the stuffy mercantile, but the boardwalks were slick, the stepstones muddy and sunken. Carrie's umbrella tottered as

CHAPTER SEVENTEEN

she slipped and re-balanced. Bale was more sure-footed in his rain slicker. Pausing to elevate her skirts above the squelching ground, she saw several young men in rather deluxe attire under the porch of the Chester Inn. They looked malevolently at Bale.

"I don't think the sheriff liked his brother all that much," Bale confided as they turned away toward North Street. "Doesn't seem too shook up."

"I noticed that too," Carrie said loudly over the rain.

"Delphius is the oldest by about fifteen years," Sav said. "There were three boys in the family. The folks are gone. The second son died of yellow fever in Cuba. I didn't realize Del and Germond were so caustic toward each other."

"It was obvious to me," Carrie continued, squinting through the rain. "They didn't exchange a word at Ophelia's wake. They stood there like two bantams in the same yard. The sheriff was disgusted when he interviewed Germond. I'd say that was accurate, Thomas."

"I don't think Worley or the Bookhoudts have any caskets left," Bale said. "I'm going to see if I can get that job. I'll be back by supper."

"Thomas, wait," Carrie said. "There were some men back there who looked daggers at you. Did you notice that?"

Bale smiled. "Ah, that's a new knock on an old door, Miss Carrie. I'm the one and only black man that didn't leave when I was supposed to. I believe some folks are still sore about that. Save me some pie!" He pulled his hat down and hurried off beneath the dripping elms. Carrie gaped at his honesty.

"He'll be fine," Sav said.

"How does Thomas know the mercantile and Mr. Worley have no caskets, uncle?" A rumble of thunder sent them hurrying home.

"Thomas is keen on lumber and furniture," Sav said, pulling Carrie along. "He knows whose timber has been cut and what's going on at the sawmill. Bookhoudt hires him to re-organize sometimes. He probably knows the inventory. He works at the post office every so often, too. If I know Thomas, he'll be working all night on Germond's casket."

"What do you think happened to Germond?" Carrie panted.

"Sheriff Morgan said he was shot. In any case, his crude attempts at philandering are over."

"Any chance his death was an accident?"

"Of course. But I don't think Delphius would have brought in Lamont if Germond killed himself cleaning his gun."

"What about suicide? Do you think he shot himself? He didn't seem to have any extraordinary guilt about what he did to Ophelia. Slow down!"

"I can't imagine a braggart like Germond hurting himself," Sav replied, easing the length of his stride. "Those who think so highly of themselves are not prone to self-harm. No, I'd wager this was murder."

Carrie's heart twanged with another reason to be fearful of the lawless tenor of this place. At least now, there were two officers of the law in the immediate vicinity. "Who might have done something like that?"

"I can't imagine any of my neighbors as murderers, niece. But I'd expect the culprit either had a long list of grievances or a short temper." Carrie remembered her own hot reaction to Germond's confession of defiling Ophelia. Was she capable of that kind of violence? What if Germond had tried to molest Marta again? Would Marta have killed him?

"What about the Grant brother? Would he avenge his sister?"

"Not Gideon. It's unlikely. He's a bit tender, I'm afraid. I can't see him confronting Germond. Sylvannia's husband is overseas, according to Mrs. Barnstable's social column. Either way, I don't know if they are aware of the strangulation. I don't know if Sheriff Morgan has discussed the results of your examination with them, only Germond. But who knows? Perhaps Gideon did take offense to Germond's treatment of Ophelia after all."

"Would that he had prior to her death, the poor thing." They rounded the corner and headed up North Street, just as a fresh gust of wind flung a heavy gout of rain through the trees. And once again, Worley's housemaid stood on their porch.

Chapter Eighteen

Marta held an umbrella the size of a small tent on her shoulder and the wet hem of her skirt above her muddy shoes. "My goodness, it's bucketing down!" she said. Sav shook out the umbrella as Marta stood dripping on the rug, and Carrie hastened to answer Worley's newest summons. She called from her suite while she collected her boots and overcoat.

"Who's at the house with you, Marta?"

"Mr. Worley, the sheriff, and the deputy, Mr. Lamont," Marta called back.

"Where's Mrs. Worley?"

"Upstairs. She doesn't want anything to do with the whole business."

Carrie emerged, clomping up the hallway in an old pair of cracked leather boots. The shoes she had worn home just now were a sodden mess, encased in clumps of mud and drying by the kitchen stove. She tugged her arms into her cold, damp jacket and looked out at the unrelenting weather in dismay.

"Worley's umbrella is a fine big one, Carrie," Marta said helpfully. "Plenty of room underneath."

"Of course, Marta. Thank you. What did Mr. Worley say when he sent you?"

"The sheriff wanted me to fetch you. He wants you to help Mr. Worley lay out Germond. He said you may be able to see something that Mr. Worley might overlook. I think he's expecting you to find things like you did with Ophelia."

"The sheriff asked for me?"

"Yes, ma'am."

Sav objected. "Goodness, Carrie. Is this proper?"

"Uncle, it's my occupation. *Lisbon & Shay* never subscribed to the idea that a female undertaker must be protected from such sights. This is no more repugnant to me than this morning's breakfast."

"Besides," she said, stretching up to peck his cheek, "Let me have my vindication."

Bundled and leaning close together under the umbrella's dome, Carrie and Marta headed into the cold, stinging rain. Their feet were soaked within a block. The umbrella protected only their heads and shoulders: their skirts were wet and heavy by the time they hurried into the shelter of Worley's back door. The warm kitchen enveloped their chilly faces like a grandmother's palms. Marta took Carrie's boots and socks and arranged them by the iron stove to dry.

"Mother of God, that was miserable! I'll let Mr. Worley know you're here, but I want to get you some dry clothes to change into. You'll fit mine easily. Wait here."

Carrie tiptoed closer to the big kitchen stove, holding her sodden skirt away from her bare legs. Savoring the warm braided rug beneath her feet, she looked around and thought *Marta must love to cook here*. A narrow work table, crowded with mixing bowls, spice jars, a rolling pin, and a crock of flour, butted against the wall. Glass-door cabinets showed off platters and stacks of plates. Rows of preserved fruits, pickles, and jellies garnished the pantry shelves, as colorful as Christmas baubles. Maybe Marta could give her some tips to improve her lagging culinary skills.

Her perusal ended when Mrs. Worley slipped into the kitchen. A startled noise erupted from Carrie before she could contain her shock. She had blown out of Worley's office last week in a fit of rage, barely acknowledging his wife's presence, let alone getting a good look at her. But to Carrie's recollection, Mrs. Worley hadn't looked like *this*.

She could have been one of her husband's corpses; so pallid was her complexion, so drawn her expression, so slack the skin on her face and jowls. Mrs. Worley looked dim-witted as she reached for the table to steady herself before letting go of the door casing.

CHAPTER EIGHTEEN

"My apologies," the elderly woman said, in a voice ruined from coughing. "Hello. Mrs. Lisbon. We haven't met properly." The wraith advanced, holding out a cold hand. Carrie grasped the twig-like fingers, her own still chilled and wet from her arrival.

"Hello, Mrs. Worley," Carrie said softly.

"I see Marta is getting you something dry. She's a dear thing. I would be lost without her." The words struggled past her pale lips.

"Yes, thank you, she is," Carrie said. "I should apologize for my conduct last week. I was most upset, and I acted rudely. Please forgive me."

"Done is done, my dear. Tell me, do you plan to look at Germond's body? The sheriff sent for you?"

"Yes," Carrie said, calculating the time Mrs. Worley had left before the 'angels carried her away.' The euphemism was clearly visible in the tremble of her weakened frame and icy temperature of her skin.

"Most improper, I say." Mrs. Worley gargled back a cough, bending with the effort. "Arthur was against it," she continued tersely. "They argued, he and our sheriff. I believe Mr. Morgan was quite insistent."

"I'm not opposed to the task, Mrs. Worley," Carrie said, holding up the woman's bony elbow. "I'm quite adept at preparation. I've laid out hundreds of people."

"It rankles Arthur to ask you. He's wholly traditional." The catarrh in her throat sounded like swirling gravel.

"I appreciate his wisdom." Carrie tried to soothe the woman's persistence. "I'll be sure to have the men present and the body suitably veiled from my view."

Even that assurance didn't satisfy Mrs. Worley. She shifted away from Carrie with a down turn of her mouth and reached out for a cabinet to stabilize her journey to the dining room. Carrie felt the dismissal, but stepped forward in order to lend the ailing woman a hand.

"Thank you, Mrs. Lisbon," Mrs. Worley said when she ran out of things to clutch, and Carrie's arm was there. "I'm failing. I just need more rest. Marta will see to me. Ah, here she is." Mrs. Worley struggled to smile when Marta arrived with a set of dry clothing draped over an arm. She and Carrie switched places. Marta pointed her chin at a door, indicating a place for Carrie to change. She turned to fuss over Mrs. Worley as she led her away.

Marta's room was a small cubby off the dining room. Her lot was to maintain the home's hot water, fires, food, and cleanliness. There was no need for her to have elaborate accommodations, nor one far from her post. A silver-plated cross held a position of honor on the papered walls. A rack held her few blouses and skirts in neat drapes; the rug under her bed was clean and dry, and a tiny mirror hung over the bureau. Carrie's reflection showed her the amount of work she'd need to do to restore her face and hair. She dressed in Marta's crisp petticoat and worn cotton skirt. The dry socks warmed her feet immediately. She took the liberty of combing out her hair with Marta's brush. As Carrie fixed a tight bun at the back of her neck, Marta returned and interrupted.

"Oh, wait, Carrie," she said. "That style fair ages you. Let's do your hair on top, like in the magazines. Here, let me."

"I'm all right with this, Marta—"

"No, no, let's have you look lovely when you go down there to take a peek at ol' Germond." Marta grinned mischievously. Carrie laughed at the Irish girl's accent and daring insinuation. Why not?

Marta crouched behind her on the bed, pulling and tying. The bed springs sagged and bounced, and both women snickered at the suggestive noises. Carrie dismissed the idea of bringing up Marta's liaison with Bale last night. Now was not the time to initiate *that* discussion. This time was better spent preparing herself properly. Her expertise had been called upon; her reputation was at stake.

When Carrie looked in the mirror, she saw Phee's wife again, the happy, confident woman who had blossomed under her husband's touch, not the skinny, pallid wretch she'd become this past year. She caught her breath before the pain of remembrance spilled over.

Marta leaned into the mirror and grinned. "Let that dead bastard get a good look at us now, eh?" she said. "He can kiss my fine Irish bum!"

Carrie descended into the cellar mortuary, where Worley and Morgan discussed their subject. Worley eyed her impassively as expected, but Carrie

CHAPTER EIGHTEEN

felt a flush of pride that her renewed appearance caused Morgan to react with a quick double-take.

Morgan cleared his throat and introduced her to Leopold Lamont, from Crown Lane in Hope Bridge, deputized at nine o'clock today. Older than Morgan, Lamont kept his hair close-cropped, but his beard and mustache grew together in a wide, rounded spade that concealed his mouth. Other than a murmur of greeting, Lamont kept silent.

The room wasn't built to accommodate a crowd. To avoid the crush and, instinctively, to provide Worley room to operate, Carrie remained standing on the bottom step, elevated enough to oversee the operation. Germond's body was the centerpiece. His cologne still clung to his clothing, but the scent of blood was heavier.

"Thank you for coming, Mrs. Lisbon," Worley droned. "The sheriff and I waited for you before we got started. I trust you are comfortable now and ready to proceed?" His cordiality included the subtle hint that he had been put out, waiting for her to tidy up. Carrie smiled and presented him with curt nod, thinking, he *insults so loftily.*

"Yes, thank you, Mr. Worley. May I express my condolences to you, Mr. Morgan?"

"Thank you, Mrs. Lisbon," the imposing man said automatically. Carrie couldn't decide if he displayed stoicism, or if his brother's death was akin to spilled milk. She remembered how disgusted and angered he had been when Germond confessed his desecration of Ophelia's body. Carrie determined he felt the latter. As did she.

"I am to act as an observer?"

"That's why I asked for you," Morgan said. "I believe you made some keen observations about Ophelia. So, if you think of anything, or see anything that we don't, just say it."

"Of course, sheriff. But, first, may I ask you something about Germond's confession? I wondered if you interviewed him after we met in Clevinger's."

"Yes, I did. That night."

"Did you ask him how he found Ophelia?"

"He said he found her at the bottom of the stairs when he came home."

"That's *where* he found her," Carrie delicately corrected him. "I wondered if he said anything about *how*. Did he say anything about her being dressed?"

"He said she was dead when he found her. He figured she had tripped on her skirts. He said lots of women trip on their skirts and fall down the stairs."

Carrie shook her head carefully. "No, we don't. We are trained to lift our skirts at the top of the stairs from a very early age. It's automatic." She paused, then asked quietly and slowly, "Did you ask him if she was dressed…when he left her that afternoon?"

The crow's feet around Morgan's eyes tightened. "I had him recite the entire timeline, from the time they left the picnic until he brought her body to Worley's."

Carrie waited. Morgan paused as well, as though considering the benefits of further discussion. Lamont turned his head to the side, listening with a good ear. Worley scrutinized them with intensity.

Morgan gave a curt, factual report. "He said he got dressed and left her in their bed, after he was done with her. He accosted Marta on the way to the Chester Inn, where he had a meal." Morgan's mouth turned down. The struggle to keep his composure about his brother's casual conduct after brutalizing his wife was obvious. "He came home after dark. Found her. Put her shoes on. Carried her to the wagon. He said he had to lean her against him, and it was a 'real bitch' to drive the horse and keep her upright. Like *that* was the big problem." Morgan clamped his lips together, fighting harder to keep his anger under control.

"He drove to Sloane Hollow. He threw her out. He picked her up and drove her to Worleys."

"What about choking her?" Carrie asked bluntly.

"He swears he didn't."

"Do you believe him?"

"No. I don't. I think he was a fucking brute. And I won't apologize this time, ma'am."

Carrie regarded him levelly. "No need to apologize, Mr. Morgan. I envy your candor." So intent was their exchange, she felt they were alone in the

CHAPTER EIGHTEEN

room.

"However," she said, "I find his testimony at odds with my initial observation. Germond said he put on her shoes when he found her at the bottom of the stairs. *Only* her shoes. He had to make her death look like an accident, so he was clever enough to put shoes on her, before he carried her out to the wagon."

Morgan's eyes narrowed. He spread his hands, palms up. "So?"

"Why didn't he say 'I got her dressed?' Why did he put on *only* her shoes?"

Morgan continued to stare at her, but his gaze had shifted from annoyance to concentration.

"Because she was already dressed, Mr. Morgan," Carrie explained. "The problem is with her clothing. She wore bloomers, a shift, a corset, a blouse, a skirt, stockings. Her corset was completely laced and tied. Please forgive my insult to your departed brother, but a man like Germond wouldn't have gone through all the trouble of *layering on* all those clothes. Frankly, men don't know how all those ribbons, buttons, and hooks work. And, it's difficult to dress a deceased person, is it not, Mr. Worley?"

The undertaker nodded sagely. Carrie turned back to Morgan.

"As far as dressing herself, I believe Ophelia's wounds from her husband's assault rendered her incapable—or at the least, unwilling—to put on all the clothing she had on when she died."

When Morgan made no comment, she kept on. "It's possible Germond found Ophelia fully dressed at the bottom of the stairs. That's why he only put on her shoes. That's all he had to put on, in order to make the wagon accident plausible. Germond may have choked Ophelia, and cooked up the story about finding her at the bottom of the stairs, but all her clothing bothers me."

"And so, your conclusion, Mrs. Lisbon?" Morgan asked.

"He may have raped her, choked her, and thrown her out of a wagon, but he didn't dress her."

The collective eyebrows of her audience shot upward.

"Who dressed her?" Morgan asked.

Carrie shook her head, shrugging.

Morgan pulled a big hand through his hair. In the close confines of the crowded room, that pleasant tobacco scent drifted warmly from him "You're saying that Germond killed her, but someone else dressed her?"

"Yes," Carrie said quietly. "He would have said he dressed her, sheriff, not just put on her shoes. He said it twice."

"And now we're dressing out Germond."

"I'm sorry, yes. Let's get started."

Chapter Nineteen

Marta fixed a small meal of tea, biscuits, and ham for Carrie, who emerged from Worley's preparation room an hour later. The kitchen smelled sharply of yeast. A table lamp created a glow over the meal, pushing back the gloomy oppression of the deluge that continued outside.

Marta kept up a quiet, cheerful monologue as she fussed over Carrie's serving, before seating herself with a contented sigh and biting deeply into her own meal. *She looks less tense,* Carrie thought. Germond's death has lifted a burden. She hesitated again to spoil the mood by broaching the subject of Marta's relationship with Thomas. She asked about Mrs. Worley.

"She's not long, I'm afraid," Marta said kindly. "The poor thing doesn't eat, and she's so cold all the time. She used to be so strong. And strict! I was afraid she'd dismiss me after Germond lied about me. Now she just slips around here like a ghost. I'm always bringing her hot stones for her bed and keeping her wrapped up. I mix up her morphine with honey for her pain."

"Those were the packages you got from Bookhoudt's the other day? I recognized the scent," Carrie said.

Marta nodded. "Mr. Worley keeps a tight lip, but he's having a hard time with her lingering on so. Not much to be done, I'm afraid. It was a galling thing for him, asking you to help with Ophelia."

By the time Bale arrived at the kitchen door with Sav's umbrella and a pair of tall rubber boots, Carrie had changed back into her own skirt, insisting that although still clammy, there was no reason to wash two sets of mud-spattered clothes. She observed Bale and Marta closely this time, but the lovers exchanged only the simple courtesies of neighbors. *They're hiding it well,* Carrie thought. She would not ask Bale about his liaison; that was not at all her place. But she surely needed to discuss it with Marta.

"These are your uncle's, Miss Carrie," Bale announced, holding up the boots. "They're from England. Damndest things for keeping your feet dry. They'll be big and clumsy, but I won't let you fall."

Heavy rain pommeled the umbrella as she and Bale slogged across the yard. The Wellingtons banged into the backs of her legs.

"It looks like Germond was shot right through the heart, Thomas." It was necessary for her to shout above the rain.

"Serves him right."

"Somebody stuck the gun right into his chest and pulled the trigger. We found that his shirt was actually scorched around the bullet hole. Sheriff Morgan says that comes from the gun nearly touching the person when it's fired."

"Is that so?"

"Sheriff Morgan had Mr. Worley pull out the bullet, too. It was a small caliber, apparently. Possibly a .38," Carrie said, proud of her new firearm terminology.

"Enough to do the job."

"Worley's got the most exquisite tools in his mortuary! He used a pair of forceps that are like knitting needles." Carrie mimed the twisting of an instrument. "Oh, I wish I had a pair like that! Did you ask about making a casket for Germond?"

"Yes, ma'am. I didn't go to the Grants; they most likely wouldn't spend a dime on that boy's box. I asked the sheriff, when he was still at the store. He's next of kin. I'll finish it tomorrow."

"Where's he to be buried?"

"Not in the Grants' plot! I think the Morgan family has a plot back in Middlefort."

"Then Digger's out of a job this time?"

Bale's heavy chuckle tumbled into the rain. "Nobody's mourning that either."

CHAPTER NINETEEN

* * *

Later that night, Carrie, Sav, and Bale finished a pot of strong tea while Carrie recited the events of the evening. She announced with pleasure that she had been accepted as a 'keen observer' by Sheriff Morgan.

Other than the grisly bullet hole that leaked blood when Worley rummaged with his long forceps, there was nothing extraordinary about Germond's body. Unbidden, Carrie had a small enamel basin ready for Worley to drop the bullet into. This garnered a surprised expression from the impassive undertaker, another feather in her cap. She rinsed the gore from the bullet and handed it to the sheriff from the folds of a clean towel. He held it up to the lamp light, then put it in his vest pocket.

Carrie emulated the gesture, and then asked, "More tea, uncle?"

Sav seemed to have envisioned the bullet between her fingers and declined in mock horror. Bale got up with a chuckle to turn up the wicks on the kitchen lamp. Carrie rose to put the kettle on for dishwater, and they all looked up and around at each other, thinking the oncoming vibration they felt was thunder. They froze, recognizing the sound was not the rumble of the storm, but hoof beats. Dozens of them.

Bale tipped the chimney off the lantern and pinched out the flame. Sav reached for his newly purchased shotgun that leaned near the stove. The hoofbeats grew louder. Surrounded the house. Torches streaked by, lighting up long guns, and spewing embers across the kerchiefed faces of a mob.

A pounding on the front door, like a booming cannon, made them all jump.

"Sav Machin! We know Bale's in there. Turn him out!" The voice was unfamiliar and angry. Shouts of agreement followed up the chilling demand.

"Machin? Ya turn him out, now, ya hear? We ain't taking no fer answer!"

Carrie hissed in the dark kitchen. "Uncle!"

Sav Machin's silhouette stood taller than she had ever seen it. Dim torchlight lit his face. His jaw clenched in anger.

A rock crashed through the kitchen door window, clattering to the floor in a spray of glass. They heard the knob on the back porch door rattling viciously.

"Turn him out, Machin. And no one gets hurt. We'll fire the place if we have to."

"*Uncle!*"

"Goddamn it, Sav," Bale muttered fast.

Overhead, Oscar squalled and let loose a string of expletives. The pounding on their front door continued.

"Machin! He's a murderer! Ya can't harbor a fugitive! Turn him out!"

"Thomas, get in the cellar," Sav commanded.

"Hell with that," Bale shouted. "I ain't letting you fight my battles."

"This isn't a battle! It's a lynch mob! We can make it hard for them to extract you—"

"No sir! Gimme that useless gun! It ain't even loaded! I'm not gonna die without a fight."

"*Machin!*" The hollow clatter of hooves on floorboards sounded on their front porch. The glass in the back door burst. Torches flamed outside the windows, ugly faces peered in, their reflections dripping down the rainy glass.

Carrie's mind swirled like the violence around her. "Get in the cellar, Thomas!" Her voice thin and shrill.

"No! Sav! Give me that gun!"

Suddenly, Sav's voice boomed above the din. "This is my house! Goddamn you all!" He barreled into the hallway and flung open the front door. "*Get that animal off my porch!*" he bellowed into the face of a man whose fist was raised to pound again. Sav reached out and jerked down the red rag that covered the man's nose.

"Hiram Stowe?" Sav shouted. He stepped onto the porch and pushed his gun into the man's belly. Stowe recoiled. Sav advanced. "What the hell are you doing? What the hell are all of you doing?" He towered over Stowe. His wavy hair stood on end. He swung the heavy shotgun at the man on the horse.

"I said get that animal off my porch! Is that you, Joseph? I'd know your nag anywhere." The horse tossed its head away from the stink of gun oil.

CHAPTER NINETEEN

The drunken rider lost his balance and jerked on the reins, distressing the animal further. It danced away, knocking the porch chair into the mud. Sav swung the gun back.

"We come for Bale," Stowe slurred, his breath laced with alcohol. The dozen or so men behind him cheered in agreement. Horses squealed and stamped the yard to mud, gagging on their bits. Riders fought for their submission.

"He's a murderer," Stowe said. "He killed Germond Morgan."

Sav hefted the gun into Stowe's face and leaned in. "You go get the sheriff, Hiram," he growled. "You tell him to come and arrest Thomas Bale." Hiram Stowe staggered away from the double barrels.

"Like hell, we will!" someone shouted. A horse was spurred forward, splashing mud. Its rider leaned over, his hat dripping heavy rain. "We ain't waiting for the law. We know he killed Germond! We don't need the sheriff. You send him out!" A drunken roar of solidarity went up.

"Is that you, Eustace?" Sav sneered. "Nobody else wears a duster that shitty! I see you, Ezra Bellinger. You can't do this and sit in my pew on Sunday."

"Burn him out!"

"*Bullshit!*" Sav's bellow rolled over the mob. "Willis? Willis Patterson? You ungrateful sonofabitch! Tom Bale helped you with your barn last fall. You're going to hang a man who helps you out?"

"We'll burn yer house down!" The threat came from the back of the mob. Sav answered by jerking the shotgun upright and pulling the trigger. The ear-splitting report blasted a shower of thick sparks into the night. Horses reared and screamed; men fell off and scrambled for swinging reins. Hiram Stowe staggered backward and fell into the mud.

"What proof? What witness?" Sav marched into the squealing horses, pointing the hot, smoking barrel into their nostrils. The herd bucked to get away, kicking at one another, sliding in the wet grass. The mob shifted in confusion. Sav pointed the gun directly into the faces of each rider around him. Each man threw up an arm and scrambled away.

"What's it like to stare into the barrel of a gun, Willis?" Sav swung the barrel again. "Kenny Bowmaker? Didn't Thomas fix your wagon when your wife was poorly? I see you Eustace Clevinger! And you, Phineas! I see you, Bert Smith!"

"And I see you, Arthur Worley!" Carrie shouted. She stood on the porch with a glass bottle and pointed to the urbane undertaker, standing in the rain at the outskirts of the mob. She held up the bottle. "Do you know what we have in this house? Any of you? I'm an undertaker! If you send one torch in my direction, the flames will ignite my embalming jars! You'll set off an explosion that will kill you before you can turn and run!"

She stepped up next to her uncle. "The flames will be so hot, half the town will burn down! Isn't that right, Mr. Worley? Tell them! The fumes from arsenic will kill you before you can run home! *Tell them, Mr. Worley!*"

Torches wavered. Sav leveled the shotgun at the crowd; the muzzle still smoked. Horses squealed and reared, defecating in panic. A gust of rain swooped down, pelting the wet men and their torches into submission.

Worley's perpetual look of disdain slid over the mob. He nodded to Carrie and without a word, turned away and walked off into the dark.

Carrie and Sav stood in the rain as the torches dropped and the yard cleared. Several men looked back, spat, and muttered threats as they left. Carrie slid her arm around Sav's skinny waist as the sucking of hoofbeats died away into the darkness. Sav trembled. He put his arm across her shoulders, and they turned as one and went inside.

Bale stood in the middle of the kitchen holding a little hand ax they used for kindling. Sav reached out without a word, took it from his hand, and laid it on the table. Carrie fumbled for a match and tried to light the lantern, but her wet fingers shook so badly she dropped it twice. Swearing, she bent to retrieve it and paused to take a deep breath before resuming. This time, tears fell as she lit the wick. The chimney clattered against the springs as she snapped it into place.

Sav sat with the shotgun between his knees. "I thought you left all your undertaker supplies back in Nanuet, niece."

Carrie's nerves broke in a burst of thin laughter. "I didn't think that gun was loaded, Uncle."

CHAPTER NINETEEN

"Holy shit," Bale gulped. "Holy shit."

Chapter Twenty

The rain persisted throughout the night, a stalled system that drenched the land, poured into fieldstone cellars, and drowned nascent crops. Just after sun up, despite a night of startled, interrupted dozing, Carrie marched down to the Worley residence, nervous energy whizzing throughout her limbs. Fighting the wind and rain aggravated her further. She burst past a startled Marta, and disregarding the closed door, banged into Worley's office, and demanded an explanation.

"Between the horse shit and the torn-up ground, our yard looks like Gettysburg! Why on earth would you become involved in a mob like that?"

Worley looked narrowly at Carrie's dripping hem and muddy boots. A sullen fire failed to warm the room.

"You presume I was there to see a man hanged, Mrs. Lisbon. I had overheard the Clevinger boys planning their violence with the Bowmaker boy outside the store yesterday. I came up *behind* the mob to your house. Although I admit my intentions were not complete, I did, however, not want to see Mr. Bale injured. I felt I could intercede on his behalf, potentially provide for your safety and that of Mr. Machin. As it was, you diffused the situation with your threat of chemical warfare."

"Coward!" Carrie shot back. "I don't believe that rubbish!"

A thin smile slid across his face. "Mrs. Lisbon, Thomas Bale saved my life. I would not see him harmed."

Carrie waited, belligerent. She was not ready to trust Worley's statement. Not when he had dismissed her so many times before.

Worley sighed and, in an uncharacteristic manner, leaned back in his

CHAPTER TWENTY

swivel chair and took a long gaze out the window. "Tom served with the 24th Infantry in Cuba in ninety-eight. You've read about the conflict. An ugly business; completely uncalled for.

"I went to prepare the dead for their return home. Heat accelerates decomposition, as you know. Embalming supplies were quite scarce. I took the names and ranks, and the personal possessions of the dead to send back home. Most of the time, I simply straightened uniforms and wrapped bodies in shrouds for the pits.

"Most of our boys died from yellow fever or typhus, not wounds. I would have been one of them if not for Thomas Bale." Worley turned painfully squinted eyes back to Carrie.

"You cannot imagine the agony of typhus, Mrs. Lisbon. Fever rages. Your bowels twist. The sick tents were foul. Filled with screaming men. The army expected you to die. Little effort was made. The doctors were overwhelmed. They simply shuffled the dying from one level to the next. You went from a bed to a litter that was carried to the undertaker." Worley's thin hand stepped down through the air. "After that, it was the pit."

"The Buffalo Soldiers were pressed into service in the sick tents. It was my utmost good fortune to have Thomas Bale recognize me when I caught the disease. He took care of me. *Me.* Personally. He kept me in the bed, by God! Not the stretcher, nor the pit!" Worley's expression grew fierce with the memory.

"He stood over me like a dog at a bone and wouldn't let any of those quacks touch me. Some still practiced bleeding a patient! I don't know where Thomas got it, but he brought me cool water to drink, and I swear to this day, I have never tasted such a sweet liquid.

"He bathed the dirt from my body and cleaned me when I soiled myself. And never did he stop filling my mouth with that sweet, clean water. He tells me it was three days of fighting before the fever broke. I remember nothing but the agony and wanting to die, and a few visions of his face and his hands and his voice. I'd have died if not for his mercy."

"When I came back to Hope Bridge, I received a hero's welcome. The picnics and the toasts and so forth. I looked for Thomas Bale to return home for months. When he did, it was late autumn, and he hadn't a coin to his name. I ordered caskets from him. I suspect my supplier in Albany still bears some malice toward me for that." Worley paused before fixing a stern glare at Carrie.

"He saved my life and made it back in one piece, Mrs. Lisbon. And I'll be damned if I let a rabble like that hang him for the murder of a wastrel like Germond Morgan."

Carrie stood quietly. Worley's tale settled over the two of them like an unfurled sheet, dropping slowly onto a fresh bed. The incessant drum of rain outside the window and a mournful church bell punctuated the silence. Presently, Worley spoke again.

"I'm to assume that you'll be staying on with Mr. Machin? If that is the case, I have need of a skilled preparer."

Carrie let his proposal square itself within her thoughts. She responded simply, nodding once.

"You're clever, Mrs. Lisbon," Worley resumed. "And you're a good mortician. You've read the *Duncan Herald*, I presume? Mrs. Barnstable's a funeral crank. She attends them simply to report on their finer points. I believe your artistry brought her to new heights of titillation."

"Perhaps my methods are simply novel to her. I'm sure Mrs. Worley has performed equally admirable tasks," Carrie said.

"Quite admirable, I assure you," Worley said.

"And you're clever as well, Mr. Worley," Carrie said. "You prepared Esther Briggs instead of your wife."

She expected Worley to react with offense. Women laid out the men of their family: their husbands or their unmarried sons, their fathers, grandfathers, and uncles. They assisted other women with this careful and solemn task. But the reverse was not true, especially not for a professional undertaker. Worley would not want his breach of mortuary precedent to be widely known. He gazed out the window again.

"Mrs. Worley was not able to lay out Mrs. Briggs. My assistance was required at first, but her strength failed very quickly. She simply didn't have the vitality to take care of Ophelia."

CHAPTER TWENTY

"That's why you called on me."

"Your arrival was fortuitous for us. Mrs. Peters is not discreet; she's simply quiet with her indiscretions. Your attention to the little girl was broadcast like seed around town within a day. Mrs. Worley will be able to rest, if you'll consider assuming her position as is required."

At last, Worley presented the acknowledgment that had meant so much to Carrie. But the context was heartbreaking. He was asking her to fill a void that was soon to be left by the death of his wife. Knowing her time was small, and in spite of his sorrow, he was making arrangements to carry on. It was admirable.

"Of course, I'll be able to assist you with preparations, Mr. Worley. We can discuss compensation for those services when the time comes."

"I am also aware of the subtle changes you made to Mrs. Peters' flower arrangements," Worley continued. "I would be able to offer you some modest compensation if you were to supply floral arrangements in the future."

Carrie smiled ruefully; the man missed nothing. "Preparing the deceased is one thing, Mr. Worley. But I won't take Mrs. Peters' egg money from her, nor her pride."

"Photographs, then?"

"Certainly."

Worley fixed a stony eye on her for a moment, then sealed their agreement with a single downward bob of his imperious chin.

Chapter Twenty-One

"Marta, I need to speak with you about Thomas."

After apologizing for bursting past her earlier, Carrie accepted a cup of tea, while Marta resumed baking. With a hot cup warming her hands, and spurred by battle nerves, Carrie broached the awkward subject of their affair.

Marta's head swiveled around with alarm. Her arms froze between the bowl of flour and the bowl of eggs.

"A lynch mob tried to kill him last night. At our house. We fought them off," Carrie said.

Marta didn't move, but her eyes got much wider.

"We were all very frightened, but I don't think they'll be back." Carrie paused; she hadn't planned a speech. Indeed, she hadn't planned to be here at all. Last night's horror had resulted in this morning's tirade. The sense of lawlessness she felt upon arrival in Hope Bridge had become a ghastly reality, one that broke into her own home. She used the flare of anxiety to launch herself at Worley, and now, she was raking through the coals of her fright as justification for bringing up the couple's danger.

"We knew the men in the mob. Hiram Stowe, Eustace and Phineas Clevinger, Kenny Bowmaker, Bert Smith. There were about twenty men. Mr. Worley was there. I spoke to him just now. He didn't mean any harm to Thomas. He was there to protect him."

"Is Thomas all right?" Marta barely moved her lips.

"Yes. We're all quite shaken. None of us slept." Carrie dropped her voice. "Marta, I saw you Friday night. You met Thomas in the graveyard. I was

CHAPTER TWENTY-ONE

at the Temperance meeting. Do the Worleys know you and Thomas are... courting?"

Marta pulled out a kitchen chair and dropped into it. She covered her face with her floured hands.

"Mother of God," she groaned. Tears slipped through her fingers and plowed tracks through the flour. Carrie pulled the girl into her embrace. Marta cried silently, her body clenching tight with spasms, then heaving open to take in more air. After a few minutes, Marta sat up, went to the sink to pump water, and washed her face and hands. She straightened her hair and took several deep breaths. Shuddering as she fought to gain control, she put a hand on her hip, another across her mouth.

"I tell the Worleys I go to see my fah-mily on Friday night," Marta whispered, her accent sharpened in distress. "I tell my mother I can only stay for supper, the missus being so poorly." Marta sniffed and stopped speaking, looking at Carrie with desperation. "I come back Saturday morning."

Carrie saw Marta's wretched predicament. They were doomed if they were found out. Socially, Marta's conduct would stain the Worleys. She'd be dismissed at once and wouldn't find work in Hope Bridge again. She'd be shunned. There would be no shelter for her, even among her own kin. Thomas would be accused of rape. The vigilantes that had been turned away last night would be emboldened and unstoppable.

But their love affair was, too. Carrie remembered the attraction she had for Phee, the longing to be near him, the desire to feel his warmth, his heaviness. To breathe in his scent. To give up her soul so he could fill the void.

Carrie shut her eyes. "Marta, my husband is gone. I miss him so much," she whispered, her lips tight against her teeth. "I would do anything, *anything*, to have him back with me right now, even for a moment. Just one moment."

Marta's tears fell again.

"I know what it's like to love someone. And my God, I know what it's like to lose him." Carrie said. "I'm not going to say a word, not a word! Do you hear me? But, you have to be much more careful. So much more! If it hadn't been me Friday night, I don't know what would have become of you."

Marta nodded, her reddened face desolate. "Mr. Worley was there? Last night?"

"Yes. He was not there to harm Thomas."

Marta's face showed a spark of hope. Carrie shut it down. "Don't think for one minute that he would approve!" Carrie warned in a whisper. "Don't think *anyone* will! He told me Thomas saved his life in Cuba, but that doesn't mean he'd abandon propriety!"

Marta hung her head and clenched her fists. She was trapped.

Carrie stood and took her hand. "I won't say a word, but Marta, please, please. Be careful! Don't ever let anyone see you!"

Marta assured Carrie with breathless, jerky nods. No doubt she would complete the breakfast and set about her household tasks as usual. But Carrie saw Marta was rattled to the core.

Abandoning the tea, Carrie left the warmth of Marta's kitchen. Back in the rain, her turmoil descended like the deluge itself. She had fought off a mob, overcome a professional impediment, and now carried a friend's mortal secret. *I should be much stronger,* she thought. But all she wanted was to run home to Phee; wanted desperately to be wrapped up in his love and reassurance. His absence stabbed her now. She used the pace of her feet, the lashing rain, and her gasping breath to drive away the ever-hungry grief.

Chapter Twenty-Two

"For Pete's sake, girl! What are you doing out in this rain?" Betsy Woodruff called from her baker's van. She hauled back on the leather reins to stop her horse next to Carrie. "Get in here, before you catch your death!"

Carrie hadn't heard the approaching squeak and chuff of the horse and cart. The pounding rain and muddy street blotted out every sound.

"Hello, Mrs. Woodruff! I didn't know you had a van!" Carrie shouted through the downpour.

"Well, I don't drive it over to your place! You're only two doors down!" Mrs. Woodruff yelled back. "Get in. I'm delivering up to the Grant's and the Manchester's."

Carrie took Mrs. Woodruff's abrasive hand and clambered into the boxy wagon. The water-streaked horse tossed its head and snorted. Mrs. Woodruff leaned across Carrie and yanked on a set of strings, loosening a tarp that immediately fell between Carrie and the pelting rain.

"Oh, that's much better!" Carrie said. "Thank you. This is lovely."

"No, it ain't. But it's better than walking in that mess. My poor Bigelow here is mad as hell, but we'll get him out of this as soon as we can. Where the hell are you going?" Mrs. Woodruff snapped the reins on Bigelow's back. Droplets spattered upward from his soaked hide. Her cursing lightened Carrie's mood.

"I was on my way home. I just left Worleys."

"He got somebody else for you to lay out? You think he'd send a carriage for you!"

"No, no. It's not that. Did you see our lawn this morning?"

"Yes! And Amos and I were loading our shotguns and heading over there last night. Looked like trouble. Then everyone lit out. What the hell was all that?"

"It was a lynch mob, Mrs. Woodruff. They came for Thomas."

The bread van reached the corner of Main and Piccolo. Rainwater sluiced down Hope Bridge's only cobbled street and formed a rivulet across Main. Navigating the slick road took precedence over Mrs. Woodruff's response. With the reins taut in her fingers, she encouraged the horse into the turn. The van tipped. Bigelow strained his way up the slope.

"Goddamn them fools," Mrs. Woodruff said when the van righted. "We don't need that kind of trouble around here. What the hell happened?"

"We managed to drive them away. But Mr. Worley was there. I was so angry; I went to his house this morning to tell him off. He told me that Thomas saved his life in Cuba. Is that true?"

"Yep, it's true. What a waste of young men, that was. Hell of a sickness, that typhus. Worley was still sick when he came home. He bought meals from me for about a month. He told me all about it, and he had mighty fine praise for Thomas Bale. Here we are."

Mrs. Woodruff grunted with the effort of piloting Bigelow another few yards into a hardpan drive and halted the horse under a portico. She set the brake and dropped the reins on the seat. "May as well give me a hand."

Carrie waved aside the flap and met Mrs. Woodruff at the back of the van. She picked up a wooden box painted with blue and white checkerboard. Similar boxes filled the floor of the van. Sacks padded the space between, holding them in place.

"Careful, that one has a crock of oatmeal. It should still be hot," Mrs. Woodruff carried a box to the door and hooked a finger into the bell pull. The door opened immediately, and a young girl in a housemaid's apron motioned them inside. Mrs. Woodruff handed the girl her box and returned to the cart for more.

Carrie followed the little maid through a short utility hall and into a wide kitchen. The Grants shared the Worleys' penchant for the latest in culinary

CHAPTER TWENTY-TWO

appliances. A Hoosier cabinet stood near an iron and silver stove. A hot water tank towered up to the ceiling, sprouting a maze of pipes at the top. The massive apparatus gave off no heat as Carrie walked by. The house itself felt smothered and inactive. *A death in the family will do that.* She set her box on the work table.

Betsy Woodruff bustled up the short corridor, puffing, and muttering. "That's it, ladies," she blared. "My God, that stove isn't even going? I won't have my customers eating cold oats! Let's get going, young lady! Go get some paper. I'll get a kettle on!"

With reaching arms and swinging hips, her big body took over the kitchen. Kettle in one hand, the pump hiccupping in the other, Mrs. Woodruff harangued the maid and Carrie into action. They stoked the big stove and slid the checkered lids off the meal boxes. Warm scents rose, and dishes clattered. The maid found trays, and Carrie rummaged for serving bowls.

The noise of commands and clattering dishes brought Rowena Grant to the kitchen doorway. Carrie and the maid froze. Once a proud matron ensconced in a hilltop manor, the death of her youngest daughter had yanked her from that perch. The matriarch wore a simple house dress, with her hair in a bun that took the least amount of energy to style. Her skin sagged like the loose folds of her clothing.

"Rowena, your maid let the fire go out, but we're cooking now," Betsy Woodruff said. "I'll have this spread on the table in a minute. Where are the girls?" She sprang about the room. Utensils, a stack of bowls, and the steaming porridge landed on the serving tray. The maid hefted it up and swept out past her mistress.

Rowena had tried to look imperious for a moment, but when the maid left the room, she pressed a kerchief to her mouth and reached out for Mrs. Woodruff. Her face crumbled as she fell into the big cook's arms.

"Oh my God, Betsy," the woman sobbed. Mrs. Woodruff patted Rowena's thin shoulders, her faded blue sleeves enveloping the silken robe.

"There, now Rowena," Mrs. Woodruff soothed, her voice lacking in volume for once. "God is blessed to have your little girl with him, honey. The angels are blessed."

Carrie stood awkwardly, a lump in her throat and tears brimming in her eyes. When Phee died, she had desperately wanted someone to hold her like that; wanted someone to gather her up in a loving embrace. Carrie could almost feel the warmth of Mrs. Woodruff's arms seeping into Mrs. Grant's shoulders, loosening the grief, causing it to spill over in a purging flow. She could imagine the release, the relinquishing of strength, while someone held her, while she melted under the hot barrage of sorrow.

The kettle whistled, jerking her attention from the women. She dashed her hands across her eyes and poured the hot water into a teapot filled with mint leaves. Mrs. Woodruff swayed side to side, as if rocking a baby, and Mrs. Grant quieted, held in the soothing cradle of the big woman's arms.

Carrie put the tea service on a tray, pushed open the door with her backside, and swung into the next room. A long dining table, covered with white linen and a row of unlit candles, presided. Two electric lights glowed on either side of a single, heavily draped window. A spray of yellow carnations erupted from a vase. *A curious color for mourning,* Carrie thought. According to the *Ladies Guide,* that flower and its color meant rejection and disappointment. The little maid held open a door on the other side, and two women entered.

The maid dipped her head away from them, a gesture that didn't look like respectful subservience. *She flinched,* Carrie thought. Maybe she's afraid of being chastised for her lapse of duty.

The Grant sisters slumped in with drawn faces and drooping shoulders. Both women wore severe black dresses, buttoned tightly up the front. The whisper of silk slipped about the room, emitting a faint scent of cedar. Their clothing had been in storage. Carrie remembered Sav saying their father had died within the past year or two.

"Hello," Carrie said, introducing herself. "I'm helping Mrs. Woodruff deliver a meal. You must be Ada?"

Ophelia's older sister nodded and sat down. She was a stunning young woman whose attitude of grief couldn't hide a trim figure or fine complexion. She wore her dark hair piled high, and her wide hazel eyes were red-rimmed under elegant brows. Ophelia had the same delicate eyebrows. On Ada, they looked haughty.

CHAPTER TWENTY-TWO

"I am," the dark sister confirmed. "This is Sylvannia. She's here while her husband is abroad. So pleased to meet you."

The two women didn't seem at all pleased to meet her. They were hollowed out, listless. Sylvannia didn't bother to greet Carrie. She just sat down at the table.

The middle sister must favor the other side of her lineage, Carrie thought. Sylvannia's brows crossed her forehead in a single pale line. While her sisters possessed slender, delicate features, Sylvannia's blunt nose presided over an unremarkable face. Her dull hair held none of Ada's wild spirit. She wore it in a severe bun, skewered to the back of her neck. Carrie agreed with Marta's advice about how that style aged a woman. The middle sister kept her hands in her lap, lacking the energy to reach for the cup of tea the maid poured.

"Please let me express my sincere condolences to you both," Carrie said. "Your mother is with Mrs. Woodruff just now. I had the privilege to prepare your sister at Mr. Worley's."

Ada Grant raised an interested eyebrow. "You did that? I thought Mrs. Worley had suddenly become an artist. Thank you. My sister looked so beautiful, so peaceful." Ada's eyes watered, and Sylvannia sniffed.

"You're so kind," Carrie said. "I was surprised when Mr. Worley asked for my services, and I did my very best for your sister. Here, let me serve breakfast."

"Won't you join us?" Sylvannia asked. Carrie placed shallow bowls of cinnamon-scented oatmeal in front of the girls. When she looked up to respond to the invitation, she caught a glimpse of Sylvannia's thin lips shifting from a sour line to a downcast bow. Sylvannia had given her a dirty look at the Whitsunday picnic last week. Carrie felt her guard come up. *Did she just do it again?*

Sylvannia continued smoothly. "I daresay, a new face may do us some good. We have to find some solace in our neighbors, isn't that right, sister?"

Ada nodded and picked up her spoon. Carrie settled into a chair. "Thank you. I have a few minutes, I believe."

The girls hesitated over their meal, sighing with disinterest. Carrie's hunger nearly overran her manners, but she ate slowly, not wanting to be rude in the face of the Grant sister's grief. She attempted a modestly cheery conversation starter. "I'm pleased to make your acquaintance. I'm from Nanuet; it's a small city, as I'm sure you know."

Only the click of spoons stirring in tea cups responded.

"This weather is so disheartening, isn't it?"

Silence.

She pressed on. "I've been to the Methodist Church and both grocers. Are there any Ladies Aid Societies in which I might enroll?" She was more willing to infiltrate her uncle's Society of Scholars than a hen party like Ladies Aid, but the anxiety of rejection coming from the two sisters was making her prattle.

Ada took the bait with a listless monotone. "The United Methodist Women meet once a month. There is a Literature League for Ladies. I believe the Crawfords host that." The tally seemed to wear her out. She took a shallow breath and sighed "We just had a Temperance meeting this past Friday. It was rousing, as always. You should attend. I believe your uncle is a supporter." Her teacup, pressed to her lips, ended the disinterested account.

"Oh, I didn't see you there," Carrie smiled, grasping at the slim commonality. "My uncle and I *did* attend. He wants to introduce me to the entire populace in Hope Bridge, hopefully by the end of the week!"

She saw the vagary fall flat. As the sister's continued silence severed the conversation, Carrie cleared her throat and picked up the sugar tongs, feeling the acute insecurity brought on by an impervious circle of young ladies.

A sudden inconsistency stopped her hand. Her arrival at the Temperance meeting last Friday had been nothing short of a sensation. Again, she felt examined as a new species. She had been put upon by every individual there, in hopes of making her acquaintance, gaining her enrollment, and of course, receiving her monetary contribution to their fervent cause. Ada Grant had not been among them.

Had Ada just lied about her attendance? What had she said specifically? 'It was rousing as always.' Did that statement imply she'd been there? She would have said, '*I heard* it was rousing' if she hadn't. And, hadn't a bunch of chin-

CHAPTER TWENTY-TWO

wagging ladies that night gossiped about the family having fits? None of the Grants had attended. Understandably so, since they were mourning their sister. She addressed Ada and lied as well. "I do look forward to attending the next meeting."

"You made the bouquet for the Reverend's table at the Whitsunday picnic," Sylvannia said. "With the maidenhair fern. That means secret admirer, doesn't it?"

"That's right," Carrie said. More confident with floral arrangements than a dish to pass, her centerpiece had included bluebells ('humility') and the delicate ferns that grew abundantly on the damp limestone edges of the hydroelectric plant at the other end of town.

"But I chose the ferns because they were lovely, not to send a message," she explained. "I make floral tributes for funerals. I'm always looking for new combinations, and I'm especially delighted at the wildflowers I've found here. Do you practice floriography?"

"No," Sylvannia said dully.

"Oh. Well, did you arrange the carnations?"

"No."

Carrie heard the final nail being driven into *that* topic.

Ada looked sharply at her sister. Sylvannia stared at her dishes. The dying conversation was like sending a bouquet of withered flowers to an earnest suitor. According to *The Ladies Guide to the Language of Flowers*, faded posies meant rejection. Carrie cleared her throat.

And then, the explanation for Sylvannia's malicious glares came to her. *She's jealous*. Is Sylvannia proprietary about the Reverend Borden? Not for herself, of course. She's married. She must be defending her older sister's interest in the chubby minister. Carrie couldn't imagine a dark beauty like Ada hitched to an unctuous man like Borden. But Sav had said Ada was flighty, had been sent away to heal her nerves. Perhaps marriage to the minister would help her settle.

The sisters resumed their attempts to eat breakfast. When the maid brought in warm bread, Carrie stood and buttered three slices, placing two on delicate plates and setting them before the sisters. Enough was enough.

"Ladies, forgive my boldness, but please, eat something. I understand your grief, as I'm widowed myself. But, I find that when we are weakened from starvation, our minds don't work as well."

Ada Grant had begun to tremble. Her eyes wide and darting, she looked as though she wanted to bolt.

Sylvannia put a firm hand over her sister's and said, "Yes, of course, Mrs. Lisbon. You are correct. Ada, please, let's take a bite together. We have always been so fond of Mrs. Woodruff's cooking. Let's not waste her efforts. She came in the rain for us."

Carrie could hear the silks of Ada's skirt rustling. Ada's knee had started bouncing under the table, but she picked up her bread and took a bite.

"Thank you, Mrs. Lisbon," Sylvannia said and rubbed her nose with a kerchief. Carrie caught a familiar whiff; couldn't place it. Not cedar. Something she had an unpleasant feeling about. Was it the scent of a stiffening agent used on ladies mourning clothes? Perhaps the Grant girls still held the belief that bathing during the initial mourning period was discouraged, but that didn't pinpoint the disagreeable scent either.

"Is that Ophelia's kerchief?" she asked Sylvannia.

"No, it's my own," the dull sister responded, looking at the wrinkled fabric in her hand. She tucked it under her leg, then looked down her undistinguished nose at Carrie. "Why do you ask?"

"Well... the scent somehow reminded me of your sister. I thought, just now, how very sentimental of you to carry it."

"It's my father's cologne," Sylvannia said evenly. The slimmest of warnings snaked through her voice. "I find it a comfort."

"I see. It reminds me of Germond. His cologne."

Sylvannia and Ada stopped eating. The bread paused midway to their lips. Sylvannia eyed Carrie with stoniness; Ada with quivering alarm.

Sylvannia put her bread down slowly. "How do you know what cologne he wore?"

Carrie stumbled. "Well, I'm an undertaker. I, uh, attended his laying out. At the sheriff's request. Mr. Worley was there, of course. And, before that, I was asked to provide, um, evidence, about Ophelia's death. Germond was

CHAPTER TWENTY-TWO

present at that time, too. I remember that scent." She omitted a synopsis of the episode involving Germond accosting her on the street, when the combined stench of cologne and halitosis had been overwhelming and still disgusted her. The sentiment rallied her.

"I have to admit to an aversion to Germond," she said. "He was not gentlemanly toward me at all."

The sisters' glares let her know she was bringing up an atrocious subject. *But they know that, surely? They must have known of their baby sister's plight with that man.* Sylvannia looked at her for a split second longer than was mannerly, her reddened eyes glinting with speculation.

"We know about that, Mrs. Lisbon," Ada said rapidly, her words tumbling over harsh, shallow breaths. "We just wondered if it was appropriate for a woman to be in attendance at the preparation of a man, not her relative. Frankly, we don't care what happens to that man's remains. Isn't that so, Sylvie?"

Sylvannia nodded and laced her fingers in front of her plate. After an uncomfortable silence, she asked, "What was the nature of the evidence you provided to the Sheriff regarding our sister, Mrs. Lisbon?"

Had Morgan informed the family of the cause of Ophelia's death? Did they still believe the poor girl had been thrown from a carriage? Carrie forced a deep breath and dug into her professional training. "My evidence was provided to the Sheriff, and as a matter of my oath of practice, I'm not allowed to disclose any particulars regarding the deceased."

Oath of practice, indeed! Carrie used the excuse her father had invented to thwart unanswerable questions. Ada stared at Carrie in alarm. Sylvannia leaned over and clasped Ada's trembling hand.

Seeking each other's comfort, or is Sylvie warning Ada to get herself under control? Carrie stood, collected her bowl and plate, and, settling them onto the serving tray, bade the ladies a good day and retreated back into the kitchen, like a well-trained and dismissed servant.

Chapter Twenty-Three

That afternoon, the wind increased in velocity, dashing rainwater against the house with a vengeance. Clattering twigs and spring leaves plastered themselves momentarily to the windowpanes before being sluiced off. Bale had boarded over their broken windows with small nails, but the wind whistled through the tiniest of cracks, like the keening of spirits.

Sav and Bale fidgeted at the kitchen table, trying to read the Sears catalog and *The Century*, respectively. Carrie stayed in the parlor, alternately fussing with the fire in the stove and leafing through the Freed files Bill Bemis had sent. Photographs, crude maps, and typed interviews with notes scribbled in the margins littered the table.

She had put the kettle on for the third time, when the doorbell jangled on its wire. They all jumped simultaneously, then realized there was no second mob. Sav stood and straightened his vest before answering the front door.

Sheriff Morgan and Deputy Lamont stamped their boots and let their coats drip onto the rug. Oscar the parrot, miserable during the past few days of dampness, shrieked overhead at the stimulation. Carrie took the men's heavy garments into the kitchen to dry before joining them in the parlor.

"Still got that parrot, I see," Morgan said, rubbing the cold out of his wet hands. "What the hell happened to your yard, Machin? Looks like you had a horse race out there."

"We had some unpleasant callers last night, Delphius."

"Looks like a cavalry of unpleasant callers. In the rain? What was so important they had to tear up your yard in a downpour?"

CHAPTER TWENTY-THREE

"They came to lynch Thomas Bale." Sav's calm reply brought the two lawmen up short.

"Not that shit again," Morgan said angrily. "Is anyone harmed?"

"No, but I have their names, if you care to hear my complaint." He pivoted to grin at Carrie. "I'll need to be compensated for the property they've destroyed, and they should be fined for not keeping their animals on established thoroughfares."

"How did you fend them off?"

"I recently purchased a Remington twelve-gauge from the Sears catalog. It made a convincing argument for the safety of my friend." Sav smiled widely. "That, and my niece threatened to blow everyone up."

Carrie had the immediate and uncomfortable attention of both lawmen staring at her. Bale had slipped into the room and, after a wordless nod to their guests, stood resolutely at her side.

"A mortician's bluff," she said lightly. She offered Lamont a towel to dry his dripping spade of whiskers and another to Morgan for his head and neck. *I'm still aggravated at you for not listening to me*, she thought. "The coffee is on," Carrie said, looking for a way to excuse herself before she thought any more about the spark she felt when Morgan's fingertips brushed hers. "I'm sure you gentlemen could use some fortification?"

"That's very kind of you, Mrs. Lisbon," Deputy Lamont said. "We've been interviewing all day. We stay just long enough to dry out, then we're soaked again in a second!"

"Let me express my condolences to you, Delphius," Sav offered. "Losing a brother is not an easy event to endure."

"Germond grew up to be a lout," Morgan said, shaking his head. "I don't mind saying it. We didn't have much in common. I'm glad my folks aren't around to see what he'd become. They doted on him."

Sav nodded sagely. "And unfortunately, he and Ophelia had no children."

Morgan frowned. "That's not a misfortune, Machin. He married Ophelia for her money. I had hoped the Grants would position him in one of their offices in Duncan. Keep him occupied. Apparently, they didn't like him very well, either. There was never an offer. So, by the grace of God, he had no children to *not* support"

Carrie listened to Morgan's calm assessment of his dead brother's character. She made an assessment of her own, still feeling the curious impact of Morgan's touch. *He looks less imposing today,* Carrie thought. Weary? Defeated? He had a shock from his brother's death, and he and Lamont must have been making inquiries since yesterday. He witnessed another family member's body being probed in a grisly fashion, and he was slogging through a gale, trying to get to the bottom of it all. She wondered who he had spoken to, who his suspects were. For suspects, there had to be, given a murder had been committed. Then, with a start, she wondered why the two lawmen were here.

Sheriff Morgan stepped over to the table strewn with the Freed photos and cocked his head sideways.

"What's all this?" he asked, pointing a chin at Bemis's black and white shots. "You've got pictures of dead women? This is how you spend your time, Mrs. Lisbon?"

Affronted, Carrie shot back. "A colleague sent these to me at my request, Mr. Morgan. I saw a similarity between Ophelia's death and those of several women in my hometown. I took it upon myself to collect information that would prove my point."

Morgan didn't speak. He considered her with the same concentration he had in Worley's cellar over Germond's body. She cleared the table, muttering, "Just trying to help."

"Just a moment, Mrs. Lisbon," Morgan said. "Is there a meaning to all this?"

Exasperated by his swing from terse remarks to curiosity, Carrie huffed. "The meaning is that I had misgivings about Ophelia's death. I knew she didn't die by accident. And I was right." She spilled the folder, splayed the contents around, and snatched up another picture.

"See this photo? See those marks? That was done by Lambert Freed." She pulled another. "This is my photo of Ophelia's neck. The marks are the same. But what good is this evidence? You won't accept my assistance. Ophelia's buried. 'Accidental death.' No investigation. Now Germond's dead. We're

CHAPTER TWENTY-THREE

quite sure someone killed *him* because you saw the bullet hole. There's a full investigation for him."

She paused for breath, glaring at him, not backing down. "But I felt Ophelia's bones. They are just as telling as a bullet hole. She died of strangulation—just like these women. Germond may or may not have killed her. But, whoever killed *him* might have. I wish you hadn't chosen to ignore my thoughts on the matter."

In the brief and stunned silence that followed her outburst, Sav interjected, effectively breaking the two apart. "This isn't a social call, I presume, Delphius?"

Morgan's gaze lingered thoughtfully on Carrie for a moment more, before he turned to Sav.

"Correct. Mr. Lamont and I are making inquiries. Regardless of his character and affiliation to me, Germond was plainly shot dead in his own home, and there's a murderer at large. We've come to question Thomas Bale."

"Why Thomas?"

"Germond often boasted about running the blacks out last year," Morgan said, turning to Bale. "Those were your people, weren't they? And your house was burned down, along with the cabins? Seems like you might have had it in for Germond."

Carrie watched Bale's face smooth to perfect neutrality. If he felt alarmed, as she did, he gave not the slightest hint.

"Where were you Friday night, Tom?" Lamont asked.

Carrie blanched. She had intended to warn Thomas of her knowledge of his affair with Marta and to implore him to be more careful. The opportunity to do so never occurred. Even this morning, when Thomas and her uncle were holed up in the kitchen, she could think of no discreet way to lure him into a private spot for a quick heart-to-heart. She caught her breath, then let it out, realizing she shouldn't look alarmed, in case Morgan noticed. What was Thomas going to say?

"I was in the cemetery," Bale said.

Carrie stiffened. *He isn't going to tell them he was with Marta?* The man was confident, she'd give him that, but she would be flabbergasted if he admitted to his dalliance.

"Doing what?" Morgan asked.

"Two things: I was listening to the Temperance Society Meeting. I'm not welcome, you see, but I always enjoy the hymns and the sermon. Plenty of places in the cemetery to rest, so to speak. And I can hear really well out there."

"A teetotaler, are you?"

Bale chuckled, "Not at all."

"And the other thing?"

"I was praying over the grave of that little girl we buried last week. Suzetta. I promised her father I'd pray for her until they could set a marker."

"Listening to hymns and praying?" Lamont said sarcastically. "In the pouring rain?"

"Wasn't raining at the time."

"Then what? Where'd you go after that?" Morgan continued.

"Just home."

"Here? You live under the same roof as Mrs. Lisbon?" Lamont cut in.

"I live in the carriage barn." Bale gave no sign that Lamont's insinuation about an unmarried black man living in the same house as a widowed white woman was unacceptable. "And you know that, Leo. You live in town. You know where everybody lives."

Lamont ignored Bale's response. Morgan turned to Sav. "Can you vouch for that?"

Sav said, "Yes, Carrie and I were at the Temperance meeting, but when we arrived home, Tom was there."

"How'd you know he was home?" Lamont asked.

"I saw the lamplight in the barn," Sav said smoothly, then followed up with annoyance, before the next, obvious question was asked. "No, I didn't go into the barn and call up the stairs and make sure he was there, Leo. But the weather was miserable, and we were fatigued. No one leaves a lamp on in their house untended."

Carrie felt the hairs on her neck prickle. That did not happen at all. When

CHAPTER TWENTY-THREE

she and her uncle got home, they came into the kitchen, hung their coats, and bid each other good night. She knew Thomas was not home, because he and Marta had disappeared into the mist by the creek. Her uncle was covering for Bale. Did he know of the affair?

"Is this true for you, Mrs. Lisbon?" Lamont asked.

Carrie nodded with wide-eyed innocence. In her confusion, she abandoned her commitment to presenting herself as a woman of independence. She was dodging bullets here, and she ducked behind the lie Sav had just told.

"I was quite done in, Mr. Lamont. I didn't notice. I came in the house, hung my coat, and went to bed."

"You own a handgun, Tom?" Morgan asked. Bale met his stare easily.

"Yes, sir. I do. A Colt. Thirty-eight."

"Go get it."

Bale excused himself and left the room. A brief roar of rain and the clicking of the kitchen door said he had left the house. They waited in silence. Bale returned, humming under his breath as he removed his coat, then stamped and scraped his feet repeatedly on the rug. Carrie watched her uncle looking down, his lips clamped together, listening to his friend taking his sweet time about it. Bale came into the parlor holding out a glossy revolver in the flat of his palm.

Morgan collected the gun and broke it open. Satisfied it was unloaded, he turned it over in his hands. He checked the cylinders and sniffed the barrel. "You keep it clean," he observed.

Bale shrugged.

"It's been fired in the last day or so?"

"Yep."

"At?"

"Rats. Bookhoudts."

"Why do you need a thirty-eight to shoot rats?"

"They're big rats."

Morgan snapped the gun back together and handed it to Lamont. "You own a pistol, Machin?"

"I do not."

"Mrs. Lisbon?"

Carrie shook her head.

Morgan slapped his knees as he stood up. "Well then. I have a man who is known to have been maligned by the deceased, owns a small caliber revolver that has been fired in the last day or so, and whose whereabouts cannot be strictly ascertained on the night of the murder. I'm ordering you to come with us, Mr. Bale."

Sav and Carrie jumped up. "Just a minute, Delphius," Sav said. "I can attest to Thomas's whereabouts! Bookhoudt can tell you he was shooting rats! There is no reason to suspect—"

"I just gave you my reasons to suspect Thomas Bale," Morgan said.

"Wait!" Carrie cried and tugged at Morgan's damp sleeve. "Wait, you can't think Thomas would kill Germond! Why on earth would he do that?"

"It's called motive, Mrs. Lisbon. People kill each other for *reasons*. And Mr. Bale has a reason for killing Germond. That's as plain as the nose on my face: revenge for Germond burning down his house last year."

"But that was last year! As I understand it, there was no complaint made! No one was accused, or for that matter, held accountable!"

"Like I said, Germond boasted of it."

"Well, maybe that's the first Thomas is hearing of it!"

Morgan rolled his eyes. "You're new in town, are you not? I'm sure in your hometown, people talk. Rumors go around. Isn't that what you said, Machin? 'That's how information is passed.' Everybody knows Germond was riding in that gang that night."

"Why would he wait, then?" Carrie persisted. "And what about the Grants? They might want revenge too, don't you think? Germond killed their sister! Their daughter! There's a motive."

"We don't know that for sure. Old man Grant is dead, and I doubt the sisters or Mrs. Grant would walk up to Germond and shoot him in the chest."

"But there's a brother. Uncle, what's his name? The one whose father-in-law lives with them. And the brother-in-law, Sylvannia's husband. What

CHAPTER TWENTY-THREE

about him?"

"Uh, that would be Gideon Grant," Sav stumbled, automatically reciting bloodlines. "Rowena's son-in-law is Peter Clarke."

"Peter Clarke is abroad, and Gideon is weak," Morgan said, reaching for the door and beckoning Bale to go with him.

"Why won't you listen to me?" Carrie shouted, angry and desperate. "Why won't you consider my ideas about Ophelia's death? Don't you think someone else was involved with Ophelia? Don't you think *that* person may have killed Germond?"

"Why would anyone *but* Germond kill Ophelia?"

"Why would *he*?" Carrie shouted. "She was a golden goose! You should go see the Grants, Mr. Morgan! Go see the Grants before you accuse Thomas!"

"Mrs. Lisbon, I hardly think the Grants –"

"What? Aren't capable of murder because they're wealthy? Of good standing? In mourning?"

"Yes!" Morgan leaned forward. His eyes, Carrie noticed in the midst of their altercation, had shown weariness a short time ago; now, they sparked with anger.

Morgan enunciated each word as though he were biting into them. "They are good citizens. They are in mourning! That kind doesn't go around shooting people they despise. They *pay them* to go away."

Carrie put her hands on her hips, civilities forgotten. Sav, Bale, and Deputy Lamont braced for the bout before them. "Carrie," Sav cautioned.

She leaned toward Morgan. "If you think for one more minute, I'm going to stand by and watch you falsely accuse Mr. Bale, you've got another thing coming. If you're worth any salt, you'll go to the Grants and give them the third degree, just like us. Unless they've paid *you* to go away!"

Morgan drew himself up and clapped his hat onto his head. He motioned for Lamont to fetch the coats, and the deputy returned carrying Bale's as well. While he drew himself into his damp overcoat, Morgan shot back at Carrie's insult.

"Your accusations are out of line, Mrs. Lisbon. I hope you find a return to propriety in the near future." He turned to Bale; his face was stony.

"Thomas Bale, I'm arresting you for the murder of Germond Morgan. Put your coat on. We're going to the post office. It's the only locked room I have."

Sav and Carrie shouted their protests, citing Thomas Bale's innocence and the pathetic defense two lawmen might put up if the mob returned.

Morgan held Bale's arm. "You know I'll keep the peace, Machin. Bring the man his meals and let me do my job." The gusty deluge prevented him from slamming the door.

Chapter Twenty-Four

"My God, uncle, what do we do?" Carrie clenched her hands and turned to Sav, helpless and furious. Sav tapped his fingertips together.

"Can you fix a big dinner for Tom?" he said. "I'll go to Mrs. Peters' house to use her telephone. I'll call Charlie Steadman. He's my attorney. He'll know what to do."

"But when those men find out Thomas has been taken to the post office, they'll come for him again."

"No," Sav said firmly. "No, they won't. The post office is a limestone building. They can't get in. Tom is innocent, and we know it. Charlie will find a way to prove that. Where're my boots?"

"Uncle, wait!" Carrie said, but then halted in wordless indecision. She could prove Thomas innocent. She knew he wasn't around Friday night when Germond was killed. She had only to break her promise to Marta to provide him an alibi.

Better yet, Marta could account for him. Surely, Marta would agree with that. What would be better: to be shamed or to have your lover hanged? But, then, the mob would hang Thomas for his liaison as soon as *that* came to light.

Could she trust her uncle with their secret? What if Sav knew another way around, with his expertise of local affairs? She pictured him fluttering at this awkward situation, but his crazed demeanor last night, blasting off a shotgun and standing down a mob, presented a backbone she never guessed he had. He could be trusted, of course, but how could he help?

Then, another impression chilled her. Perhaps, Thomas *did* have a motive, but not the one Del Morgan had recited. Thomas had been in Clevinger's back room when she told Morgan about Germond accosting Marta. Thomas was a steady man, but surely, he felt as passionate about protecting Marta as he did Bethy Hays. And he'd made barely any response last night when they'd walked home from Worleyss' when she recounted Germond's wounds, the burned shirt, and the extraction of the bullet. What if that wasn't news to Thomas Bale? What if he knew all about the peppering of gunpowder on a man's shirt because he had stood that close and fired the gun? He had a gun; he had a grudge. *Someday that boy will learn his manners.*

"What, Carrie?" Sav stood waiting.

What would he say? Would he condemn Thomas and Marta? Would he be an ally or would he shun his friend? Carrie looked away and sat back down, her indecision and its weight suddenly too much. Sav sat next to her and put an ink-stained hand on hers.

"What is it, niece? What's the matter? I assure you; we will help Thomas."

Carrie exhaled slowly, gaining a moment to think straight and steel herself. "I can provide Thomas with an alibi for Friday night."

Sav sat up straighter. "I thought I had."

"Well, I've got a better one," Carrie said drily. She got up and paced, rubbing her hands together. The rain drummed; thunder boomed closer. The house felt chilled and empty, like it was missing a piece. Thomas's forced departure had the finality of an amputation.

I'm not so brave after all. Maybe independence wasn't for her. Maybe not having agency over her future wasn't the goal to pursue. The humiliating encounter with Germond, the mob circling the house on screaming horseback, the weight of indecision, the insecurities of social navigation, now the morality of secrets. When had she ever faced such things alone? Why did she think she should do so now? A dull pain crept over her head. She opened her mouth to speak.

"Wait, Carrie," Sav said. "Let's get some tea. Let's take a minute to think."

Carrie nodded gratefully. Sav seated her in the kitchen, and set about plumping up the fire and filling the kettle.

CHAPTER TWENTY-FOUR

"Did I ever tell you how Thomas and I met?" he said over his shoulder, a boyish grin on his face. "I went to the Burr Street schoolhouse in Duncan when I was a child. I was an adroit student, of course. I passed every exam. I was excellent at memorization, and the school plays, especially. But my real talent was my orations." He shook his head in wonder. "I could recite Proverbs and Shakespeare better than my masters. I won every prize." He dug into a jar of dried tea, spooned the crumbled leaves generously into a china pot, and rummaged in the cupboard for honey.

"Of course, that got the attention of the Cooke brothers, who reasoned that, by virtue of their age and size, they should be the recipients of all prizes and the meager monetary awards, which, to a twelve-year-old stick like me, was the wealth of the Sultans.

"Anyway, the Cooke boys determined that I was in a good position to apportion my winnings with them. And by apportion, I mean the ratio was all for them and none for me. So," Sav made a wincing grunt as he reached for the highest shelf, "they stood me up against a brick wall and made their proposition. Of course, I agreed immediately, in favor of avoiding some broken ribs, plus other injuries and insults, which I can't repeat, they being of the more indelicate nature. In addition, I was to write any future papers the headmaster assigned for them. I was on the verge of concurring heartily, as I valued my ribs and didn't want any objects put into places that might be painful, when a savior appeared."

Theatrically, Sav paused to retrieve the kettle and poured boiling water into the teapot. He spooned a generous dollop of honey into the brew, grinned at Carrie while stirring like an alchemist, then poured the aromatic concoction into their cups. Fragrant steam filled the table space. Carrie already felt warmer.

"Thomas Bale came walking into the yard." Sav shook his head and inclined a bony shoulder in a gesture of disbelief. "A black boy. Half my size. Whistling. With his hands in his pockets. Bare feet, bare shanks, and cool as they come. He regarded us all with a rather surprised expression, as if we'd interrupted *his* stroll through a schoolyard he had no business being in. I, of course, being pinned by my lapels, was in no position to greet him, but I remember being shocked he was there.

"He then proceeded to ask what in the hell the Cooke boys were doing to his, pardon the expression 'skinny-ass friend'? I had never spoken to Thomas prior to that day. I was as stunned as the Cookes to know I was considered his friend. The Cookes were as shocked as I was, and it was at that precise moment I felt their grip on me relax, which gave me an opportunity to get a knee in the brisket of the one in possession of my lapels. I credit Thomas afterward for giving me the courage. That was the extent of combat for me; my one and only experience!" Sav blew across the surface of his teacup before he bent and slurped the brew. His spidery fingers gripped the minuscule handle with the barest of pincers.

"The knee was effective for securing my immediate release, and I wasted no time in running for my life. I heard a brief melee behind me, and in a moment, Thomas was running beside me. We ended up under the railroad trestle, skimming stones for the rest of the afternoon. Turns out, Thomas sneaked away from the Duncan Inn each morning to listen to our lessons outside the window. He knew the Cooke boys were up to no good just then. He had my back the whole time. We've been friends ever since."

Warmed by the tea and Sav's tale, Carrie pictured her uncle as an even more rawboned youth in the rough and tumble school yard, with Thomas Bale whistling in to the rescue.

"When Tom was burned out last year," Sav said, not looking at Carrie, "I gave him a place to live. But I should have done more to help his people. I didn't pursue it."

Carrie waited. She had always known this man to be charitable with his goodwill and exuberant knowledge. But a glimpse of his personal failures was rare. He had a full view of her darkest hours when Phee died. Now he trusted her with his own heartache.

"I hope I redeemed myself last night," he continued. For once, a smile didn't frame his long teeth. "That those young men are *still* pursuing this stupidity is beyond my tolerance! I acted purely out of fright, of course. But the righteousness of my conduct has settled on me, and I'm *bound* to see them answer for their actions. I can't do anything about last year, but I will hold them accountable for this."

"That's as it should be, uncle," Carrie said. "Can he be forgiven, if he's made an unforgivable mistake?"

"Of course. But, I can't think of any mistake Thomas might make. What do you know, niece?"

Time ran out on her indecision; she closed her eyes and grimaced as she stepped over the line. "I saw Thomas and Marta on Friday night. Together. Embracing. They met at the edge of the Presbyterian graveyard and walked together down to the creek."

Sav sat back, letting his eloquent hands drop into his lap. Carrie let the news digest. The disclosure was enough; the blanks could be filled in easily, as could the ramifications.

"I suspected," Sav said, smiling sadly. "They should have been much more careful. Thank God it was you who saw them."

His words elicited a relief so profound she felt light-headed. The burden of her knowledge had been heavy. Shedding the load brought on near joy. Her indecision about not trusting her uncle now felt scurrilous.

"I can provide an alibi that proves his innocence, but at what cost? Thomas may be saved from the noose as a murderer, but the mob will lynch him for his affair," she said. "I hope no one else saw them. They're in serious danger. I can't expose them. But I can't let him be locked up either."

"Understandable, Carrie. Let me think."

"Well, think about this, too, uncle," she went on. "Thomas heard me tell the sheriff about Germond accosting Marta after the Whitsunday picnic. That day in the store when Thomas stayed with me? He heard me say Germond harassed Marta—tried to grope her—the same day Ophelia died. What if Thomas... well, what if Thomas decided to put an end to that? What if he really did kill Germond?"

Sav sat, unstirring. "The 'unforgivable mistake?'"

Carrie nodded solemnly. "One or the other. Take your pick."

"I can see Tom courting Marta," Sav said slowly. "And, God help me, I can understand him shooting the man for bothering her." He and Carrie considered the quandary silently.

"Do you think Sheriff Morgan will be able to keep him safe? Treat him fairly?"

"I do, Carrie. Del Morgan is not like his baby brother. The mail room at the post office is as good as a barred cell. He'll be safe. And fair? Del Morgan is untested as a sheriff in a murder case. We haven't had a murder in the county for many years. Not since the Borthwick murder, which was nothing like the Taylor case. And Del wasn't sheriff in either of those events." Sav shook his head quickly, recognizing his own off-topic meander. "But, at the moment, I'm afraid Delphius and Leo may have their hands full with the flood."

"Flood?" Carrie said loudly. "What flood? We're flooding? My God, like Johnstown?"

To punctuate Sav's ominous prediction, thunder crashed and rumbled, as if a barrel filled with boulders had been suddenly dropped and rolled only inches above their heads. Carrie felt the shudder in her belly. Ghastly images of the Johnstown Flood in Pennsylvania blazed before her eyes. A wall of water had annihilated an entire town in a matter of minutes eleven years before. She had been eighteen then, planning her wedding. The papers, periodicals, and photos at the time depicted a nightmarish end for thousands of people. Sav's announcement pricked her with fear.

"No. Not like Johnstown," he said. "The Duncan is an innocuous creek most of the time. But, like all of the valley creeks, when it rains heavily for several days straight, the feeder streams all empty into her. I'm afraid the water has risen dangerously already. Now it's a problem."

"What do we do? Should we get out? What's going to happen?"

"Well, the electricity won't work; the hydro-plant will be overwhelmed," Sav said thoughtfully. "We won't be able to use the phones. I'd better get to the Peters house to use theirs, as soon as I can." He stood, listing his tasks while he collected their teacups. "The folks in the bottoms will be herding their stock onto higher ground; that always causes a fuss. Two years ago, the Holloway's ewes were bred by an inferior ram when they had to put their flock in with the Grossman's—"

"Uncle! For Christ's sake! What are we to do about Thomas and the flood?"

CHAPTER TWENTY-FOUR

"Ah, well, for one, let's get him some food. We'll get Emmet Cross to let us in. He's the postmaster."

"Should we get to high ground?"

"We *are* on high ground. The Duncan is rising, but the valley flattens out north of town. Plenty of river bottom to fill up. We'll be alright."

Carrie was already up. Her uncle's assurances, thin but trustworthy, were enough. She pulled a basket, bread, and jars together. "I'll get the food prepared. We'll get this to Thomas. Can you get your shotgun ready?"

Chapter Twenty-Five

They struggled against the wind and rain. North Street's stone walkways were slick. Small branches fell around them. Carrie held a basket of pickles and bread, pie, and books in one hand and kept Bale's slicker draped over it with the other. Sav carried his shotgun under his coat to keep it dry.

Carrie shouted above the torrent. "On the subject of liaisons, uncle, are there any ladies who meet your fancy?" As she expected, Sav began to fidget about the subject.

"Well, no. I've given up on that sort of thing...my age. Not to say I'm *not* the object of some coveting. The Peters sisters are smitten. To no avail, I assure you."

Sav danced over a puddle and threw out an arm to help Carrie leap over it as well. "Mrs. Woodruff's sister comes from Albany every summer to pick hops. She's a positive nuisance! Ophelia's sister may have made an overture. But, ah, here we are!" Their arrival at the post office ended the topic.

Carrie lingered over the idea of her uncle as a love interest while Sav tried the door. *So, Ada Grant had designs on Sav, not the chubby Reverend Borden?* Ophelia's eldest sister was a beautiful woman, poised, wealthy, with a touch of flair, perhaps a little bit on the nervous side as well. Why would Sav not have fostered that relationship? Why, then, had Sylvannia thrown her such malignant looks?

There was no response to Sav's pounding on the post office door, and he twisted the knob back and forth. "Another sound reason for building a bonafide constabulary," he muttered. "Well. Delphius must have locked

CHAPTER TWENTY-FIVE

Thomas in and left again. Clevinger's got a spare set of keys. Wait here. I'll fetch them."

Carrie nodded, pulling a wet tendril of hair off her cheek. "Leave your gun with me. I'll keep it dry." She watched her uncle trot down Main Street, his figure blurring in the distance and the rain. Making the turn into the general store, he slipped, grabbed his hat, and splayed his scarecrow limbs before grabbing a post, swinging around, and disappearing inside. Alone, Carrie looked around. Rain poured down in a perfectly straight curtain. No one was about.

Hope Bridge was in sodden disarray. Would she be warm and dry in this deluge in Nanuet? Would her view be any different? Her former hometown's streets would be awash with debris: manure, papers, hay, and trash that looked just as unsightly as Hope Bridge's weeds and mud. Would she be worried about a flood washing them all away? She would be alone, for sure, but unlike now, she wouldn't have a purpose. She surely wouldn't be toting a shotgun. She tightened her hand around the cold barrel, picturing Sav blasting it off in the air above the mob. It had, indeed, 'made a convincing argument.' Grasping it now, she felt a strong sense of resolve to keep protecting Tom Bale, to get Morgan to see his innocence.

Sav trotted back through the heavy rain, his drenched coat flapping. He produced a brass key and popped it into the keyhole. They stepped into the vestibule, depositing Bale's basket and Sav's shotgun. The heavy door thumped close behind them. Sav crossed the tiled floor, leaving muddy footprints behind. He unlocked the postmaster's door and slipped into the barred room. He came back out quickly, his face grim.

"He isn't here."

Carrie went rigid, her voice shrill. "Where could they have gone?"

"I'm sure there's an explanation," Sav said, turning for the door.

"But what if they were waylaid? That mob? Weren't they all townspeople? Local men? What if they saw them coming down the street and—"

Sav held up a hand, cutting her off. "No one peeks out their window and sees the sheriff with someone in tow, in the pouring rain, and thinks, 'gee wilikers, I've got to go get my lynching pals and finish the job!'" Even so, he pulled on his hair. "I'll find them. Leave the basket here. Go home."

At that moment, the door burst open. Carrie and Sav jumped. Morgan swept in with a splatter of rain, followed by Bale and Lamont. The men were winded, and mud-spattered. Lamont pulled the door shut. Bale stood beside the men who arrested him. He was not being guarded.

"The creek's over its banks. It's bad already," Morgan said. "We took the long way around to look at the bridge. I need to telegraph Duncan. Damn. Emmett's across the creek. Machin, can you send a telegraph? How'd you get in here?" Morgan spoke three subjects at once as he hung his sopping overcoat on a hall tree. Carrie found herself looking at the way his shirt clung to his arms.

Why? she thought, *why am I staring at him like a courtesan?* Thomas's arrest, the impending flood, and the bedraggled men in front of her were by no means conducive to *those* thoughts. *Enough of that!* she scolded herself and dropped her eyes when Morgan turned.

"Sam Clevinger has a set," Sav said. He made a gesture of humility and stepped behind the postmaster's desk to the telegraph set. "And I'll be happy to oblige your telegraphic requirements, Delphius. As a former member of the National Telegraphers League, I'm at your service."

"Clevinger's got keys?" Morgan said, exasperated. "Leo, put Tom in the mail room," he added wearily. Carrie made a sound of protest. Bale shook his head at her, collected his food basket, and walked into the tiny room. He sat down in the postmaster's chair in front of a desk topped with pigeonholes. Lamont shut the door. The click of the lock echoed through the room.

Carrie turned to Morgan. "I have misgivings about your arrest, Mr. Morgan. I believe you need to be more diligent in your pursuit of the man who may have killed your brother," she said.

"I've arrested a man who may have killed Germond," Morgan said. "I believe your thoughts on the matter are still relevant. I'll have plenty of opportunity *in the near future* to look into your misgivings. But, right now, I've got to get a telegram to Duncan to let them know your goddamn bridge is going to collapse in the even nearer future. Now, if I can get to it, Mrs. Lisbon!"

CHAPTER TWENTY-FIVE

Burning, Carrie turned to Bale. He stood facing her through the brass bars of the postmaster's window.

"Thomas, I was so worried you'd be lynched. When we came in, and you weren't here, I thought the worst."

"Nah. Del's going to keep me safe. I was the one who suggested we better take the long way around. I needed to see the bridge. It's not going to last. Likely it'll be swept off its foundation. East Hope is already under water."

"Oh, no! What's happened to all the people? The Scuttles?"

"They've all gone to higher ground. Yesterday, most likely. People know what to do. We're used to it; we've had freshets before."

"But you're arrested for murder. Why would Mr. Morgan let you go see the bridge before he locked you up?"

"Del and I have an understanding," Bale said with a small dismissive wave. "I know more about that bridge than anyone else."

"Did you save his life, too?"

Bale smiled broadly. "No, but he saved mine. There was a time, a while back, when he and I used to box. You ever been to a fight, Miss Carrie?"

She shook her head and laughed. "No."

"It's a thing of beauty." Bale's eyes warmed with his recollection. "It's a dance in there. A hundred men lining a ring. The whole crowd yelling their heads off, so loud you can't hear yourself think." Bale's hands came up in loose fists, and he jabbed the air a few times. "Me and Del were circling around, fists up. I let him hit me a few times, just for show. I let him go five rounds, just so the bets piled up. Then I let him have it.

"He fell kind of slow, like he had to think about it," Bale laughed. "But there was no thinking; he was a goner. The bet master didn't like it. Well, nobody liked it. The thing about being in a ring, is that when you need to, there's no way to get out." Bale smiled again.

"Fair of foul, didn't matter. I had to resume my match, so to speak. Men jumped in the ring and came at me. I got in some licks, then there were too many. Somebody fired a gun. Everybody stopped pounding on me and looked up. Del had a pistol aimed at the barn roof. He still didn't look like he was thinking, but he aimed that gun at the pig pile I was under, and just like that, they left me alone. 'Fair and square,' he says. 'He won fair and square.' He and I collected our stakes, and he rode with me until we were clear. I still trust him."

"You shouldn't be in here."

"I know," he shrugged. "It's all right."

"Thomas," Carrie's voice dropped to a barely audible murmur. "I saw you Friday night. I can give you an alibi."

He turned his head a fraction; his dark eyes slanted quizzically. Lamont had left them, disinterested in their conversation, to stand beside Morgan. A few steps away, Sav had gotten the telegraph to work, and the machine clicked out Morgan's report.

"Marta," Carrie whispered. Scarcely breathed the word. Bale's expression hardened.

"I'll die first, Miss Carrie," he said so quietly, the words barely made it to her ears. He stepped back, his eyes never leaving hers, never letting her doubt his sincerity for a second.

"Stay dry, Miss Carrie," he dismissed her conversationally. "I'll be home soon. Del will see me safe. Keep Mrs. Woodruff's pie coming!"

Chapter Twenty-Six

The storm lingered over Hope Bridge like an idle god toying with a maelstrom, callous of the carnage below. On Monday, no commerce was conducted at either general store; folks hurried to get under shelter. The druggist hung his closed sign at noon. The creamery man swore constantly, unloading wet cans in the rain. By that afternoon, the rutted roads became quagmires. With no more earth to soak it up, groundwater spilled into the Duncan. And the Duncan swelled.

Vicious with volume and speed, the creek smashed through the slender valley of Hope Bridge like a freight train through a marketplace. White caps churned across the appalling expanse. Trees clattered to their demise along the banks. The hapless battering rams boomed against the bridge's stone abutments. *Hope the bridge holds* was no longer a joke.

Struggling against the rain under an umbrella that never dried, Carrie delivered a dinner basket of fried egg sandwiches to the post office. Bale sat in the mail room, behind its locked door, with his feet up, reading postcards to Sav before popping them into their respective slots. The two gossiped like farmwives at a Sunday social. The pot-bellied stove kept the damp away.

Sav had taken up the job of telegrapher since Emmett Cross remained stranded on the east side of the creek, but one by one, the lines went down, severed by fallen poles and shorted out from rain-soaked branches. Last night, Hope Bridge's ticking machine, too, went silent. Sav reported the electricity failures as they ate their lunch.

"And you're sure there is no threat of any dams breaking?" Carrie asked.

"None. Although, in the future, we have to look into setting power poles more securely. The lines have to be clear of trees, as well...." While he planned aloud, Carrie collected a pile of telegrams meant for the Chester Inn and headed back out into the rain.

Hurrying up the hotel steps, she narrowly missed bumping into a man who stood on the porch. He squinted at her from under a bowler hat. Every inch of his face was covered with cinnamon freckles. Tufts of red hair sprouted from underneath.

Carrie stopped in her tracks and stared. *"Bill?"*

The freckled face burst into a smile "Oh, good heavens! Carrie! What a magnificent stroke of luck!" He waved her in and under the shelter of the high porch. Carrie dropped her umbrella and hugged her friend from the *Nanuet Daily*.

"What on earth are you doing here?" she asked, brushing happy tears from her eyes.

"What on earth are *you* doing here?" Bemis gestured to the mail packet she carried, then to the village and the rain in a single encompassing motion. "I was dropped at this hotel, unceremoniously, I might add, by the most cantankerous driver late yesterday. He said he had to leave me by the side of the road and get home. Something about sheep mating? I don't know. What an awful day! And that bridge? I was never so scared in all my life! That thing is *not* going to hold. What are you up to?"

"You came over the bridge?" Carrie said, aghast. She could hear the overwhelming roar of rushing water and a desperate moan of timbers under stress.

"God, no! We saw it yesterday morning, and the driver turned around. We had to go south—Middle Town or some such place? We crossed there. Then we came in from the west."

"Well, thank goodness. I think I know that driver. I have to deliver these telegrams. Here, let's go inside."

The two crammed through the Chester's front door, chattering over one another with disbelief. The hotel had filled to capacity with travelers who could no longer make their way through the impassable roads. She and Bill wove their way between crowded tables. Farmers in rough clothes, travelers

CHAPTER TWENTY-SIX

in better attire, and tradesmen in muddy boots groused about their delay, the ghastly weather, the condition of the roads, and the fate of the bridge. Chairs were littered with clothing hung to dry around a fireplace in the dining room. Short marble pillars topped with explosive ferns now held discarded glasses and dirty plates as the overwhelmed staff darted about, unable to keep up with the demands of the refugees.

An end table, still littered with someone else's meal, was the only surface available. Carrie put the plates on the floor. She hung her damp jacket on the back of her chair while Bemis managed to flag down a harried maid to ask for coffee and sandwiches for them both. Carrie caught up her friend's hand.

"I'm so very glad you're here, Bill. I have so much to tell you!"

"Well, get started with your tales, my dear. Now that I'm here and soon to be fed, I am, as always, all ears!" When Bemis grinned, his spotted ears flared outward. Carrie had always thought he must have been the ugliest child, but she likewise found him completely endearing. They sat knee to knee, clutching hands, and she started her tale.

A teen-aged boy, wearing the clothing of the hotel's stabler, finally brought their coffee, and with a helpless shrug in regards to the whereabouts of their sandwiches, hurried away. As Carrie went on, Bemis's expression went from gleeful to gleaming, his reporter's ears keen as a wolf.

"Floods. Murders. Lynch mobs?" he said in conclusion. "My God, Carrie! You didn't get out of Nanuet for all this, did you?"

Carrie laughed "No. I was expecting a life of leisurely gardening, at least to begin with. Why are you here?"

"Well, there's a great story here. A fair damsel in the idyllic countryside, strangled and violated," he said dramatically. "A killer as yet to be apprehended."

"I'm afraid the story gets awfully sordid, Bill. The husband was believed to be the murderer, but someone killed him this past Friday—"

Bemis's ears flared anew. Freckles stretched at the corners of his mouth. "That's fantastic!" he whispered quickly. "What a twist!" He used his thumbs and forefingers to delineate the headline in the air. 'Murderer murdered!'

This is rich, Carrie."

She smiled despite herself and shook her head, her sympathy for Ophelia at odds with Bemis's excitement. "Not so fast, Bill," she cautioned. "Ophelia was cruelly violated. And there is some evidence that the husband didn't do it. He certainly abused her and desecrated her body, but he may not have killed her."

Bemis lit up with enthusiasm. "A desecrated body? A double murder? Are there two killers?"

"Good lord!" Carrie laughed quietly. "If we have two killers in Hope Bridge, we have more to worry about than a flood."

"So, the husband killed the wife, but someone else killed the husband. Therefore, one murderer is taken care of, and another still exists."

"Or, there was—and still is—only one person who's committed both crimes. We don't know why anyone other than the husband would kill Ophelia. But he swears he didn't. *And* there's some plausibility to that. *And* I know he didn't dress her after her death, which makes me think there was someone else involved."

Carrie looked around and lowered her voice. "I have to say, while I have sympathy for Ophelia, Germond was a brute, and God help me, good riddance to him."

Bemis threw back his head and laughed. "Carrie, you'll never cease to delight me! You must marry me straight away!" He busied himself in his case. "Here, I brought the whole Freed file to show you. I didn't send you all the interviews; there are too many. But I talked to family members and the neighbors. We could review those interviews; see if there's anything in there that helps. I was after anything that might shed some light."

Bemis stacked their coffee cups on the floor among the other dirty dishes and spread his files across his knees and the small table. "There is a *mountain* of gossip and innuendo after a murder. Everyone accuses their neighbors of everything, from illicit affairs to damn near witchcraft. And families are so vicious among themselves, especially after a death.

"To my point, here's an interesting interview," Bemis said, warming to his subject. He passed a stapled set of pages to Carrie. "The interview of Miss

CHAPTER TWENTY-SIX

Margaret Carter, sister of the deceased Mrs. Elizabeth Chatterton, Freed victim number three. Miss Carter indicated some jealousy toward her sister. Elizabeth had a home and a husband, and the sister was a spinster. My guess is that she was lonely and bitter."

Carrie picked up the page and read aloud. "'My sister's announcements were always in the headlines. She always had something to crow about. Our period of mourning is nearly complete. I anticipate my trip to the dressmaker and the color lilac with some eagerness.'" Carrie put the paper down. "So? Sisters are jealous of each other. That's hardly new. I don't know how you managed to listen to so many tawdry family details."

Undeterred, Bemis handed over another yellowed page. "And here's more. Mrs. Hester Whitcomb, neighbor of the first victim, described her as 'an actress' who 'played false with her neighbors.' She supposedly behaved coquettishly to the husbands in the neighborhood, like a trollop to the sons, and like a shrew to the women. I spoke with several of Mrs. Whitcomb's neighbors, who said something similar. It's amazing what people hide."

"What were you looking for?"

"Anything. Any angle. I thought strangling a woman was a terrible violence. How does that happen? How does someone carry that out, unless you're looney or enraged?"

"Lambert Freed was simply insane, wasn't he?" Carrie said. "He was a monster with a blood lust; unreasonable, inhuman. That's the kind of person who puts their hands around another's throat."

"All of that, yes, but he was reasonable enough to hide his insanity until he killed again. He committed his crimes for years without being caught."

"Except you did catch him, Bill," Carrie said fondly. "You're a downright pest!"

Bill Bemis's freckles collected in the corners of his eyes as his face wrinkled mischievously. "Oh, yes. Pest I am. Let's keep looking."

Chapter Twenty-Seven

An hour later, when the hotel door blew open, Carrie looked up from her reading. Sheriff Delphius Morgan came in, followed by an angry spray of rain. A maid hurried forward and took his coat and hat. Morgan made for Carrie and Bemis, then stood near them with his back to the fire, drying his clothes.

"Mr. Morgan," Carrie said. "May I introduce Mr. William Bemis, my associate, from Nanuet."

Morgan dropped Bemis's hand after a single shake. "Are you an undertaker, Mr. Bemis?"

"No sir!" Bemis shivered in mock horror. "The deceased are beyond my comprehension. I'm a reporter with the *Nanuet Daily*."

Morgan frowned. Carrie watched his fatigue disappear as he braced for a new challenge.

"Mr. Bemis sent me the photographs you saw Sunday at my house, Mr. Morgan," she added, feeling an inexplicable need to ease this man's burden. *Never mind he argues with you at every turn?* She nudged aside the sentiment. With Bill here, and her uncle and Thomas safe, she could turn her energies to the puzzle of Ophelia Morgan, and this man was in charge of that enigma. "He was instrumental in the capture of a man who killed multiple times in Nanuet."

"Won't you join us, Sheriff?" Bemis swept his hand to a nearby chair, just as the stable boy brought a cup of coffee for Morgan. The young man and the sheriff exchanged a few words regarding lunch. Morgan sat and sighed, as though dropping a heavy load.

CHAPTER TWENTY-SEVEN

"What brings you to the Chester in such foul weather, Mrs. Lisbon?" he asked, sipping his coffee.

"I was delivering lunch to your prisoner, Mr. Morgan, and to my uncle. He asked me to deliver some telegrams to the hotel. I met my friend here by happy accident."

"So, you've come to scribble a few words about our humble town, Mr. Bemis?" Morgan asked.

"Indeed, I have, Mr. Morgan. There is a great deal of material here that will please the *Daily's* readership to no end!"

Morgan looked from Bemis to Carrie. "And, Mrs. Lisbon, you'd be complicit in splashing our town's good name across the headlines?"

Carrie offered him a wide smile. "I think, Mr. Morgan, this would be a story about the triumph of a little country town and its peace officers who restored law and order to its citizens."

"You think we're so lawless here?" Morgan returned her smile, and this time it was a warm and handsome expression. He sat back to receive a generous slice of steaming shepherd's pie from the stable boy, who had no further news regarding Carrie's sandwiches. Morgan arranged himself before his meal and snapped a napkin onto his lap. Carrie watched him take up a fork and pause. "You don't mind if I eat?" he asked. While he chewed slowly, Carrie responded to his challenge.

"Unless your question is rhetorical, permit me to reply, Mr. Morgan. I've witnessed incidents that put a citizen ill at ease. I've heard about events that caused great damage to a close friend. I've observed the murders of two people within a week and, not to put too fine a point on it, my uncle and I had to defend our home with firearms against a mob. So, yes, my perception of our town is one whose law*ful*ness comes into question."

Morgan stopped eating and looked at Carrie for a moment. "And that's just the first week," he said, and popped more pie into his mouth. Carrie noticed Bemis's ears flaring outward and shot him a glare.

"I'll not be mocked, Mr. Morgan."

"And I assure you, Mrs. Lisbon," Morgan said as he gained another forkful of pie with a decisive scoop, "my levity was not to be taken as mockery. But,

I believe you said you 'envied my candor?'"

Well, damn, so I did, Carrie thought. If she were honest, his comment was a well-timed quip. She huffed a grudging bit of laughter and watched him put away another mouthful. She noticed the stubble on his jaw. He kept his hands clean and used a napkin with good manners. Carrie put her elbows on the tiny table, laced her fingers together, and leaned forward. What was it that erased her initial assessment of him? His wary bonhomie? His pebble-colored hair drying in unruly tufts? Crammed in beside her, she could feel the heat of his leg under the table, next to her skirt.

"Has Mrs. Lisbon apprised you of our situation, Mr. Bemis?" Morgan asked the reporter.

"All of them, Sheriff," Bemis said. "I offer my humble expertise on the chance Mrs. Lisbon and I might prove useful again to law enforcement."

"And what is your field of expertise? I thought reporters wrote lurid observations and slanted opinions under sensational headlines."

Bemis nodded enthusiastically. "Interest is income, Sheriff. We are also prone to ask far more questions than anyone else, and we follow leads to get more stories. Indeed, there are occasions when my quest for information has been very useful to the police."

"You refer to the homicides Mrs. Lisbon mentioned?"

"The Freed murders, yes. I determined they had commonalities that lead to the killer's arrest."

"And how did you contribute, Mrs. Lisbon? I assume you and Mr. Bemis discussed these murders?"

"I prepared the body of the first victim. Our association began there."

Morgan didn't respond to their *curriculum vitae*. He put his empty plate aside, sat back, and regarded them both.

"And having achieved success in Nanuet, you believe your methods will be appreciated here?" Morgan asked.

"Is that so bad?" Carrie said. "Are not professionals and their services welcomed? I should think any and all opportunities for the swift and *accurate* dispensation of justice would be appreciated."

Morgan made a conciliatory gesture. "It's not unwelcomed. It's unex-

CHAPTER TWENTY-SEVEN

pected, especially from someone who just arrived. My position doesn't always create an immediate relationship of trust. I tend to be no one's friend."

Carrie huffed another laugh. "How would you like to be the daughter of a man who kept dead bodies in the house?"

Morgan smiled. "So, you see my hesitation. Nevertheless, I can see that Mr. Bemis has researched his cases thoroughly. I see now, Mrs. Lisbon, that your professional credentials are without flaw. I just wasn't prepared for your methods."

Morgan set his cup down and rested his big hands on the table; his jaw muscles clenched and relaxed. He came to a decision. "I'm glad I ran into you today. I wanted to tell you that you were wrong."

Carrie frowned hard at him. "What?"

"I *will* accept your assistance."

She couldn't help herself. She felt like that afternoon at Ophelia's funeral when Worley told her the Sheriff wanted to talk about Ophelia's death. She leaned back in her chair, crossed her arms, and gloated. "Do go *on*, Mr. Morgan."

"I don't need my balls busted, I'll thank you very much," he glared at her.

"Heaven forbid!" she laughed. His salty language did not offend her; she found it refreshing in the midst of etiquette-bound citizens, after the hushed and stifled treatment she'd endured over the past eight months; after a lynch mob and the arrest of Thomas Bale. A boundary between them dissolved.

"Look," Morgan went on, "that you, of all people, had doubts about Germond's story carries some weight. Given that he was such a Philistine toward you last week, I would have thought you'd be eager to have him stand for murder. People wronged don't care if they're right. A finger pointed is as good as a fact.

"But, you're right. Germond wouldn't have put all those clothes back on her body. I couldn't get that out of my mind. It was not only beyond his capacity; it was too much work."

Morgan spread his palms and dropped his chin, as if to ward off a rebuttal. "He *was* my baby brother. I was fourteen when he was born. My parents didn't expect him; my mother had a terrible time. But they coddled him until the day they died. Germond was a spoiled brat, then a lay-about, then a married rich man. Never worked an honest day in his life. So, knowing him, I concur," he said as Carrie held her breath. "He didn't dress her."

Bill Bemis leaned in, his expression wolfish for details. Morgan invoked his authority quietly. "Mr. Bemis. This is going to be a privileged conversation between us. Not a single letter of this goes into print until I say so. Is that completely clear?" Bemis nodded assent. He and Carrie exchanged looks of triumph.

"And I don't think she dressed herself," Carrie said.

Morgan looked at her steadily. "So, who? What woman would be complicit with Germond? Who would come in after he left Ophelia, help her get dressed, and then leave?"

"Someone who wanted to keep up appearances," Bemis said. "Keep the situation from getting to the neighbors."

"You have to talk to the Grants," Carrie said earnestly. "One of the sisters may have helped her."

"Leo and I already have. Yesterday morning," Morgan said. "Mrs. Grant was quite aggravated at my inquiry. Both sisters swear they were not at Ophelia's house after the picnic. Their little maid said they were home all afternoon. I have to take their word—for now—as there are no witnesses who can say otherwise."

"Ada was awfully nervous when I was there," Carrie said. "Is she usually like that?"

Morgan nodded. "She's high-strung, for sure. Impulsive. Ophelia was sweet, Sylvie's a recluse, and Ada's prone to drama. So much so that she's been in and out of rest homes to restore her nerves several times."

"But they could have gone to help their sister," Carrie said. "Tended her wounds; gotten her dressed?"

"But you said no one tended her. She hadn't bathed. And, you thought someone dressed her after she died, isn't that right?"

"That's true," Carrie said. "But I wonder if both sisters dressed Ophelia and left her there so that Germond could be held accountable for her death."

CHAPTER TWENTY-SEVEN

"Not possible," Morgan concluded. "They didn't leave the house Sunday night."

"What about Germond's killer?" Carrie asked. "Could any of the Grants have done that? What about the brother or the brother-in-law?"

"The Grants hated Germond, but Ada had an alibi for that night, and Sylvannia never leaves the house. Her husband is away on business, and the brother lives in Albany."

Carrie remembered Ada's misstep at the awkward breakfast. "What *was* her alibi? Ada said she had been at the Temperance meeting on Friday night. But I was there. I met everyone. We sat in the back and could see everyone. Ada was not there."

Morgan stifled a grin. "No, she was not."

"You know where she was?"

"She asked me to step into another room with her, so she could speak to me in private. She goes to Temperance meetings, but she's not abstinent. Not by any stretch. She said she was with George Louis Friday night."

Carrie slapped the table in disbelief. *"Digger?"*

Morgan laughed. "Where'd you hear that nickname?"

"My uncle. Good lord! That's repugnant."

"Well, I didn't ask if they were doing anything other than drinking. But that's a hell of a thing to admit. The Reverend Borden's wife—"

"I know, I know," Carrie chuckled, waving a hand. "Is Digger's sister. My uncle gave me the genealogy of the entire town." Her eyes narrowed. *So, Ada hadn't missed my comment about her absence at the Temperance meeting.* "Digger confirms this?"

"Digger has only a vague memory of seeing Ada on Friday night, but that's all."

"So, Thomas is still your main suspect?"

"I'm afraid so."

Bemis cut in. "What about itinerants? Tramps? Someone completely unrelated to either person. Perhaps a vagrant woman tried to rob Ophelia, and there was a struggle? If Ophelia died, the woman may have dressed her before fleeing?"

Morgan frowned. "It's a bit far-fetched."

"And biased, Bill," Carrie said. "Isn't it unfair that itinerants are always a little suspect?" Carrie told them about her interactions with the Scuttles. Wyatt's grief, his dogged determination to have his little girl buried properly, and his tenderness toward his stricken wife spoke volumes about his character.

"But we know they can be," Bemis said.

"I'd vouch for Mr. Scuttle," Carrie said firmly. "He is not like Lambert Freed."

"Well, maybe a woman came to the house trying to sell something or asked for a hand-out, found Ophelia dead, then dressed her and left."

Morgan and Carrie shook their heads. "Even more far-fetched," Carrie said. "I'm sure anyone happening by would run away quickly or alert a neighbor, not enter, dress a dead body and leave."

Morgan said speculatively, "I remember a bunch of men looking for work around here last year. They alluded to some women in town who could offer them something other than monetary compensation. I have no idea what that meant. It's not like Hope Bridge ever had a whore problem. I thought that rumor was just to lure them into town to work."

Carrie held up a hand. "It's the same thing Mrs. Scuttle said. She said Hope Bridge had a sinful reputation among the itinerants. She didn't want to come here."

Morgan nodded, regarding her for a while. Carrie flushed at its duration.

"Every so often, I get a complaint of that sort of thing in Duncan," Morgan said. "But not Hope Bridge."

He shook his head in frustration. "I'm thinking in circles here. I believe Germond killed Ophelia, but I can't get past who would have dressed her. I keep asking myself: who had a motive other than Tom Bale to kill Germond? The only thing is, Tom's revenge wouldn't take on that kind of finality. He'd want the men who burned him out to live a long life, full of guilt. That's more his style."

"Who else, then?" Carrie asked.

"I thought of Worley's maid. The Irish girl. Marta."

CHAPTER TWENTY-SEVEN

Bale and Marta's dilemma leapt suddenly at Carrie with the menace of a springing tiger. She remembered Bale's voice crooning an intimate word to his Irish lover that misty night. She saw again their embrace and their joy. She felt the dread of their secret and its hellish repercussions. She remembered the vehemence of Thomas's whispered vow 'I'll die first, Miss Carrie.'"

"Why Marta?" she said carefully.

"You said that Germond accosted her after the Sunday picnic." Morgan rubbed his cheeks and chin while he spoke. "I heard some talk of it happening before. You know the Irish have tempers. Maybe she lost hers."

With relief, Carrie saw her way around having to disclose her knowledge of the affair. "Really, Mr. Morgan, blaming Marta for murder just because she's Irish is like blaming Thomas just because he's a Negro. Or Mr. Scuttle because he's homeless."

Bemis leaned forward, pointing at his carroty hair and pale, freckled complexion. "This Irishman doesn't lose his temper, sir."

Morgan tossed his head with exasperation. "Fair enough, but it's possible. I'm sure her family owns a gun."

"Then it's possible that Sylvannia Clarke left her house," Carrie said. "No, Mr. Morgan. Marta tends Mrs. Worley like one would tend an infant. The woman is dying. Marta rarely leaves her side. Germond may have assaulted her, but I don't see her traveling to her family to get a gun, coming back, going to Germond's house, and shooting him in cold blood. Especially in this weather."

"Her family said she left them shortly after dinner because she had to tend to Mrs. Worley. She could have gone to Germond's before she got back home."

Carrie clenched her fists under the table. Morgan had gone so far as to interview Marta's family to determine her whereabouts on Friday night. He was close to uncovering her affair with Bale; he had only to question the Worleys. She used her own interview with Marta to steer him from the truth.

"Mr. Morgan, may I tell you something?" she asked patiently. "Marta was petrified of Germond. She avoided him. Crossed the street when he approached. When I went to Worleys to lay out Ophelia, she was terrified that Germond would once again resume his pursuit of her. And she was right: Germond accosted her after the picnic. He said so himself. I cannot conceive of her plotting to get so close to the man in order to shoot him."

Morgan folded his hands on the table and sat back, looking defeated. "There were no witnesses to Germond's killing. No one heard anything with the rain that night. I can't say for certain that Germond didn't kill Ophelia. I don't know how another woman comes in to dress her. I'm at a loss."

They were quiet for a moment, digesting Morgan's summation. The drumming rain continued. Cheers and taunts came from another room. Carrie craned her neck to see through a set of connecting doors. Several young men, dressed in clean vests and nice shoes, moved in and out of her view. One carried a billiard cue, another leaned on the mantle with a drink, another blew a stream of smoke upward. All laughed. Young men of leisure.

Bill Bemis, still considering the problem, said, "There are phones here, right? What if Ophelia called one of her sisters? But then she fell and died before the sister got there. The sister saw an opportunity to accuse this Germond fellow of her death, and they could be rid of him. So, she dresses Ophelia, maybe to preserve her dignity. Forgot the shoes. Leaves her alone. Lies about it."

"Ophelia was strangled," Carrie said. "She did not die from a fall down the stairs or otherwise."

"Why wouldn't Germond help Ophelia get dressed, then choke her, then cook up the story about her falling?" Morgan asked.

"A man who treats his wife like that isn't going to be helpful to her afterward," Carrie said quietly, recalling Ophelia's wounds. "He told you he left her in bed, naked and alive. Thomas said he was too stupid and scared of you to lie. If he didn't lie, then he didn't choke her. I assure you; he didn't dress her. A woman dressed her." Carrie sighed. "Let's get back to the sisters. Why isn't Sylvannia considered?"

"Sylvannia doesn't come out of the house," Morgan countered. "She's a shut-in. She's just...."

CHAPTER TWENTY-SEVEN

Carrie mulled over the middle sister. Plain, pale. Hardly a presence. "Unlikely?"

"Exactly. Unlikely."

Carrie scoffed, remembering Sylvannia's cold rebuttal about floriography. She knew enough about the meaning of flowers to insinuate that Carrie made an offer of courtship to Reverend Borden with her picnic arrangement. And Sylvannia's nasty looks? Didn't that indicate some malice? "Except hadn't Sylvannia demonstrated her devotion to Ophelia by overseeing the remodeling of her sister's home? She would have ventured out of her house then. Are you saying she doesn't even answer the phone?"

Morgan said, "We don't know there *was* a phone call. No phone. No sister. I'll ask Ruth."

"Who's Ruth?" Carrie asked.

"Ruth Nickerson, the operator. She works the switchboard on Elm Street. Good thing the phones are out; she can't handle more than one call at a time. She'd be spitting mad by now. Everyone who's stranded here needs to call their people to let them know where they are. She's ornery when she's hungry too."

Carrie sat upright. "There's only one phone operator?"

Morgan looked at her quizzically. "We've only got a dozen phones in the village. But the hotel makes a lot of calls. Ruth gets angry if everyone wants to call at—"

"I had no idea!" Carrie exclaimed. "In Nanuet, there are *a hundred* operators! When you make a call, any one of them can connect you. There were thousands of calls every day. But, we only have Ruth? She'll be able to tell us if Ophelia made a call or not."

She clenched her fist in victory. "Del," she said, hearing the diminutive escape her, but dismissed it instantly in her zeal. "Do you think Ruth will remember? Can you go see if she connected Ophelia to anyone that day?"

"Elm is on my way to the post office. I'll go now."

Carrie stifled an impulse to watch Morgan leave. She and Bemis ate the sandwiches that finally arrived and cleaned up the files. She told Bemis to stay dry at the hotel; there was no need to see her home. She waved her umbrella at him and lifted her feet, demonstrating the clumsy but effective rubber boots. "See, completely impervious to the rain!" she said. "We'll talk again tomorrow."

Outside, Carrie was surprised to see how dark the evening had become while she was entertained by Bemis's company and Morgan's investigation. The weak daylight had simply faded away to a murky twilight, then to night, cold and thick with rain. Carrie hustled under the umbrella, holding her skirt up and out of the mud. She decided not to check in with Sav and Bale, and crossed Main Street, a morass that sucked at her boots. Once she reached the stability of the flagstone walks, she glanced up and saw Ada Grant entering the side door of the Methodist Church.

Carrie squinted through the dark. *Ada must need some serious spiritual guidance if she's out in this weather.* Or, maybe the good Reverend Borden knew where Ada's drinking fellow could be found? Carrie shook her head, chiding herself for her pettiness. But...

An idea prompted her in a new direction.

Chapter Twenty-Eight

The puddles on the flagstones glinted in the diminishing light thrown from Main Street's gas lamps. Carrie found her way to the back of the annex and reached for the door handle. She hesitated. Either swollen with summer moisture or needing a few drops of oil, every church door announced a visitor. She thumbed the latch down slowly with one hand and braced the wet door jamb with the other. The heavy door didn't protest. She pulled it open and slipped through.

She half expected to see Mrs. Peters lurking like a noiseless guard dog, emerging from the gloom of the hall, growling a challenge to her presence. Thankfully, the room, which had been lit and buzzing with Temperance fanatics on Friday, was now an abandoned, chilly place. Carrie remembered crossing a short hallway to enter another vestibule that led to the Reverend Borden's office when she and Sav bargained for Suzetta's plot. *In for a penny,* she decided, and retraced her steps, took the short hallway, and started across the vestibule. She placed her feet carefully and quieted her breath as she closed in on the office door. A woman's anguished voice stopped her.

"I need to be rid of this!" Ada's sob was sharp. "I can't carry it!"

The Reverend Borden murmured a response to Ada's lament. Carrie eased her foot down and leaned in closer to listen.

Borden's voice rose and fell, a practiced cadence. He had spoken the same way when she had asked for help with Suzetta in this very office. He wielded it again during his scant service by the child's graveside, and during the Temperance meeting, as if the ups and downs of his delivery inspired greater piety. Carrie found it grating.

Ada continued to sob and snuffle, and Carrie pictured Borden's hand on her shoulder. Couldn't carry what? Needed to be rid of what? Ada's absolution was not Carrie's business, but if she was lying about being with Digger Louis Friday night, what else was she lying about? And why come to Borden? Hadn't Ophelia been interred in the Presbyterian cemetery?

A cold dash of recognition jerked Carrie to attention. Was Ada talking about a pregnancy? Realizing her shameless eavesdropping, Carrie eased her foot back and leaned away from the door.

"You'll need to confess your crime to the sheriff, my dear," Borden's voice rose and fell. "This is the way of justice. You'll stand before God and man with a clean soul."

Carrie stopped her retreat. *Crime?*

Ada wasn't burdened with a pregnancy? She was confessing to a crime? Too curious now and, feeling justified in her voyeurism, Carrie cast about once more for Mrs. Peters and crept closer.

"Oh, I can't!" Ada wailed. "I can't. He's Germond's brother. I'll be jailed. Oh, I don't want to go to jail. I don't want to die!"

"There, now, Miss Grant. Perhaps I can escort you home. A good meal and a good night's sleep may be helpful in seeing your way clear. Nothing will come of this tonight." Borden's voice rose and fell. "I can keep your confession for you. I can give you sanctuary. You are most brave to come to me in your hour of need. All will be well."

Carrie felt slightly offended about Ada's assertion that Del Morgan would not be fair to her predicament. Hadn't he invited her to discuss two murders just this afternoon? Accepted her opinions? Treated her like a colleague? Ada was distraught, yes, but her bias against Del Morgan's impartiality was flawed. As Morgan's 'keen observer,' she had a duty to find out what this was all about.

She knocked quietly on the door. The sobbing and the droning ceased instantly. No one moved to answer. She knocked again and called the Reverend's name.

"It's Carrie Lisbon, Reverend. I-I can't find my uncle." She blurted the first lie that came to her mind, hoping her quavering voice appealed to Borden's

CHAPTER TWENTY-EIGHT

magnanimity. She hoped to sound breathless as well, like she'd just arrived and hadn't been snooping by the door. "Can you help me?"

The office door opened, and the room expelled a heated burst of sweat and perfumed air. A flash of lightning lit elongated, mullioned windows. Borden held the door tightly against his side, blocking her entrance.

"Mrs. Lisbon. What's the trouble? Your uncle?" Borden attempted an expression between concern and surprise; it didn't quite mask his confusion and anger.

"I can't find him," Carrie spoke quickly, continuing the impulsive charade. "We met with the Sheriff about an hour ago. We were supposed to meet back at the house, and he hasn't shown up. Mr. Bale suggested I try here. Has he come by?"

"No, I haven't seen him. Isn't Mr. Bale jailed in the post office?"

"Is Mrs. Peters here?" Carrie hurried on, hoping to present as frantic. "She is so fond of my uncle. Would she know if he had stopped by?"

"Mrs. Peters isn't here. Why don't—"

"Is there anyone else here? Has anyone seen him?" Carrie craned her neck around Borden and peered into his office. "Oh, Ada, have you seen my uncle?"

"Mrs. Lisbon!" Borden protested, stiffening upright to block Carrie's search of his office. She squeezed by him, feigning desperation. Borden sputtered and stumbled back.

"Ada, have you seen my uncle Sav? I know you're fond of him. Did you happen to see him when you were coming by?"

Ada Grant's former arrogance had crumbled. The rain had drenched her clothing and her glorious dark hair. Wide-eyed and trembling, she turned to face Carrie with a kerchief held to her mouth.

"You saw the sheriff just now?" Ada asked.

Carrie felt suddenly sure Ada had something to do with Ophelia. Ada was the big sister; she'd have known what to do if Ophelia called for help. Had Ophelia called? Did Ada dress her? Pressing the intrusion, Carrie reached toward the dark sister. "Yes, he was at the Chester."

Ada squeaked and twisted away. She pressed the kerchief hard against her open mouth. Carrie pushed to the front of the chair. All pretense gone, she tugged at Ada's stiff forearms.

"What is it, Ada? What's wrong? If you know something, you must tell the Sheriff. Poor Thomas will hang if you don't! Please, if you love my uncle, please come with me and tell the sheriff what you know."

"I don't love your uncle!" Ada squealed in distress.

The situation had gotten completely out of Borden's hands. He hustled over and stood over the women, protesting Carrie's intrusion. "Mrs. Lisbon, Miss Grant has asked for my confidence this evening. You've interrupted—"

"You opened the door, Mr. Borden. You let me in."

"You pushed your way inside!"

Carrie ignored him. "Ada, it's true the sheriff was at the Chester. We can go there now. It's also true that our friend Thomas Bale has been arrested. He'll hang Ada. Please, if you know something about Germond, please tell me. Come with me. I'll help you tell the sheriff. Mr. Morgan has proven himself quite fair to me. But you must come and tell him. What happened to Ophelia?"

"Ophelia?" Ada said. "Germond killed her! He killed my sister."

"Mrs. Lisbon," Borden waded back in. "Mrs. Lisbon! Miss Ada is upset enough as it is."

"How do you know, Ada? Were you there?"

Disbelief widened Ada's eyes. "What?"

Carrie pushed on. "Were you there?"

Ada winced with incredulity. "No, I wasn't there!"

"Miss Grant, wait!" Borden insisted, but Ada pitched forward onto his desk, her face buried in her arms. Borden took Carrie's arm firmly and pulled her to her feet. "I must insist, Mrs. Lisbon. You can see Miss Ada's distress. She has come to me for comfort, and I'll not have that sanctuary violated! You must leave!"

Carrie called back to Ada as Borden hustled her toward the door. "Ada! Whatever it is, you can tell Sheriff Morgan! You can tell him, so Thomas won't hang! Ada!" Reverend Borden shoved her well into the hallway and pulled the door shut behind them.

CHAPTER TWENTY-EIGHT

"How dare you stick your nose into the business of my church!" he hissed. They could hear Ada continue to sob as they squared off.

"Our dear friend Thomas Bale is arrested for Germond's murder," Carrie shot back. "Ada might be able to help him if she knows something. Does she know something?"

"Mr. Bale's affairs are not my concern. Miss Ada's are. You have no place here, Mrs. Lisbon. I insist you leave at once. Miss Ada is distressed beyond tolerance. I need to resume my ministry of comfort and confession—"

Carrie held up a hand. Borden stopped his tirade in confusion. They heard silence from behind the closed door, then another sound: the splattering of rain on a wooden floor. Carrie barged past Borden and back into the office. The tall windows behind the desk had been flung open. The curtains blew inward; papers lay in shodden sheets on the floor. Carrie ran to the window and leaned out into the storm.

Needles of icy rain pricked her skin as she squinted into the gloom. She glimpsed Ada's skirt disappearing into the dark. Carrie shouted after her. She turned to Borden. "Go to the post office, Reverend, and get the sheriff. Can you tell him to come quickly? I'll stay with Ada." She bolted past the stunned man and, panicked by his inaction, shouted over her shoulder, "Go! Now!"

She dodged around sanctuary pews and ran down the center aisle. An exit through the front door would head off Ada. Borden, chubby but stronger, could catch her, but then, he'd protect her information. Better he fetches the sheriff.

The rain soaked her as soon as she burst out of the church entrance. Ada stumbled ahead of her, making for Main Street. Carrie called to her as she cut across the church lawn. With no stable flagstones to secure her footing, Sav's rubber boots were a hindrance in the spongy grass. She fell, gave up calling, and began cursing.

Gas lamps lit up Main Street on either side. Once derisive of the quaint illumination, Carrie felt whole-hearted gratitude for whoever braved the storm to light the street lamps tonight. She spurred herself forward, clutching her sodden skirt high. Elm trees reared and shook like great shaggy beasts in torment. Leaves shredded from their branches hit her with the same impact as the rain.

"Ada! Please! Stop!" Carrie screamed. Ada disappeared in the gloom between the lamps and reappeared in the next frail glow. "Stop!"

Ada fell in the mud, tripping on her own wet clothing. Carrie gained on her, but Ada sprang up and kept going. This time, Carrie added reason to her cries. "You haven't done anything wrong," she gasped, tiring. "Ada, stop!"

Rain swallowed the oldest Grant sister. Carrie glimpsed her, struggling against the gale, heading for the bridge before the last lamplight faded. *Why isn't she running home?*

Fighting to keep from floundering in the mud and the big boots, Carrie heard Sav's voice describing Ada. "*She's imprudent.*" Imprudent was another term for impulsive, impetuous. Did he mean insane? Had Ada completely lost her mind?

A wall of sound roared up ahead, the howl of the flood. Carrie tried to keep running, but she was soaked and heavy. Her chest burned. Her skirt weighed down her legs. She stopped and gathered a handful of the wet material. She stood below the last lamplight. If she stepped past the comfort of that little glow, she stepped into hopeless darkness. Lightning and thunder cracked simultaneously and lit up Ada's form. She clutched the frame of the bridge. Flood water swirled around the entrance.

"Ada, no!"

The volume and violence of the water stunned Carrie. She ran into the darkness, screaming for Ada to come back. She stumbled in the mud, went forward, and stopped at the entrance of the bridge. Clinging to the slippery wooden frame, terrified to go any further, she saw Ada in the next flash of lightning.

She had waded onto the bridge, into the water, and stood only a few yards away. Her skirt was tugged horizontally. She turned back, her face a mask of open terror, and threw out her hand toward Carrie.

"*Help me!*"

The bridge shuddered as it collapsed downward, sideways, and away. The grinding and squealing of ripping wood overwhelmed Ada's screams.

CHAPTER TWENTY-EIGHT

Carrie's feet sped backward. She fell, grasping uselessly at the mud, and slipped downward with the heaving structure.

The icy water claimed her legs, tugged greedily at the oversized boots, yanked them off. Suddenly she was wrenched backward, clenched in an iron grip. She spun over to clutch at the saving hands just as the creek raised her up to bear her away. Del Morgan lay on his belly, pulling at her forearms, grimacing with strain.

Stalemate. The creek had her. Morgan shouted in her ear; she screamed into his. The water consumed both sounds. Then Thomas Bale had his feet planted, hauling back on Morgan's belt, roaring with effort. And Carrie was pulled away from the dark, hungry flood.

Chapter Twenty-Nine

They stumbled together; bent refugees covered in ooze, barefoot and hobbling through the drenching rain. Bale and Morgan hauled Carrie up onto Bookhoudt's wide porch and collapsed on either side of her. They lay there gasping for a few moments before Bale rolled over and staggered to his feet. He disappeared around the side of the building.

Carrie breathed hard and shook, still feeling the icy water sucking at her legs. If she had slid into its grasp, she would have been ground up in an instant.

She thought of Phee. He would have been there, at the end. She would have been back in his embrace, gathered up and soothed forever. It would have been all right. Shivering and desperate for a haven, she reached out for him. *Just get up; just get that far. Then we'll see.*

She found Del Morgan's hand, icy cold and wet. Her fingertips brushed past the bristly knuckles. The big hand turned over; hers burrowed in. He squeezed gently and held on. Carrie burst into tears.

"Ada," she sobbed, covering her mouth. They lay there while the muddy street filled with people. Alerted by the catastrophic sound of their namesake going down, Hope Bridge responded. Shouts of alarm and warnings rose; an iron wheel clanged, calling up the fire brigade. Dozens of thudding feet vibrated the floorboards Carrie lay on. Morgan heaved himself up, releasing Carrie's hand and leaving her colder than before. Bale reappeared from inside the building. He and Morgan helped Carrie up and inside. Bale lit a lamp and opened the grates on the pot-bellied stove, reviving a fire banked for the evening. Bookhoudt came down from the residence upstairs,

CHAPTER TWENTY-NINE

carrying a brutal hickory stick and an equally ugly scowl.

"What the hell?" he said.

"We needed to get in, Gene," Morgan said. "Can you get us some blankets? We're freezing."

Bookhoudt turned and went back up the stairs. Carrie stood with Morgan, shivering, staring vacantly, while Bale fussed up the fire in the big stove. Bookhoudt came back down with heavy wool blankets and a quilt. Morgan draped the quilt over Carrie and one of the woolens over that. Bale led her to the fire.

"How'd you get out of the post office, Tom?" Morgan asked. He had peeled off his coat and vest. His shirt clung to his skin as he swung another blanket over his shoulders.

"Shit, Del, you forget I work there," Bale said. "I know where all the keys are stashed." With that, he handed a small brass key to Gene Bookhoudt, who frowned and pocketed it. Bale looked cynically at the Sheriff. "You complaining?"

Morgan raised his wet eyebrows and rubbed water from his face. "No."

"The bridge," Carrie said. "Ada was on the bridge."

"I know, Mrs. Lisbon. What the hell is going on?"

Carrie told him about the interview in the church office through chattering teeth. "I told the Reverend to go find you."

"He did. I ran out. I saw you both running toward the creek."

Carrie shuddered and leaned closer to the fire. "We left the room for a moment, and Ada went out the window."

Bookhoudt's wife came down with a tray of cups and a pot of coffee. She put one into Carrie's hands. The hot liquid jumped and belled in time to Carrie's shivering. Mrs. Bookhoudt held her hands over Carrie's to assist in getting the cup to her lips. The coffee was strong and sugary. It coursed through Carrie like a balm.

"She confessed something to Reverend Borden. I think she was there. With Ophelia."

"She should have come to me," Morgan said quietly.

"I tried to get her to come to you. I told her I'd stay with her." Carrie's eyes welled again. "She shouldn't have gone onto that bridge." Mrs. Bookhoudt put an arm around Carrie's shoulders and pulled her close; she held Carrie's hand around the cup with the other.

"Ada's gone?" Mrs. Bookhoudt asked softly. "Ada Grant?"

Morgan nodded. "With the bridge. Bale saved Mrs. Lisbon and I. Are the 'phones working, Darla? I need to use the 'phone."

"No, Del, they still aren't. I suspect they won't be for a while."

"All right. All right." Morgan had started pacing. "Can you loan me a raincoat, Darla? Do you have one?"

Darla Bookhoudt unmoored herself from Carrie and went to fetch the coat from upstairs. The fire in the stove roared, dissipating the chill in the room.

"Where are you going?" Carrie asked Morgan.

"I need a work party. I need someone to ride to Duncan. Let them know." Carrie had seen him speak aloud his mental lists before.

"I'll see you home first," he continued. "Gene, can you go get the boys? They may still be at the Chester."

Bookhoudt scowled. "Them boys ain't no good at working. They're only good for cards."

"I don't give a damn, Gene. They're the closest able-bodied men, and I need them *now*."

Bookhoudt grumbled off into the rainy night, his hickory cudgel held firmly in hand. Morgan fumbled with his heavy badge, his fingers too numb for the task of unpinning it. He finally got it off and handed it to Bale.

"Put it on, Thomas. Can you get them organized? I need men to keep a watch, keep the lamps going." Bale took the heavy pin without a word.

Morgan kept planning. "Get posts and rope up. And lanterns. Keep people away. As far away as Bookhoudt's. I'm worried about the bank collapsing."

Reverend Borden burst in, his cassock, pants, and shoes plastered with mud. Carrie looked dully at the indignant man, despairing of another prickly encounter, one she had no reserve to endure.

"Sheriff Morgan, I must speak with you," the reverend said. "I just heard Miss Grant was on the bridge when it went down. Is that true?"

CHAPTER TWENTY-NINE

Morgan nodded, pulling on the oilcloth coat Darla Bookhoudt handed him. "Mrs. Lisbon tried to stop her. She was nearly lost, too."

The chubby man glanced at Carrie sharply. "Miss Ada had come to seek my counsel, Sheriff. While we were engaged in a private conversation, Mrs. Lisbon interrupted us most rudely. If she hadn't come in, Miss Ada would not have run away. Indeed, she would not be dead right now."

Carrie gasped at the pain of his cruel accusation. Ada had been distraught and panicked; she was known for her histrionics. She may have done anything *imprudent*. She could have run anywhere.

"I tried to stop her! I tried to get her to see the sheriff. She had confessed to something! It may have saved Thomas."

"She *was* in a high state of distress," Borden said. "Your interference was uncalled for."

"What did she see you about, Reverend?" Morgan asked.

"It's a confidential matter, Sheriff. I need to maintain the sanctity of that pact with my parishioners."

"I believe that confidence is moot once the confidante has died, Reverend."

Borden swallowed; his tense body stalled.

"Isn't that so?" Morgan pressed.

"It is. But it's the pastor's discretion to disclose the contents of the discussion. Is there a circumstance that warrants my disclosure?"

Carrie wanted to scream, a residual impulse from being nearly swallowed by an icy flood coupled with frustration from this self-important man's stonewalling. The circumstance was dire enough: an innocent man stood accused of murder, and a woman had just died hideously with information that could potentially save him. Her shivering doubled with righteous anger.

"There is," Morgan said evenly. "Keep your confidence, for now, Reverend. We've got to manage this flood. Think on your 'discretion,' won't you." He gently pulled on Carrie's arm. She reluctantly left the heat of the wood stove as Morgan moved her toward the door.

Bookhoudt's porch and Main Street were lit up with lanterns and crowded with villagers. Bundled up and huddled under umbrellas, they gathered outside the store, peering through the gloom at the new and wretched landscape. Carrie pulled Mrs. Bookhoudt's quilt tightly to her throat and stepped outside behind Morgan.

Bale barked instructions to the group of sullen young men Gene Bookhoudt had rounded up. The store man clenched his hickory stick as he stood behind the reluctant gang. Carrie recognized the dandies from the gaming room at the Chester. They were the same young men who had surrounded her house with fire and hatred.

"Thomas!"

Bale turned to the sound of Marta's voice a split second before she pushed her way through the crowd and flung herself at him. He caught her, strapped his arms around her, and lifted her off her feet. Their lover's embrace was unmistakable.

Carrie and Morgan froze, as did the crowd. Ina Barnstable's eyes gleamed. Reverend Borden scowled. Hiram Stowe's plump wife gasped next to him, and Hiram turned away, shaking his head. Someone murmured, "oh, my!" Thomas and Marta stood in the light spilling from Bookhoudt's door, surrounded by stunned attention. The destroyed bridge was forgotten. Then, Thomas Bale turned, his face hard in the silence.

"What?" he said. "What? This here?" He held up Marta's hand, clasped tightly in his own.

"This is a problem for you? You'll put up with a man who abuses his wife, but *this* don't work for you?" He dropped Marta's hand and took a step into the void. He turned full circle, a mud-covered contender, looking everyone in the eye.

"You'll put up with a drunken mob that tries to *murder* a man, but *this* you can't abide?" No one spoke.

"You burn out people?" He shouted, pointing a finger at Eustace Clevinger, the grocer's entitled son. He pointed again at another young man. "You kick a woman who's with child, Bowmaker?" The young men who had hidden behind kerchiefs on Saturday night looked away as their names were called. Bale's finger jabbed at another. "You ride a woman down! You keep a man from worship, *but you got a problem with this?*" He stared down the mob.

"I'm not finished!" he bellowed. "You don't have a problem with me

CHAPTER TWENTY-NINE

anymore. You've got a problem with the law," he stormed, pulling his soaked vest forward. Morgan's badge winked dully in the lamplight. The crowd wavered. Marta put a shaking hand over her mouth.

Thomas Bale stood a moment more, then stepped forward. "Get the hell outta my way," he snarled to the young men. They stepped aside. Bale and Marta walked through. Carrie, suddenly feeling weak beyond words, passed a cold hand over her face.

Chapter Thirty

Morgan hurried her in silence, her bare feet and chattering teeth notwithstanding. The roar of the Duncan receded behind them. She shivered under the weight of her sodden garments and heard Ada Grant screaming over and over again. Morgan opened the front door to her house, pushed her through, turned, and hustled away into the night.

Moving rigidly toward the kitchen, she wondered where Sav was. If he was still holed up at the post office, he would have come to her aid with Morgan. *Keep moving,* she counseled herself, her brain dull with cold. *Just get that far.* The fire had gone out. Cursing the damp newspaper, she struck a bundled trio of matches before succeeding with a spark. Tinder, kindling, and small staves fed the precious flame until she knew it would thrive. She dropped her wet garments on the floor of her bedroom and stiffly pulled on a cotton shift, dry socks, and a housecoat. Still, her body refused to warm up. She shuddered in front of the kitchen stove until the doorbell jangled on its thin wire.

Her mind skittered. *Dear God! What now?* She glanced around for a weapon and startled herself by doing so.

Why not? She was alone in the house, and two people had been murdered within a week. A lynch mob had encircled her and her family a few days past. Bill Bemis might be the one at the door. That would be expected, but what if it wasn't him? Rain storm be damned, she decided. Whoever it was could wait a blazing minute until she found a cudgel or a knife. She realized with dismay that Sav had taken the shotgun. The doorbell jangled again.

CHAPTER THIRTY

She remembered her threat of using embalming chemicals to create a blast of fumes and white-hot fire Saturday night. She pictured herself answering the door with a table lamp in one hand and a bottle of arsenic in the other. She'd been bluffing that night; there were no embalming materials here, just developing solution. She bolted down into the cellar and scrambled around for a similar bottle, careened back upstairs, and thumbed off the glass stopper. She hurried down the hall, setting the kerosene lamp on the hallway table, as the bell jerked and bobbed angrily for a third time. She yanked open the door with the bottle cocked back, ready to soak the threatening intruder.

Delphius Morgan took up the whole doorway, an imposing, dripping mess. He pulled his hat off his head impatiently and made to step inside.

"Stop!" Carrie cried. "What do you want?"

"Christ, to get out of the rain, for one. May I come in?"

Carrie held her ground.

"Mrs. Lisbon. This is highly irregular—"

"I'll tell you what's highly irregular," Carrie shouted. "Murder, floods, lynch mobs! No police force, no phones, nobody around."

They stood at an impasse, exchanging wary looks. Then he simply shook his head and slumped in defeat. He cupped his hat in his big hand, touched it to his head, and turned to walk away. "I have to get back, Mrs. Lisbon. I'm sorry to have frightened you."

"Wait," Carrie said.

She was struck with pity for the big man drooping under the downpour. His wet pants bagged and puddled over his shoes; the brim of his hat was a tiny basin filled with water. It spilled over onto the borrowed raincoat. She remembered his grip on her arms, pulling for all he was worth against the freight train power of the flood. Her hand in his on Bookhoudt's porch. The rain drummed loudly, the percussion of a billion tiny impacts. Carrie stepped aside so he could come in.

* * *

She hung his coat on the back of a kitchen chair and pulled it close to the stove. She added wood to the fire until the air wavered with heat. She sat down without a word, regarding her guest. She put her jar of developing solution on the table. Morgan jutted his chin at it.

"What did you propose to do with that?"

"Set you on fire."

"Jesus," he winced. "Your uncle said you threatened to blow up everyone Saturday night."

"Yes. I told them I had embalming supplies in the house, and they'd go up in intense flames if they threw one torch."

"Would that really have happened?"

"I've never tried it, but arsenic is flammable. I let them think I had some. We were afraid for our lives, Mr. Morgan. If it came to it, I'd probably try it. Why did you come here?"

Morgan's face turned bleak. "I've just come from the Grants, Carrie. When I told Mrs. Grant…she…just fell down. I sent for Mrs. Woodruff. I didn't know what else to do."

Carrie felt pity again when he spoke her Christian name. A breach of etiquette, certainly, but it meant familiarity, and had they not just survived an ordeal that sealed their familiarity?

"That's a summary of *your* affairs, Mr. Morgan. Why did you come *here?*"

"I came to see that you were all right," he said gently. "I saw you home; I just pushed you inside. And now I think you were almost lost." He paused. "Are you all right?"

"I'm all right," she said and settled her hand over his. The comforting touch was automatic. Why did she employ it now, to this man who had held her in contempt at one time, who jailed her friend, who refused her expertise? Because he exhibited that which she had been trained all her life to relieve. Grief and distress. The hand, above all things, had the power to connect the grieving to the support they needed.

"I haven't thanked you for pulling me out," she said.

He blew out a breath, withdrew his hand from beneath hers, and pushed himself up, reaching for his damp coat.

"I've got a flood to contend with. I'm glad to see you're safe. Will you be

CHAPTER THIRTY

all right?" he asked again.

Carrie stood as well. Would she? Didn't she want to fall down, like Mrs. Grant? Didn't she desperately want someone to hold her up after all this? Why was she the one to provide the comfort? Why was comfort denied her?

"No," she croaked.

Morgan looked down at her, his arm still outstretched for his coat, creating a natural invitation. They stood facing each other. He needed to go out the front door. The front of the house was behind her; she had to step out of his way, otherwise, he would have to step forward, too close to her, in order to get by. He stepped forward anyway, and she wanted him there, wanted him to close those big arms around her, to complete the invitation. His scent of rain and warmth overtook her. She remembered his hand around hers as they lay on the wet boards of Bookhoudt's porch and her body simply emulated her hand. She stepped into his embrace, and he gathered her in.

* * *

There were no plans, no words, no thoughts. What started as shelter from the storm became a torrent in itself. Where there had been a set of individuals, in the quiet of her suite, they created a new one. One that gave and received; one that held and surrendered within the same breath. Heavy gave way to frail; icy limbs found fire. Recognition fused with secrets. Life asserted itself with sparks and simple need.

Afterward, he sat in her bedside chair, his long cotton shirt half-buttoned, pooling in his lap. His bare legs fell slack, waiting for socks and trousers. "I've never been unfaithful, Carrie," he said quietly. "Never. I don't know why this happened."

She sat with her legs over the side of the bed, close to him, still warm and replete from his weight. "I've never been unfaithful, either," she said. "But I *do* know why this happened."

She reached out and took his hand. "You and I almost died together. That's a bond we now share. I've heard of this. One doesn't expect it to happen. But now that it has…I'm…"

Carrie considered her feelings, looking hard into his eyes.

"...not sorry."

With small, decisive nods of her head, she rose and stood naked before him. She leaned forward, her hair unfurling across his chest; she pulled both of his hands around her again.

"And I won't be sorry this time either."

Chapter Thirty-One

He snugged his hat onto his head before he opened the door to go back out into the night. They hadn't lit any lamps; the darkness would hide his departure. He had almost turned away when Carrie put a staying hand on his sleeve.

"I have no claim on you, Del."

He looked at her with a stunned expression that turned resolute. He bumbled over his words. "I understand. Still, I apologize. You're a widow. You're still in mourning."

"Maybe not so much now," she said quietly. He shook his head and turned away. She watched him trot off into the darkness, his stamping feet hurling up sprays of water and mud like mortar shells. Carrie closed the door behind her and blew out a breath.

"Damn!" she said, expressing a sentiment of appreciation, lurid memory, and misgivings. She returned to her bedroom, her limbs loose and tingling. Her suite was wrecked. A shirt sagged from a bedpost; tonight's muddy skirt and bloomers lay in a pile in the middle of the floor. Her mattress slumped; blankets cascaded onto the floor. A matter for later, she decided and sat down.

That she and Del Morgan had just consummated an affair was not the most grievous thing. She knew a line had been crossed, but she didn't feel like a trollop, a whore. The engagement with Del was not sordid; he had not pursued her; he was not lascivious. She had not simpered her way into his bed, either. Theirs had been an acknowledgment of triumph, an embrace between victors. By society's measure, it wasn't an acceptable manner of celebrating achievement, but their battle with the creek had warranted an equal affirmation of life. *Good lord, how we toasted* that *win!*

But Mrs. Morgan—what was her name?—was now a consideration. While she and Del hadn't plotted their liaison, Mrs. Morgan didn't deserve it. Carrie had no idea about Del's wife. She had seen her standing next to Del at Ophelia's funeral; she looked practical and sturdy. Carrie remembered the couple lived in Duncan, the county seat. There would be little opportunity for their paths to cross. She knew nothing of the larger town, other than the train station and the dusty road that led her to Hope Bridge. Del would worry about his unfaithfulness. Carrie just had to hide it.

What kind of wanton had she just become? Since her arrival, her need for comfort seemed to have flared. Had she, over the past few weeks, felt less of a longing for Phee and more desire of the physical nature? Did she and Del truly act out a post-battle congress, or did she just fulfill a baser need with a willing and available man?

That man was the county sheriff. A married man. A man with a great deal to lose should his indiscretion become known. And he now had the burden of trusting her, a woman he barely knew. She had wanted to ease his travails yesterday. Instead, she had made herself a liability.

And what about Phee? Dear lord, what had she done? How could she be so callous to her husband?

The longing for Phee, like a waking demon, lifted its head but did not approach. Instead, she had the distinct impression that the upwelling of grief merely bubbled, as though through cold molasses. It did not burst upon her, did not cause her to clamp back a sob. She remembered there had been a moment when the hairy roughness of Del's legs and the tightness of his embrace had pushed her into sparkling oblivion. She had left her consciousness thinking minutely of Phee's picture on the mantle. Just a flicker, before twinkling stars and agonizing pleasure blotted it out. Unable to process her new dilemma any further, she lay down, thinking of Phee's kind face and of Del's weight and scent. Sleep came in a peaceful moment.

Chapter Thirty-Two

As if satisfied with its efforts, the storm gave up and moved away. Ragged clouds shouldered their way across the sky, hurrying, as if to avoid the impending sun. Broken branches, frayed debris, and dead birds littered the muddy ground around Hope Bridge.

Carrie pulled open the front door and stepped out onto the porch. She held the post and leaned out as far as she could, squinting through a brief glare of sunshine she hadn't seen in almost a week. Birdsong announced a return to business, but this time, Carrie didn't find it delightful.

She was worried about Sav. He should have come home at some point last night. Del Morgan had said they couldn't get any messages through. Why would Sav still be at the post office? She couldn't remember if there was a place to sleep in the building. When Thomas pulled her and Del out of the Duncan, and they all retreated to Bookhoudt's, Thomas hadn't said anything about Sav remaining at the post office. He said he had keys; he had unlocked the mail room door and let himself out. He and Marta had stood against the crowd, their affair exposed, their safety ensured by Bale's fury and Morgan's badge, and with Ada Grant still screaming in her head, Carrie hadn't thought to ask about her uncle.

What if he fell in the river? What if one of Germond's gang had assaulted him and he lay seriously injured in the mud somewhere? With mortification, she recalled she had feigned her uncle's disappearance to gain access to Reverend Borden's office to question Ada. What if he were really lost?

She hadn't been off the mark with her suspicion about Ophelia's demise. She had the same bad feeling now. Sav would not be away from Oscar, his warm kitchen or his books for so long in this weather. Wasn't he an apprehensive man? Wouldn't he want to remain secure in the face of this chaos?

Carrie pressed her chest and drew a deep breath. She tried to settle herself and think rationally. Sav was probably safe from the lynch mob, since Bale had pressed them into service, erecting barricades and ropes around the wreckage of the bridge. Her uncle knew everyone in town. It was quite likely he stayed at someone's house, enjoying a hot meal and waiting for his clothes to dry, as she had done for the sheriff last night. Sav would be home soon.

She thought of Del Morgan. Of his heaviness and intimate warmth. She caught her breath, her indecent recollections colliding with that of icy river water enveloping her legs and sucking her in. Del's hands like iron, straining and failing to pull her out. The river tugging at them both. If it hadn't been for Thomas Bale…

Oscar screeched overhead, and she jerked herself into the present. She hurried up the stairs, realizing the big blue bird needed tending.

Oscar's room faced southwest. Floor-length windows lit up two walls, gaining sunshine from the shredding clouds overhead. The big bird scratched its chin with a fleshy gray foot, before waddling unhappily along the perch. "Cookie? Cookie?" Oscar croaked at her.

Carrie marveled again at his size. From his long tail to his battering ram head, he was easily three feet long. Oscar's beak curled like a thick snail shell on his wrinkly, white-leather face. "Cookie? Cookie?" He bobbed his body vigorously up and down, a mix of beggary and annoyance.

"Aw, you miss your pal, Oscar?" she murmured. The bird spread its bright orange wings and clacked its beak. Carrie smiled. No wonder her uncle loved this bird; its unexpected animation was so like his own.

"I'll take care of you," she said, and bending to pull the lid off a bucket of birdseed near the door, she caught the scent of Germond Morgan's cologne.

She stood up quickly and swung around. The open can of bird seed wafted up a hay-like scent; she smelled the bird's guano and damp woodwork. Had she imagined it? How had that brute's scent invaded her home? She

CHAPTER THIRTY-TWO

cautiously bent again to retrieve the distressing smell.

The odor drifted away between the door and the jamb. She stepped into the hall, turning her nose side to side like a dog. She caught the faint scent again in her uncle's library.

Cabinets and bookshelves on two walls housed Sav's collection of histories, genealogies, mathematics, and classics. Carrie had intended to browse his shelves one day but had instead been caught up in Hope Bridge's intrigues. Now, she canted her head to the side, catching titles and authors stamped elegantly on beech-colored bindings: Thoreau, Dickens, Twain, Franklin. Sav used a worn out, leather chair to do his reading. It sagged in a corner. The writing table and chair were opposite the books, situated with an unobstructed view onto his beloved village.

Among the clutter of his desk lay a list of Hope Bridge's vigilantes and the scribbles of the first draft of a complaint. Carrie felt a pang of affection for her uncle. This room, of all, seemed to be the heart of his home. The intrusion of Germond Morgan's scent puzzled and disturbed her.

She knew her uncle's fragrance by now. Other than a hairbrush and tooth powder, Sav Machin was unencumbered by fashionable demands. Tidily, he went unscented, un-slicked, and clean-shaven. The tang of ink and mild sweat permeated his clothes. Carrie sniffed again. A concentration of the offending cologne centered on a small waste basket.

A folded sheet of stationery lay on top of the litter. Carrie pulled it out by a corner. Germond's scent drifted up. Elegant handwriting was scripted across the page. It was dated yesterday.

Dear Mr. Machin,

As you know, our family is suffering a profound bereavement. Further, we find ourselves in a state of perplexing circumstances, and we have concluded we have need of your counsel. Would you kindly call on us this evening?

In all Sincerity,

S. Clarke

Sylvannia sent for Sav yesterday? It must have happened when Carrie was at the Chester Inn with Bill Bemis and Morgan. Sav must have come home and found the note in the hallway. He would have gone straightaway to assist the family with whatever counsel they needed. But Carrie couldn't see him staying the night at the Grants' home.

She examined Sylvannia's stationery closely. It was inscribed at the top with only *S. Clarke*, and decorated with a simple illustration of a marigold at the bottom. Puzzled and wary, Carrie laid the letter on the floor and gently lifted the matching envelope from the trash can. She regarded the offending papers, disliking their presence in her uncle's room and the feeling of trepidation they inspired.

When she was thirteen, she had purchased her first set of lady's calling cards. She agonized over how the inscription should appear, having learned that choosing the typeface, and the inclusion of full names and titles was as important as the construction and color of the paper. The card represented the character of a woman. A first initial followed by the surname implied austerity and a certain amount of anonymity.

And the marigold? Of all the flowers listed in *The Ladies Guide,* the marigold was special. They symbolized cruelty. As an undertaker, she'd never use them in a floral tribute, but privately, every time Carrie was snubbed by a peer, every time she saw a chatty group of women stop speaking and lean away when she passed by, and every time she proudly made a plate of ginger crackles for her father and Phee, she thought of sending marigolds to each and every one of them. She longed to remind them of their cruelty.

Sylvannia's envelope was unmarked, an intriguing blank. Who delivered it? Carrie swept the back of her fingers over the envelope to get a feel for its dampness. Perfectly dry. Perhaps the little maid at the Grants' home had run it over yesterday, just as Marta had been sent from the Worleys to summon her. The little maid would have kept it dry under her garments and herself dry under an umbrella. She would have slipped it into the mail slot on the front door and run home again. A quick errand that would take a sprightly girl no more than half an hour to complete. Sav must have come home at some point, found the letter, and then gone to the Grants. But why hasn't he returned?

Carrie tapped a knuckle against her chin, thinking. Sylvannia was the spokesperson of the family, now? She must have sent the letter before Ada

CHAPTER THIRTY-TWO

left for the Methodist church, before she died. What was the perplexing circumstance she wanted to discuss with Sav? Did Sylvannia know the same thing Ada did? Had she calmly written for Sav's guidance while Ada, nerve-wracked, fled to the church for shelter?

She put the letter back in the waste basket, cracked two windows to help dissipate the offending smell, and left the library. Why would Sylvannia have stationery that carried Germond's scent? Carrie remembered another time Sylvannia had possessed the cologne: at their home, last Sunday when she and Mrs. Woodruff had delivered a meal. Sylvannia said the scent was not Germond's but was, in fact, her father's perfume. Maybe that's why Ophelia took a liking to him. But given Germond's brutality, Carrie thought the remaining Grant girls would have abandoned the scent, whether it brought paternal comfort or not.

If Uncle Sav had responded to the summons and gone to the Grants' house, where was he now? Hadn't Sylvannia concluded her business with him by the time Del arrived to tell them that Ada had been swept away? Del didn't mention Sylvannia or Sav being there, but he had been distressed, then quite distracted, when he came last night. If she and Sav weren't at the Grant house, where were they?

Carrie had become still, poised at the window, looking out over the yard and beyond to North Street, remembering snatches of conversations with Bill at the Chester, with Del at the funeral, with Sav when he rambled on about everyone's family trees. She saw Ada Grant's confusion. *"I don't love your uncle!"* She thought about Sylvannia's invitation. Sylvannia, the recluse, who practiced floriography but lied about it. *Sisters are jealous of each other.* Sylvannia, so devoted to Ophelia that she took over the remodeling of her house... bought her soothing medications.

Carrie turned and hurried to her bedroom. Snorting with impatience at the perpetually haphazard state of affairs, she rooted for clean and dry clothing. She pulled on her last set of bloomers and socks, snapped her work shirt off its peg, and stepped into a damp gray skirt that had been flung over her dressing table chair at some point in the last day or so. She hastily tied on her shoes that had stiffened with heat and dried mud overnight and hurried out the kitchen door.

Chapter Thirty-Three

The post office door was locked; Carrie banged hard, shouted Sav's name. No answer. She had hoped her uncle would still be behind the telegraph desk, but knew deep down he was not. Her anxiety growled from a deep place, like a dog warning of danger. She bunched up her skirt in one hand and skipped over puddles and mud all the way to the Methodist Church.

Even at this early hour, Mrs. Peters was sweeping debris off the flagstone pads with a curled witch's broom. Her face, etched with determination, turned to dislike when she saw Carrie approach.

"Good morning," Carrie panted, offering the suspicious woman her good graces. Her uncle's tutelage was clear: she had bigger fish to fry today than Stingy Peter's attitude. Nevertheless, Mrs. Peters put up her broom like a postern guard.

"The good Reverend isn't in this morning," she said without hiding her annoyance. "He's on Main Street. Seeing to those that need his counsel."

"Thank you, Mrs. Peters. I need to speak with him as soon as I can. Would you please let him know I'd like him to call on me at my uncle's house as soon as possible?" Carrie stopped short of asking the church guardian if she had seen Uncle Sav this morning. The Peters sisters might spread the word if it came to a manhunt, but they could just as easily scatter unnecessary gossip. She turned without waiting for a response and left the spare woman to her broom and disapproving scowl.

Main Street was crowded. Hope Bridge residents came out to see the damage, to spread the news of Ada Grant's demise, and to turn their faces toward the sun. Carrie felt self-conscious. How much of her involvement in that debacle did they know? Fighting back the urge to ask each passerby if they'd seen Sav, she dodged around onlookers, slipped on the wet boardwalks, and used lamp poles and porch posts to swing by knots of people. She spotted Leopold Lamont coming out of Bookhoudt's. She hailed him and hurried over.

"I haven't seen your uncle, Mrs. Lisbon." Lamont looked surprised at her request. "But I'm glad I happened upon you. Mr. Morgan asked me to get a statement from Reverend Borden regarding Miss Grant. He said you knew something about what I'm to ask him."

"Yes, I do, Mr. Lamont. Mrs. Peters said he's giving a service in town, but I don't know where. Can you help me find my uncle afterward?"

"We'll get a search party together. Borden's giving a sermon with Reverend Moore at the creamery. Main Street was too much of a mire to get through. We'll find him there."

They wove back through Main Street to Creamery Road, slogging through mud, dodging puddles, and side-stepping wind-blown debris. On the creamery's loading dock, the two clergymen had found an unmuddied, high spot to minister. The thanksgiving service had concluded, and the crowd was dispersing when Lamont and Carrie approached.

Reverend Moore, the Presbyterian minister who'd presided over Ophelia Morgan's committal service, finished shaking the last hand and turned to Carrie and Lamont. A man well into his middle years, with a bloom of vigor on his clean-shaven face, Moore looked friendly and purposeful. Borden stood near Moore. His benevolent expression slipped when he saw Carrie.

Lamont explained his inquiry to Borden. "Sheriff Morgan wants me to take a statement from you, Reverend, regarding the events of last night that lead up to Miss Ada's death on the bridge. He's asked Mrs. Lisbon to witness."

Borden let out a derisive snort, abandoning pretense. "Of all people to act as witness!" he ranted. "Mrs. Lisbon is the *cause* of Miss Ada's demise! Why is it that she is the witness? Why not my colleague?" Borden jerked a petulant hand to indicate Reverend Moore. "I haven't discerned the spiritual

CHAPTER THIRTY-THREE

guidance I need in order to breach a parishioner's confidence." He paused, staring angrily at Carrie.

Carrie leaned toward him, just as angry. This interview delayed her quest for her uncle, and she was desperately impatient. "Reverend, you're in possession of information from a confession that could absolve a man of murder charges. Please, don't you think it's appropriate for you to dispense with sanctimony and tell us what you know? You had no such qualms regarding a breach of confidence when I paid you for a pauper's grave. Do you remember? Or should I continue with the details, which smack of impropriety?" She and Borden eyed each other fiercely.

"If I may, Reverend," Moore put a hand on Borden's arm. "Ada Grant was a parishioner in my church. I'm told she tried to see me last night, but I was at the Patchin's home. Mrs. Patchin is gravely ill. Ada may have needed to unburden herself quite badly, so in my absence she sought you out, Reverend. We have enough tragedy. Please, let us provide our sheriff with the information he needs."

Borden rolled his eyes, stepped away, and paced around. The smell of sour milk crept over the platform as he completed his circuit. He lifted his chin with pudgy dignity. "Ada Grant confessed to killing Germond Morgan."

Lamont grunted in disbelief. The Reverend Moore shook his head sorrowfully. Carrie spoke up. "What did she say?"

"She was inconsolable, poor thing. She was always high-strung. Sent away for nerves more than once. But she was overcome by guilt. She said that Ophelia was in love with that monster, even though he thrashed her. Even though he..." Borden looked away before speaking again. "'Used her like he did,' she said." Great splotches of crimson crept up Borden's cheeks.

"But Germond approached Ada after Ophelia's funeral. She said he told her he 'needed consolation.' He came to the Grants' house, saying he thought it would be proper for *her* to 'continue in her sister's role,' since she was unmarried and his period of mourning was over." Borden paused and took a deep breath. "She said Germond put his hands on her. She said he was...."

"Seeking congress?" Carrie asked, finishing his sentence. Borden made an uncomfortable noise.

"She made him leave, but when it happened again, she put him off by agreeing to come to his house Friday night. She brought her father's gun. He opened the door, and she shot him in the heart."

Borden looked down at the cement floor, then back at his audience. "She said 'because that was the blackest thing about him.'"

The roar of the Duncan carried over the silence. Sunlight poured down, warming the scent of milk and manure. Carrie spoke first. "Sheriff Morgan said Ada told him she was with your brother-in-law, Digger, that night. Why would she say that?"

Borden responded with a shrug. "Better a scandal than the gallows. And he is always too drunk to remember anything."

Chapter Thirty-Four

The desk clerk at the Chester Inn tried hard to maintain a civil level of deportment, but his austerity had taken a beating overnight. The crush of delayed travelers grumbled openly about their need to send communications, to have their bags and horses tended to, to have breakfast. Small bells rang cheerily on the wall behind him, but their insistent chimes turned sour the longer they went unanswered. Carrie had a desperate thought that Sav might have stayed at the Chester with Bill Bemis. The clerk regarded her request peevishly.

"You can wait in the dining room while I ring for the page to call up to Mr. Bemis."

"Or, just tell me if he and my uncle are still up there," Carrie insisted.

"I don't know if Mr. Machin is a guest of Mr. Bemis," the clerk retorted. "Please wait while I send for a page."

"Or, just tell me his room number!" Carrie said impatiently. "I'll just go up by myself."

The clerk huffed, glanced over his shoulder at the irritating bells, and turned back to Carrie. "We don't allow ladies into the gentlemen's rooms. I'm sure you understand. It would be unseem—"

"Oh, for heaven's sake! I need to see Mr. Bemis. I'll get to him faster than your page."

The knot of travelers, as impatient as Carrie, ganged up on the clerk. "Just let her go up, man! It's not like women aren't up there all the time. Let's go!"

The clerk reached behind him and pulled a bell wire with short vicious yanks. He glanced at the registry, and as his cheeks tightened, he spat, "Room two ten!"

Carrie gathered her skirts and flew up the grand staircase, dodging people coming down. Two flights up, she was gasping when she knocked on Bemis' door. He answered quickly; his expectant face changed swiftly to concern when he saw her. She barged in, breathing hard. "Is my uncle here?"

"No. Good morning. As usual, you're on another mission of some gravity?" Bill's attempted smile melted as she hurriedly scanned his room. Bemis had pencils and paper piled around his breakfast tray. A plate with breadcrumbs and a smear of egg yolk marked him as one of the lucky guests who'd eaten this morning.

"I can't find my uncle," Carrie said rapidly. "He didn't come home last night. He's not at the Post Office. I don't know where he is."

"All right, all right. Slow down. Let me get my hat and coat. Tell me what's happened. It's not enough the bridge collapsed? Now there are missing persons?" With headlines to be made, Bemis snatched up his notebook.

Carrie was already at the door. "Ada Grant confessed to killing Germond Morgan last night before she died. But that's not important. Bill, stop writing and listen to me!" Her hands flapped in emphasis as she continued. "I know it will make good headlines, but I can't find Uncle Sav. I need your help."

"Of course. Of course. I can't file an article anyway until the phones are on again. What's happened to Sav?"

"When he didn't come home last night, I assumed he was still at the post office. But he wasn't there when I checked this morning. I found a letter from one of the Grant sisters, asking him to come over to talk about a family matter. It must have been delivered yesterday afternoon while we were here, having supper. He must have come home from the post office, found the letter, and gone to the Grants."

"So, we go to the Grants to see if he's there," Bill said. "It was beastly last night before it blew itself out. Maybe he stayed there?" Bemis looked at her steadily as his eyes grew rounder. "Good God, Carrie! What if—"

"Don't say it!" she cried and swallowed a lump of dread before speaking again with resolve. "Let's get to the Grants and see if he's there. I know it's early, but he may have stayed there, giving comfort to Mrs. Grant."

CHAPTER THIRTY-FOUR

"This is the same family whose girl went down with the bridge? The sister of the strangled wife?"

Carrie saw Bemis constructing the tragedies into bold font headlines.

"Yes," she said, tearing up. Ada's screams renewed inside her head. She realized she was trembling with exertion and anxiety. "I think Sav went there while Ada went to the church. Sheriff Morgan brought me home, then went to tell Mrs. Grant about Ada." She stopped herself before confessing that Del hadn't mentioned Sav when he came back to her house.

"God, if we could just call!" Bill said. "It's impossible to operate in this town without a phone. We have to walk to our sources."

"We have to walk to find my uncle, Bill. Please, can we go now?"

Back down in the lobby, the harried clerk fended off angry breakfast requests. The smell of coffee as yet undelivered, added to the general agitation. They ignored the melee and hurried to the front door. Delphius Morgan reached for the knob as Bemis pulled it open.

He was haggard. His eyelids drooped along with the stubbly skin of his face. He tried not to shiver, but Carrie could see his clothing sagged with wet weight. He held up a hand as she stammered an alarmed greeting.

"Are you going out?" he asked.

"Uncle Sav is missing," Carrie said. "We're going to the Grants. I think he went there last night."

Morgan frowned "I didn't see him there. I thought he was at the post office."

"He was," Carrie said impatiently. "But he didn't come home, and he's not there now. I found a letter from Sylvannia this morning, asking him to come over to talk about something urgent. I need to see Sylvannia. She may know where he's gone. If she doesn't, we need to get a search underway. Where's Thomas?"

"I sent him to assess the damage upriver this morning."

"He's free to go, then?"

"He's free to go."

Something in the way he said it made Carrie pause. He looked at her guardedly, some sort of warning coupled with pain. She followed the unspoken meaning of his words and placed a shaking palm over her horrified mouth.

"You knew Thomas was innocent," she stated between her fingers. Her eyes widened as the knowledge dawned on her. Sharp-edged remorse cut into her chest. She doubled over; she couldn't breathe. Morgan stepped to her side.

"If...if I knew," Carrie said, as short breaths burst from her lungs. "I wouldn't have tried so hard to get Ada to talk. She wouldn't have run away. She wouldn't—"

Morgan took her hands and drew her upright. "It's not your fault. Tom Bale *was* a suspect. He met all the criteria."

She jerked away, angry now. "I forced Ada to talk because I thought Thomas would be hanged. But you knew! For days! Why didn't you tell me?" Ada's screams resumed inside her head. She clapped her hands over her ears.

"Why did you lock him up?" she groaned in despair. "Why didn't you tell me?"

"Mrs. Lisbon, you had a bunch of liquored-up young men attack your house Saturday night. I put Tom in the post office to keep him safe. To keep you and your uncle safe."

It was all she could do not to shriek. Her words came out in a rapid whistle. "I thought he'd be hanged! I had to do something!" Overwhelmed, she turned away and covered her face to hide the surge of guilt and horror. Morgan led her gently to a corner of the hotel stoop. She stood with her back to him, fists clenched, shuddering and sick.

After a while, the mantra floated upward. *Just get up....*

Carrie wiped her eyes with shaking hands. "The secrets this town keeps," she muttered.

Morgan looked at her sharply. She stepped around him. "I have to find my uncle."

Morgan spun on his toes and fell in beside her. "I'll go with you. Bemis, can you send telegrams? Good. Get to the post office. Break in if you have to. The lines are the priority for the crews this morning. I need an operator

CHAPTER THIRTY-FOUR

there."

Chapter Thirty-Five

They walked quickly. Carrie, to get away from the painful guilt of her misguided role in Ada Grant's death, and Morgan to keep up with her. She did not want to keep hearing Ada scream. She did not want to admit to being so zealous about freeing Thomas Bale, that she acted so rashly. The pain of knowing Ada's death was the result of her foolish heroism was heavy. She needed respite. She needed her uncle's counsel. She had to get to Sylvannia.

In addition, she was acutely aware of being alone again with Del Morgan and his sturdy legs, his wet, borrowed clothing, and his sweaty scent. She wanted to feed him, clean him up, dry his skin, and, God help her, explore him some more.

"Mr. Morgan," she said, fighting to regain control and choosing formality to shield her from her thoughts. "Did you see Uncle Sav at the Grants' last night?" She stopped before adding 'before you came back.' He'd know what she meant.

"No, I didn't. Sylvannia wasn't home, either, now that I think about it."

"Sylvannia wasn't home? But she invited my uncle to go there to meet her."

"That's odd." He changed the puzzling subject. "I found Leo just before I got to the Chester. He said you witnessed the interview with Borden?"

"Yes." Carrie recounted Borden's reluctant telling of Ada's confession. She left out the part where she bullied the Reverend with a threat of scandal in order for him to do so.

"I didn't consider Gerry being killed for anything other than revenge for

CHAPTER THIRTY-FIVE

Ophelia's murder," Morgan said. "But it wasn't vengeance. Ada killed Gerry because of who he was."

Carrie couldn't think of anything to say. Her emotions writhed. Her fear for Sav grew. Her role in Ada's death crushed her with remorse. She was angry at Morgan for not telling her Tom Bale was never going to hang for murder, and she was regretting the awkward situation she and Morgan had created. Above all, if she was honest, she felt a strong desire to repeat the performance. She decided to clear the air of at least that. She stopped Morgan with a light touch under the shelter of a hedgerow of privets.

"I have no claim on you, Del," she said quietly, repeating last night's vow. "What happened was an aberration. It won't happen again. You can trust me to keep my mouth shut. I'm an undertaker. We call it the 'oath of practice' when it's prudent to do so. I'm sure you employ the same measures?"

Morgan drew a deep breath. "Mrs. Lisbon, I apologize again for my actions last night. If you wish to consider me reprehensible, I would agree."

A puff of incredulous laughter escaped her. "Good lord, Del," she said drily. "If that's your reprehensible, I'd like to see your incorrigible."

"God, Carrie!" Morgan threw back his head. "I'm married! You're widowed! These are small towns."

"And I told you I wasn't sorry. Didn't seem like you were sorry, either. The first or the second time."

"Goddamnit!" He took her arm and resumed walking "Let's get to the Grants. We'll deal with this another time. I didn't get a chance to tell you I spoke with Ruth Nickerson."

"Tell me now," Carrie said shortly.

"Ophelia called the Grants' house around 5 o'clock Sunday night."

Carrie nodded with satisfaction. *Right again!* She asked the obvious follow-up. "A lot of operators stay on the line. Eavesdropping isn't allowed, but they do it all the time. Did Ruth?"

"I asked about that too, at risk of offending her. She got a call from the Valley Star Hotel almost as soon as she connected Ophelia. She said she couldn't tell who answered at the Grants', or who Ophelia spoke to."

"Damnit," Carrie said. "What if Sylvannia answered the phone? What if she went over and dressed Ophelia?"

Morgan considered for a moment. "Why wouldn't she have said as much? She hated Germond as much as Ada did. I think she would have relished the opportunity to throw him under if she saw how her sister was abused. You're saying Sylvannia was the woman who dressed Ophelia? All right. That makes sense. Germond choked Ophelia. Sylvannia dressed her body. Or, Sylvannia helped her get dressed. Then Germond came back and killed her. Germond is still the liar here."

"It seems to fit," Carrie said with some dejection. Was she wrong, after all, to believe Germond's claim of innocence? Was even Del Morgan duped by his repellant brother?

But it was Sylvannia who seemed duplicitous. Carrie continued doggedly. "I was thinking about Sylvannia's disposition. Do you think she may be genuine with her avoidance of society?"

"I don't know her that well. She has always been..." Del searched. "...distant. Except at her sister's wedding, I've never met with her socially. Why?"

"I think she's been disingenuous. She acts like a recluse, but you said she was frequently at Ophelia's house to assist with the remodeling. She carries a kerchief scented with Germond's cologne, but she claims to hate him."

Morgan did not reply, and Carrie understood he waited for her to go on with her logic.

"I wonder if my uncle was referring to *her* when he told me the other day that 'Ophelia's sister' was pursuing him amorously. I assumed it was Ada, since she wasn't married, but what if he meant Sylvannia? I remember Uncle Sav saying he thought there was a rivalry between them. He wasn't specific, and I wasn't paying attention, but what if he meant Sylvannia and Ada? What if she was a rival with Ada for my uncle's affection?"

"Why would she pursue Sav Machin? Sylvannia's married," Del said.

Carrie stopped short and searched his face to see if he was serious about the sanctity of a marriage vow. "Really?" she said.

Morgan's eyes danced around for a second before he regained control. "Present circumstances notwithstanding," he said quickly.

"Her husband is always out of town, isn't that right?" Carrie resumed.

CHAPTER THIRTY-FIVE

"Maybe she feels like she can get away with trifling with other men. Maybe she's the one the itinerants refer to."

Morgan responded with a frown and two palms up.

"Another thing," Carrie said, " I think Sylvannia practices floriography, even though she denies it. She has yellow carnations in her home. In the funerary business, we discourage the use of yellow at a funeral, even if it was the deceased's favorite color. Yellow carnations, especially. Their popular meaning is rejection of a potential sweetheart."

Morgan shook his head again in perplexity.

"Furthermore, the stationary she used in her letter to my uncle was adorned with a marigold. The marigold is the symbol for cruelty in flower language."

"Flower language?" Morgan's response was heavy with skepticism.

"Undertakers rely heavily on *The Ladies Guide to the Language of Flowers* if we are to assemble an appropriate floral tribute to the deceased. Ladies especially, want to express their feelings through their arrangements. One sends a bouquet of lilies to represent purity, roses for eternal life, ivy for fidelity, that sort of thing.

"Her choice of flowers to decorate her home and her stationery indicates to those who know the language that she's a rather nasty piece. That she's not to be trifled with. She's been spurned by someone. Maybe by my uncle? And she keeps yellow carnations in her house to remind her of that rejection. She writes letters on paper with a marigold as a subtle warning. But only those proficient in the language would know. Uncle Sav didn't know."

"Maybe she just likes marigolds?"

Carrie ignored him. "I wonder if she has used Ophelia's death as a ploy to get close to Uncle Sav. Did she lure him somewhere? Why are they *both* missing?"

"We don't know that they're *both* missing," Morgan said. "Carrie, you've just laid the blame for a lot of ills on a woman who couldn't turn a man's head if she had ahold of it. A woman who never leaves her house."

"And who says she never leaves? Anyone could slip away, at night perhaps, without the household knowing. She cleans the druggist out of laudanum.

She oversaw the remodeling of Ophelia's house. Sav says she stays at her mother's home when her husband is away. That doesn't sound like a recluse to me. I know she has a maid run errands for her. Who knows what other arrangements she makes?"

Chapter Thirty-Six

They hurried up Piccolo Hill under a placid blue sky. The soggy mourning wreath on the Grants' front door dripped black dye down the wooden panels. They hurried to the back door where Mrs. Woodruff's bread van and the ever-suffering Bigelow were parked under the portico. The little maid answered Carrie's knock. She looked exhausted and kept glancing around worriedly. She bobbed awkwardly to Morgan, the big man's presence unnerving her.

"I kept the fire going this time, miss," she informed Carrie with timid pride as she led them into the house. Carrie murmured a kindness and peered about the Grants' home. The expansive dining room where Carrie had met and served the Grant sisters was on one side of the front entrance and a formal parlor on the other. The parlor's wallpaper displayed a pattern of weeping willows and swans. A plush burgundy carpet covered the floor, but the room smelled of vomit. Betsy Woodruff sat with Rowena's head in her lap, stroking her hair. She looked up at Carrie and Morgan and shook her head.

"She's in shock. I've given her some Soothing Syrup in some tea. I'm putting her to sleep," she reported quietly.

"Have you seen my uncle?" Carrie whispered. Mrs. Woodruff shook her head.

"Sylvannia?"

"She's steeped in laudanum by the smell of it," Mrs. Woodruff responded, her brows knitted together. "Maybe opium. I haven't seen her." Rowena made a querulous sound, and Betsy bent her attention to the old woman.

Carrie and Morgan stepped out of the room.

"You can try Miss Sylvie's house, ma'am," the little maid said bravely, then dropped her gaze to the floor when Morgan looked at her intently.

"Why?" he asked.

The maid blinked in fear. "She goes there…she went there…last night. With Mr. …your uncle…miss…sir." She turned and fled down the hall.

"Sylvie's house?" Carrie asked. She and Morgan stared at each other, then she quickly followed the little maid, holding up one hand to prevent Morgan from coming too. Clearly, the girl was terrified of him, of his authority. She was better off alone, calming the girl so she could gather information.

The little maid had squashed herself into a small space between the big stove and the new Hoosier cabinet. She sat on a stool, her shoulders hunched. She hung her head and kept her clasped hands in her lap. Carrie knelt in front of her.

"Hello, there. Don't be frightened. We've met. You remember? I was here the other day with Mrs. Woodruff. I don't think we've been introduced. There's been so many dreadful things happening. I'm Carrie, sweetie. What's your name?"

The little maid's chin shook. "Louisa, miss," she mumbled.

"Oh, what a lovely name. Are you warm here, Louisa? You kept the fire going; it's a real comfort to be warm, isn't it?"

Louisa nodded her head; her shoulders loosened.

"Give me your hands, child. My goodness! Sometimes I feel like I'll never be warm again, don't you?"

Carrie held the girl's clammy hands inside her own palms, warming them. "Louisa, this house has had some dreadful shocks. You look quite worn out. Mrs. Woodruff is here now, child. You can rest. I'll tell her you've gone to get some rest. She'll understand."

Louisa nodded jerkily. She kept her fists balled up. She took in a sudden deep breath, and her shoulders relaxed. Carrie smiled. Her ministrations were working. "Louisa, you said, Miss Sylvie might be at her house? Why is that, dear?"

Louisa turned her face away. Her mouth drew down, and she blinked

CHAPTER THIRTY-SIX

rapidly. "She goes there, sometimes. With…with her men. The workmen."

Carrie's eyebrows perked up. "Her men?"

"She has me bring her invitations to them. Then they go off. When Mr. Clarke isn't home." Carrie's puzzled look spurred more explanation.

"Oh, but I never go there!" Louisa said. She burst into tears. "I'm sorry I lied to the sheriff about where Miss Ada was!"

"You've done nothing wrong, Louisa. The sheriff forgives you." Carrie recalled the girl's cowering when she held the door for the sisters last Sunday. "Are you afraid of Miss Sylvie, Louisa?"

Louisa nodded and sniffed. Her resolve broke, and her words spilled out quickly. "She'd pinch me. She put l-lau-denum in my tea once, and when I woke up, I was on the floor. She scratched me… scratched my…." Louisa pulled a hand out of Carrie's grasp and gestured to her thin chest.

"Louisa, did you bring a letter to my uncle yesterday?" Carrie's alarm made her words rapid. Louisa quailed.

"I went right over, Miss Carrie," she babbled. "I went right over. She gets so mad if I don't. I was glad Mr. Machin wasn't home. I didn't know what to do, so I left the letter in the slot." Tears spilled from her eyes. "I didn't dare not!"

"It's all right, now, darling. It's all right. You didn't do anything wrong." Carrie bounced the girl's hands in her lap for emphasis. "Did my uncle come here yesterday, Louisa? Did you see my uncle?"

Louisa shook her head emphatically. Tears sprayed. "No. No miss. I didn't. I heard the bell ring, but Miss Sylvie answered it. She waits there, for the men, after I bring the letters. It was raining so hard, and I was trying to make the supper. Miss Ada was gone to the chur – ur—urch. Oh! Miss Ada!" The girl broke down completely and fell forward into Carrie's arms. As she held the sobbing girl, she looked up to see Del Morgan standing in the doorway. He no longer looked tired, but he did look worn.

Chapter Thirty-Seven

"Charter Street," Morgan said as they stepped out into the increasingly hot day. A warm breeze stirred the air, and maple trees shook off their residual raindrops. Carrie had to trot to keep up with him as he cut across a corner yard. He hadn't slept in a day, but he seemed to have found some reserve of energy.

"Their house is just up here," Morgan gestured.

The well-kept home of Sylvannia and Peter Clarke was two stories high, above a wide porch and cement walk. Its pristine clapboards were plastered with torn-off, wet leaves and splattered with mud at the downspouts. Del knocked at the front door, then walked to the back, pulling a set of brass keys from his vest.

"You have keys to Sylvannia's house?" Carrie asked.

"No. I have keys from Tom Bale. Apparently, he can get in anywhere." Morgan selected a brass key and fiddled with the lock. It turned easily. He pushed the door open. Inside, Sylvannia's kitchen had a vacant feel. Unlike the Grants, she had neat, serviceable appliances, but they appeared unused. Cupboards housed regular stacks of dishes; no plants were tended in the parlor. The upstairs rooms were immaculate and cold. No footprints smeared the dust. No scents of perfume or tobacco or lingering cooking odors. No one had been here for quite some time.

"Gerry and Ophelia live on Garnet Street. We'll try that next," Del announced, taking Carrie's elbow. "The house was an old pile when they were married. They had work done. Sylvie was always over there, giving advice. I've never been there."

CHAPTER THIRTY-SEVEN

Out on the street, steam rose from the drying flagst
asked, "did you know how awful Germond was to Ophei

Morgan's mouth turned down. "I should have known, Ca
was not kind to her, but I didn't realize he had been so brut.

Carrie let a few paces go by before she responded. "I'm su
have put a stop to it."

"I should have known," he said again. "There's always so mu
didn't take the time."

There was nothing to say to that. A few hastened steps more, an
said suddenly. "Del, what if Sylvannia and Germond ganged up on C
Louisa said Sylvannia has an awful mean streak. She used laudanu
incapacitate her. Then she hurt her."

Morgan looked down and took up her arm, hurrying her even more. Th
reached the dead couple's house. Morgan pounded on the front door, thei.
twisted the handle. None of Bale's keys worked. Morgan drove his elbow
through a thin window pane, reached in, and thumbed the lock open.

Ophelia's wedding photograph stood on the parlor mantle. Germond's
scent spilled across the furniture, as did Sav Machin's long overcoat. Carrie
shouted out to Sav as she darted through the rooms, scanning quickly,
spinning around, and racing to the next. "Sav? Uncle Sav?"

"Let's try the cellar," Morgan said. In the kitchen, they clattered through a
shellacked door and down the cellar stairs. They split up at the bottom and
threw aside firewood and old cider barrels in the dim light. They slapped
cobwebs out of the way. "Uncle!" Carrie shouted with frustration.

Morgan and Carrie met eyes for a split second before he bounded back
up into the kitchen. Carrie swept up her skirts and followed; caught sight
of him as he rounded the newel post and went upstairs two at a time. She
caught up with him again as he stood, panting, outside the only closed door
on the second floor.

Sylvannia Grant Clarke answered the bedroom door barefoot, in a pale
gray, flouncy nightdress. She leaned on the doorframe and smiled at their
sweaty, cobwebby faces. "Hello," she said in a sleepy, sultry way.

Carrie stopped short. A woman of Sylvannia's standing didn't entertain parlor; did not entertain anyone, did not show herself unclad. remembering Louisa's

Not expecting the brusque immediately smelled a combination cologne hit her with its sweet ugliness, seeped throughout the room.

Morgan said, throwing open the window. "Mrs.

low, languid sound. Her eyes were heavy-lidded, her pinpoints, and her colorless hair hung loose. She held hand to her throat. Dreamily, she slurred, "Whatever do Sheriff? I heard you bash your way in. And you're shouting, Mrs. What is the meaning of all this?"

Morgan advanced on the slender woman whose attempt at seduction seemed as washed out as her features. "Your maid suggested we might find Mr. Machin here. The room reeks of laudanum. Too much for treating the vapors."

"Is he here?" Carrie butted in. The interview was already taking too long.

Sylvannia smiled sidelong at Morgan and turned her body so that her thin garments outlined her nakedness beneath. She dragged a pointed finger across Morgan's chest as she sauntered past him and sat down on the bed. Stunned, Carrie watched the girl pat the coverlets invitingly.

"Can't we talk first, Mr. Morgan?" Sylvannia purred.

Morgan stood speechless, a thunderous, red expression on his face. Carrie was no less appalled at the woman's behavior.

"You're the ones who burst in here," Sylvannia pouted and leaned back on her arms. Her breasts poked up from the posture. "Any way you can make it up to me." She dropped her jaw and slid a long tongue over her lips. Carrie gasped. Germond had used those exact words.

Morgan jerked Sylvannia upright and marched her over to the boudoir chair. She fell forward, boneless, her elbows scattering bottles and mother-

CHAPTER THIRTY-SEVEN

of-pearl powder boxes. Morgan pulled her upright, one big hand squeezing her exposed arm. Raised, Sylvannia changed hideously. She pushed out her chest and leaned into Morgan.

"Ahh, do that again," she breathed. "I don't mind it!" She smiled at Morgan intently, all teeth. He backed away from her. She swung her hips seductively. He hit the wall behind him, and she came on. "Make it hurt, Sheriff. Come on. Hurt me! You'll like it too."

"Now see here, miss—"

Sylvannia crouched, then pushed against him, scraping her body upward across his buttons, his belt buckle catching on her sheer clothing. She pulled his hands around her and clung tightly as she jerked herself backward. He fell forward with her. She clung to him as he fought to disentangle himself, to scramble up and away.

"Stop that!" Carrie shouted. She snatched up a pitcher of water and upended it over Sylvannia's face. Sylvannia sputtered and coughed, settling on a series of horrid, laughing barks as she sat up, bedraggled. Morgan distanced himself, chastely trying to straighten his clothing. Carrie flung a blanket from the bed over Sylvannia, and as the girl pulled it around her shoulders, Carrie's patience ran out.

She pulled Sylvannia's chin upward. "I've had enough of your nonsense," she said angrily. "Where's my uncle, you nasty trollop?"

Sylvannia jerked her face away. Now sullen and uncooperative, she stared down at the floor.

"Ada's dead, Mrs. Clarke," Morgan spoke as if his chest was being squeezed. "Your sister was on the bridge when it went down last night. Your mother is near death from the shock. I have no idea what you've done with Mr. Machin, but goddamn it, we're here to find him."

"Ada?" Sylvannia's face twisted. "Ada's dead?" The sultriness vanished. She trembled badly. "Ada's dead?"

She collapsed forward, hunching over the floor, covering her face with shaking hands. "No! No!" she moaned, again and again, the words vibrating against her cupped fingers.

"That's enough!" Carrie said sharply. She was disgusted by this woman and her wanton performance. Her grief was more of the same unhinged farce. "You can mourn all you want later. I want to know where my uncle is!"

Sylvannia hitched several breaths and looked at Carrie with vacuous eyes. Her flattened, wet hair and bland features seemed to muddy and blur her whole being.

"I need Ada," Sylvannia bleated.

"She's dead," Carrie said heartlessly. "Where's my uncle?"

Sylvannia dragged a hand across her mouth. "He'll save me. He'll keep me out of jail."

"*What?* Sav will save you? What are you talking about?"

"He knows people," Sylvannia said flatly. Then she giggled, a guttural bubble from her slack mouth. "I just had to get him on my side. People will believe me if he's on my side."

Sylvannia's voice strengthened with drug-induced confidence. "I never take Ophelia's calls. Ada always takes Ophelia's calls. I heard her crying, asking for help, and I knew. I knew it happened again."

Sylvannia mocked her little sister. "'He doesn't mean to be so rough with me,' she said. 'It's just that I don't like it. I'm not a good wife,'" Sylvannia shook with fury, a complete turnaround from her dull state a few moments ago. Spit flew as she thrust the words from her mouth. "I couldn't stand it! The silly little bitch! I slapped her. She cried harder. She wouldn't *shut up!*"

"I got so *angry!* I tried to shake some sense into her. How could she not like it? She shouldn't have married him! He was too big. Too mean. He wanted things she'd *never* be able to give him. But *I* could have."

She stopped talking and looked at Carrie, her eyes flattened into the gaze of a snake. "Your uncle never saw me. Germond never saw me!" she hissed. "He saw *you!* He saw that Irish slut! He never looked at *me!* Ophelia was sweet and pretty. He hounded after Ada. But me? Ho, no!" Sylvannia breathed hard in her resentment.

"Don't even think of Sylvie!" she mocked in a hag's voice. "She doesn't have the looks! All this time, I've been married to a milquetoast! Peter should have married Ophelia." She bared her teeth. "God! How I *lusted* for him! *I*

CHAPTER THIRTY-SEVEN

would have liked what he did to her!"

Sylvannia stopped talking and stared into memory, her body heaving with exertion.

"When I saw she was dead," she resumed dully, "I thought, good, now I'll have him. So, I dressed her. I dragged her to the top of the stairs and threw her down. People would think Germond killed her. Serves him right. He didn't know what he was doing, anyway." She took a deep breath and muttered a bitter conclusion. "He picked the wrong sister."

Carrie stood paralyzed by the woman's admission. Sylvannia Grant, the featureless middle sister; plain and unremarkable, uninspiring and married off. Not the eldest and most striking, not the sweet baby sister. Passed over by a fiend because Ophelia made an easier target and dazzling Ada, an unattainable one. Where her sisters carried the more physically appealing features, Sylvannia harbored *carnality*. How could she crave depravity, the kind of violence that every woman shrank from? And admit to it!

"Where's Mr. Machin, Sylvannia?" Morgan asked. He stood nearby, just behind Carrie's shoulder. She felt embarrassed that he should have been assailed in such a manner. But he spoke clearly, not with the huskiness of a man influenced by the woman's antics, but of a man focused on his task.

"Please, Sylvannia," she echoed. "What have you done with my uncle?"

Sylvannia cast a hand toward a wall panel, and Morgan went to it immediately. He pushed on one side. Hinges, cleverly hidden at top and bottom, swung the panel out into the bedroom. Morgan squeezed through the narrow opening. Carrie pressed in behind him. He put his arm out to stop her progress into the small chamber, but she pushed by. She saw a sharply sloped ceiling, a single bed tucked against the knee wall, and a long naked man lying upon rumpled sheets. She gasped into her hand as laudanum and cologne swept into her mouth. She and Morgan rushed forward to see if Sav Machin was still alive.

Chapter Thirty-Eight

There was no help for it: Morgan used the belt from Sylvannia's robe to tie one of her delicate wrists to the leg of the bureau. She moaned languidly as he knotted the sash, and he moved quickly away. He hoisted Sav's slack body out of the secret chamber and onto Sylvannia's bed. Sav's sweaty head thumped against the door. He grunted sleepily, giving Carrie both a pang of horror and a thrill of encouragement. She pushed aside Morgan's attempt to shield her from her uncle's nakedness.

"I've seen this more than you, Mr. Morgan. Step aside." They restored Sav's decency with the application of the depraved woman's sheets and quilts. While Carrie bundled up her uncle, Morgan flung open another window to let in more fresh air.

There was no help for it: Carrie had to assist Sylvannia with dressing into something decent. Morgan left the door ajar and advised Carrie to call out if she needed him. She hated to get near the woman. She wanted to be out of Sylvannia's presence just as much as Morgan. But whatever had burned in Sylvannia a short while ago had turned to cold ashes. Wrung out and docile, she resumed weeping for Ada while Carrie tugged simple clothing over her head. Morgan cut her bonds and stiff-armed her out of the room. Sylvannia would be taken to the post office and locked in. Morgan asked Carrie to come along.

She passed the back of her hand gently over Sav's bristly cheek, praying he'd be all right alone. But there was no help for it: she could not call someone to come over and keep watch. His ordeal would remain as unknown as possible. She left the bedroom door open and followed the Sheriff and his

CHAPTER THIRTY-EIGHT

prisoner down the stairs.

"I would have let him go this morning," Sylvannia explained casually when they were on their way down Garnet Street. "He'll have vague memories of me. All the workers certainly seemed to appreciate my efforts." She laughed, but elicited only silence from her appalled escorts. She smiled drowsily down her shoulder at Carrie. "They never say a word afterward. Much too embarrassed."

She looked across her other shoulder at Morgan. "You'll put me in prison, sheriff? Hang me?"

"Christ, no!" Morgan swore as he propelled her toward the post office. "You're for Utica if I have anything to say about it." Carrie approved of his declaration. Sylvannia was exactly the type of criminally depraved woman the state's insane asylum took in.

"I always have a little opium," Sylvannia persisted idly. "It's always been so easy to lure a man upstairs. Your uncle was willing after a while, you know. Able, if sparingly so. Not entirely satisfying."

"*Shut up!*" Carrie and Morgan said in unison. Morgan burst through the post office door and shoved Sylvannia into the mailroom with distaste. He locked and rattled the door, testing its security.

They retreated outside and leaned against the stone building, turning their faces to the blue sky and steamy air. They both breathed as if they hadn't in a long time. Around them, battered and muddy, Hope Bridge was quiet, its roads impassable, its populace taking stock. Even Bill Bemis was elsewhere. Presently, Morgan spoke.

"Carrie, forgive me," he started, then cleared his throat. He brushed his eyes and tucked in his chin. "In the discharge of my duties, I am obliged to manage unexpected circumstances. You've witnessed one of the more repellent."

When he stopped talking, Carrie glanced up at him, saw his face working itself out of embarrassment and into regaining control.

"Please don't consider me one of the delicate feminine souls you must shelter from disagreeable facts, Del. Remember, I'm an undertaker. I've encountered a great deal of nefarious and heartbreaking circumstances."

She didn't smile; their world wouldn't allow that just now. "No one can be quite prepared for what we confront. We have no choice but to do our best, do we not?"

Theirs had been a battle each had flung themselves into, headlong, not knowing their opponent. As it turned out, their enemy had knocked them both for a loop. An unexpectedly garish face had been revealed once the vanquished helmet was removed.

Morgan let out a shuddering breath. Carrie wanted to pat his hand. Although there was no one on the street, any physical contact in public would be construed as unseemly, and this town knew how to cultivate its skeletons. She kept her distance.

"I'd like to return to Ophelia's house and retrieve my uncle," she said, straightening away from the wall. "I'm going to commandeer Mrs. Woodruff's bread wagon to bring him home. I should be able to manage his care for the next day or so. Will Sylvannia be secure?"

"Yes. I'll arrange for her to be transferred to Utica Asylum as soon as possible. Emmett's going to need his post office back." He stood away from the wall.

"Carrie," he said." I think it's best we come to an agreement."

She nodded, but kept the sinking feeling hidden. "Of course. Let me begin." She stood straight and looked at him squarely. "I won't say anything about our indiscretion. You have my word. I can expect the same?"

He nodded and continued haltingly. "I believe we sought a measure of comfort from each other. I believe we are recovered now. I am most assuredly to blame for my lack of control. I assure you, it will never happen again."

Carrie regarded his tired face and his uncomfortable stance. She remembered how his warm hands had thawed her cold body, and how she slipped wholly into the safety of their ultimate act of trust. Again, her desire for independence had been thrown to the side in favor of shelter. In favor of comfort. Was it petty? Was the closeness of another human being truly what she had been seeking when she left Nanuet? To have that sanctuary found, and now lost, crushed her. *Am I to have no comfort?*

CHAPTER THIRTY-EIGHT

Not with this man, an inner voice reprimanded. This man is taken. This man has too much to lose. She locked unbidden tears behind a gate of eyelashes, and murmured, "Agreed, Mr. Morgan. Let us resume our association as professionals without any consequence. Now, I need to get to my uncle."

"Will you be all right?"

His question shocked her. It had been the invitation to their lovemaking. She drew a ragged breath and nodded decisively.

"We'll all manage, Mr. Morgan."

"We will." He dipped his chin to her, his eyes glistening as well. "Good day, Mrs. Lisbon."

Morgan stepped off the landing and walked east. Carrie stood against the stone wall of the post office for a moment, watching him. Duncan County's sheriff moved with exhausted determination toward the roar of the Duncan Creek and the crowd that had gathered at its edge to watch the mighty water hurling away, carrying all its broken, looted debris with it.

Chapter Thirty-Nine

Carrie flew up Piccolo Street, hardly noticing the new glistening landscape, how the sun tried to put a dewy face on the muddy destruction. She rushed through the Grants' kitchen door and snatched the little maid into a swinging embrace, whispering gratitudes and a scant explanation.

"She's to be locked up, sweetie. Miss Sylvie can't hurt you anymore. Oh, thank you, dear heart! We found my uncle because of you."

The girl responded stiffly to Carrie's emotional spillage, her big eyes bewildered. Carrie went to fetch Mrs. Woodruff. She would need the big woman's muscles to load Sav into the bread van and to drive Bigelow. Betsy could be trusted with Sav's condition. Louisa would stay with the prostrate Mrs. Grant for an hour until Mrs. Woodruff returned.

Betsy drew the horse and cart to the back door of the Morgans' home. Sav staggered between the two women, his long arms dangling over their shoulders and his big feet dragging through the hallway. He sank onto the floor of the bread van, and Bigelow lurched forward under the snap of Mrs. Woodruff's expert reins. The horse and cart struggled and lurched through the mire until Mrs. Woodruff directed the horse illegally onto the flagstone walks.

They staggered up the stairs with Sav and dumped him into his bed. Oscar fretted at the hullabaloo. Carrie opened the windows and pulled off Sav's shoes. He had resumed snoring before the women left the room.

"Keep them windows open," Mrs. Woodruff warned in the hallway. "And see that he has lotsa water to drink. You got coffee?"

CHAPTER THIRTY-NINE

She patted Carrie briefly, a gesture of understanding, but she left her hand on Carrie's shoulder for a moment longer. "Nobody needs to know, Carrie. You come and get me if you need anything."

She lifted her skirt and bustled back down the stairs, sweating in effort and the new humidity. Carrie returned to Sav's room and looked down on her lanky uncle with pity. What torment would he endure when he woke up and remembered? She knew that he was a private man, fatuous with his books and papers, skirting liaisons in favor of scholarship, yet so likable, so...*innocent!* She clenched her teeth, remembering the sultry dismissal Sylvannia had given him.

Delicately, she pulled her uncle's limbs from his clothes and washed him in warm water, soaping the scent of depravity from him. She saw with despair that Sylvannia had left her trademark scratch across his breast. She would see to it that the minor mark didn't leave a scar.

Sav responded to her touch with the animation of one of her cadavers. Frightened at the drugs Sylvannia had used, angry, and determined to restore his dignity, she cleaned his face of any possible kisses Sylvannia may have planted there. Finally, she washed his hair back from his forehead and covered him with his own blankets.

That afternoon, when she heard Sav rustling and splashing around, she brought up a pot of strong coffee and a warmed plate of eggs and fried potatoes. He stood in a long nightshirt, steadying himself, then gingerly got back into bed.

"I'll be fine, niece," he exclaimed after eating the plateful in quick, snuffling gulps. But his hollow eyes told Carrie otherwise. She sat at the edge of the bed and took his hand.

"Uncle Savoir," she said gently and firmly. "Listen to me. I will take care of you until you're well. But you've been through an ordeal that will have consequences with your judgment. Please don't think you can simply *be* well because you wish it so. Sylvannia killed Ophelia. She may have killed you while you were drugged and helpless. Even I need time to recover my wits about that."

Carrie told him of Ada and the bridge, of her own near demise and rescue from the Duncan, of the standoff and triumph of Thomas Bale. The sun had lost its intensity, and shadows had begun when she finished with the story of little Louisa, Sylvannia's confession and arrest. She purposefully omitted two lurid aspects of the last twenty-four hours. Her affair with Del Morgan would never come to light, and Sylvannia's lecherous attempt to seduce the sheriff would remain unmentioned. She and Del had secrets to keep.

Sav sat under the covers with his knees drawn up and his coffee cup perched on one knobby peak. Carrie had refilled it several times. Surprisingly, he made not a single comment. At the conclusion of Carrie's story, he no longer feigned brightness. He shook his head as if drowsiness set upon him again.

"I presumed to know a great deal about the inhabitants of our town, niece. I have preferred to maintain a rigorous pursuit of the niceties rather than the seediness." He looked at his hands. "It seems I have been foolish not to have seen so much. I had no idea about Sylvannia. None."

"How did she overwhelm you, Uncle?"

Sav shook his head, his voice quiet and slow. "It was most curious. She met me at the door, which I thought odd, but in light of her compelling missive, I thought no more of it. She insisted we seek the privacy of her own home. I found that odd, too, but she fell into a distraught state immediately, so I agreed."

"We took a drink in the formal parlor; she insisted she needed fortification. I wanted to be polite. My brandy tasted just a bit odd. I thought it may have turned, but again, at her insistent distress, I drank it, not wanting to add to her suffering." Sav trailed off, looking out the window. His countenance was dreamy.

"It was rather pleasant. I felt overly warm, and…Miss Sylvannia was attentive when I seemed to fall back in the chair. After that, we were walking in the rain. I remember thinking, 'this can't be right.' Then it floated away." Sav's misty recollection turned to embarrassment. He said quietly, "Well, I believe you are privy to the rest."

"Sylvannia took you to Germond and Ophelia's home. She had a clever half wall and a large closet built into one of the bedrooms when she directed

CHAPTER THIRTY-NINE

the remodeling. You were hidden. I don't believe she intended to hurt you, but she did want you to be…willing with her."

Carrie hoped her avoidance of the sexual details spelled out what Sav may or may not remember. But her hedging made its point. Sav's mouth turned down in a trembling bow, just a split second before he threw himself over the side of the bed and vomited into the chamber pot.

"Who…who knows?" Sav retched, his eyes streaming and panicked.

Carrie wrung out a cool cloth for his face and covered the bowl. "Del and I. Mrs. Woodruff," she said quietly. "I have no doubt Betsy will be able to keep your confidence. Sylvannia was the sister that had made amorous advances toward you?"

Sav nodded and slumped into his pillow. "I was appalled. She was married to Peter Clarke. He's always away." He waved his fingers shakily. "She took an interest in me that I found unsettling. I have a hunch she pursued Leo at one point. Not that I can ever bring it up to confirm."

"It may have been part of her scheme to have Ophelia's house remodeled. There is some scuttlebutt about traveling workers coming here to be paid with favors, as well as cash," Carrie said.

Sav looked down at his hands. "Seems I'm now a member of another secret society."

Carrie's heart broke. She smoothed his bedding and kissed his damp forehead. "I'm going to Worley's to help Marta with some baking. There's to be a relief effort."

When Sav didn't acknowledge her, she took up his hand. "Uncle, get up. Please go see Oscar. He missed you. And get yourself dressed. I believe we will need your expertise if we are to help our town recover."

Chapter Forty

The last time she'd seen Marta, the Irish girl was terrified until Bale parted the crowd brandishing his new badge and his old anger. They had both walked away with their heads high.

Now, Marta answered Carrie's knock at the kitchen door with a sad smile. "Mr. Worley's dismissed me," she announced after she provided Carrie with an apron and resumed her kneading.

"No!" Carrie said, dismayed. "He can't do that! He's beholden to Thomas. Let me speak with him."

Marta held up a hand, smiling sadly. "I told him no. I'm not leaving until after Mrs. Worley...well, until after she's gone. She's not long, poor thing. She can't breathe anymore, with the rain and damp. I'm not going to abandon her. But I'll not be the cause of Mr. Worley losing business. I agreed to go. After."

"But he's the only undertaker in town!" Carrie said. "It's not like customers can go anywhere else."

Marta held up her chin, her blue eyes fierce. "It's fine, Carrie. I can take up work at the Alms House in Duncan. They can't keep good help. There's the answer. Thomas and I will be fine."

* * *

Bill Bemis telegraphed two days later, having made it to Duncan on foot and on the back of several wagons that he abandoned when they became hopelessly mired. His cheeky message read: ALL HEADLINES MINE STOP

CHAPTER FORTY

IN DUNCAN ALL SUMMER STOP MARRY ME STOP

* * *

From the Duncan Herald, June 20, 1900.
Death Notice
HOPE BRIDGE- Mrs. Arthur Worley, aged sixty-one, departed this realm for her heavenly reward on June the 15th, of consumption. Mrs. Worley was attended at the hour of her death by her husband of forty-three years, Mr. Arthur Worley, and Doctor Jonathon Horton Wells. Mrs. Worley was born December 17, 1839, and was a longstanding member of the Hope Bridge Presbyterian Church, the Devout Ladies Aid Society, the Duncan Temperance Society, and the Society of Perpetual Prayer. The funeral was attended by many whose generous respects were complimented with arrays of the finest seasonal blossoms. The Reverend Elias Moore performed the committal service. Mrs. Worley's mortal remains were prepared by the talented hand of Mrs. Carrie Lisbon, who endowed the deceased with such bloom in her cheeks, she appeared to be living among us once again.

* * *

Marta wept as she helped Carrie prepare the frail body. She made sure the water was warm, and the dead woman was wrapped and dressed in soft, comfortable clothing. Carrie sought out the husband afterward. Arthur Worley sat in the light of a single lamp in his office. One hand rested on his desk, dry fingers encircling a forgotten glass half-filled with amber whiskey. The other hand lay in his lap, curled around a pipe that had long gone out. Only his eyes rose to acknowledge her admittance.

"We've finished, Mr. Worley," Carrie said quietly. "Marta and I will clean up, and I'll call on Mrs. Peters in the morning." When he made a scant movement with his head, Carrie came further into the room and sat before him in the client's chair.

"Mr. Worley? I'm capable of making all the arrangements for you so that you can grieve without having to do the work. Please, let me inform the clergy and make the arrangements for you. Marta and I will handle all there is to do."

He said nothing. Carrie reached out and placed her hand over his icy fingers. Worley looked at her with his usual expression of impassivity, but this time his demeanor was played-out. Then the formal man spoke.

"Thank you, Mrs. Lisbon. I am not myself at present. I've had the most disconcerting lapse of thought just now."

The man had snubbed her, dismissed her, and berated her like a child. He had deliberately sought to undermine her professional ability and judgment. Yet a wave of pity for him could not be denied. The cold bastard had loved his wife, and now his grief was sharp and powerful, so much so, his usual hauteur had deserted him.

Carrie knew the feeling. She rose and took the cold pipe from his hand, squeezed the bony digits gently, and gestured toward the whiskey.

"It's late, Mr. Worley. Drink that down. Marta is making up your guest bedroom. Go see your wife. Then get some sleep. I'll be back in the morning."

Worley rose, straightened his vest, buttoned his suit coat, and drained his glass. Carrie accompanied him to the stairs, and Marta met him at the top. She gently took his arm. She and Carrie exchanged a nod of understanding. The rituals for the dead would continue.

A Note from the Author

This story is fiction, but many of its details are true parts of American history. It is my hope to have treated that history with respect.

Duncan County and the Duncan Creek are fictitious. I patterned both after the rural counties, small villages and the many beautiful creeks that are found in a corner of New York State south and west of the Hudson and Mohawk Rivers. Hope Bridge is a mash-up of them all.

Nanuet is a real place in Rockland County, New York. In 1900 it was not the bustling small city mentioned in this story. It was a small town with dirt roads much like my fictitious Hope Bridge. But I love the name Nanuet. When I crafted Carrie's life I wanted her to come from a city with such a pleasant name. Nyack is another real place along New York's Hudson River, also in Rockland County, and I took the extraordinary liberty of switching the name Nanuet and applying it to the city of Nyack. Apologies to the citizens and history of both places.

Covered bridges were everywhere in the early years of our nation. They functioned as a means of advancing commerce and easing travel along major and secondary thoroughfares. Roofs kept the wooden structures dry, preventing the timbers from rotting, but in the winter, snow was brought *into* the structures to enable sleds to slide over the frozen surface. Richard S. Allen's *Covered Bridges of the Northeast*, Eric Sloane's *American Barns and Covered Bridges*, and Ward E. Herrmann's *Spans of Time: Covered Bridges of Delaware County* are wonderful resources for these marvels of engineering and craftsmanship. By all means, look into the Oxford Memorial Library's Theodore Burr Covered Bridge Resource Center in Oxford, New York.

Back in Carrie's day, floods were called "freshets," a term that sounds quaint, when in fact, raging floods are terrifying and catastrophic. Floods routinely washed away roads and bridges in the early twentieth century, and that destruction still happens today after hurricanes and torrential downpours.

Embalming practices can be traced back to the Egyptians. The practice became, let's say, "standardized" during the Civil War, when thousands of men died, hundreds of miles from home. Technology existed that would preserve the body so that it could be shipped back home for burial. The early procedure was, by today's standards, grisly and dangerous. The chemicals caused harm to the practitioners. By 1900, embalming schools, safer chemicals and medical knowledge advanced the techniques, and the educated mortician was considered a unique and legitimate professional.

Throughout time, women prepared the bodies of the dead. But in the Victorian era, it was popular sentiment that women were weak and unable to comprehend, or carry out unpleasant tasks. (Tell that to the millions of women who worked outside their homes, in addition to working constantly *at* home to keep their families alive!). By America's Gilded Age, women prepared the deceased, arranged the home for the funeral, cooked the reception meals, and managed the guests. If an undertaker's services were used, a woman could lay out any gender, but it was taboo for a male undertaker to prepare the body of a woman. Hence, professional women undertakers were in demand.

Lina D. Odou, a female undertaker and a friend of Florence Nightingale, trained under Auguste Renouard, and A. Johnson Dodge, two morticians who worked to standardize embalming procedures. She founded the Lina D. Odou Embalming Institute in Manhattan and the Women's Licensed Embalmers Association around the turn of the 20th century. I've made Carrie a proud member of this organization, but the Association of American Funeral Directors (and its *Index*), The National Floral Décor Association, along with all of Sav Machin's clubs and fraternities, are fictitious.

I've taken liberties with one or two expressions for this story. *Curriculum vitae* is an expression of "one's life work" that was first coined in 1902. The first occurrence of "scuttlebutt" meaning "gossip or rumor" is indicated to

A NOTE FROM THE AUTHOR

be circa 1901. The other expressions are solidly entrenched as American idioms prior to 1900.

The Wilmington Massacre occurred in Wilmington, North Carolina, in 1898. Originally described as a race riot caused by blacks, over time and with more facts publicized, the event has come to be seen as a violent overthrow of a duly elected government by a group of white supremacists. A mob of 2,000 white men expelled a legitimately elected local government. They ran opposition black and white political leaders out of the city, destroyed the property and businesses of black citizens, including the only black newspaper in the city, and killed an estimated 60 to more than 300 people.

The Ladies Guide to the Language of Flowers is a fictitious book. But floriography, the language of flowers, was quite the rage in the Victorian era. Women passed messages, insults and invitations to suitors and rivals by sending a single bloom or bouquet along with their calling card. For example, yellow carnations meant rejection, a jonquil meant affection returned. Nuts meant you're stupid. A dried bouquet meant rejected love, and dried leaves meant sadness.

I made up the use of wax for sealing a deceased person's eyes. In 1900, morticians had glue for that.

The Utica Asylum for the Insane was established in 1836, with a massive building completed in 1843, which still stands today. The treatment of the insane during the mid to late 1800s was awful, and Utica is infamous for a variety of its treatments and for the unmarked graves of patients who died while in care. However, Utica was New York's attempt to house, and treat people with serious mental health disorders. Utica originally took in patients from all over New York State, but in 1890 limited its service to a handful of upstate counties. Naturally, I included Duncan in this roster.

Acknowledgements

Writing alone is a large part of how words get on a page, but polishing those words and turning them into a book is a group effort. No better crew ever assisted a writer, and I offer my sincerest gratitude to the following people who supported my efforts to bring this book to life and who provided grit for the final polish.

My editor at Level Best Books, Harriette Sackler, whose patience and spot-on direction have put *No Comfort* in your hands.

Huzzah to my beta readers Pam O'Connor who feeds me wine and cheese with her critique; Helen Thomas, who wrangles the best words and ideas from me; John Mullins, who also shoots shirts for me; Marlie Wasserman, a woman who knows her stuff; and Gary Earl Ross who gave me a professional thumbs up.

My writing buddies at the Cobleskill and Schoharie Libraries Writing Groups who provide the feedback and encouragement I always need to keep writing. Without their support, I'd never have gotten this far.

Sisters in Crime, and the Guppies subgroups who provide the very best support and education a bumbling mystery writer like me truly needs.

My gal pals and pond-floating enthusiasts Victoria Stewart, Paige Consalvo and Diane Nicolai, who are forever championing my efforts.

Trish Kane, curator of the Theodore Burr Covered Bridge Resource Center at the Oxford Memorial Library who opened my eyes to the wonders of covered bridges, their construction and their characters. I'm so sorry the bridge went down!

RuthAnn Williams for her excellent resources regarding funeral rituals, symbols, flowers and early embalming.

Gratitude goes to my husband Dave, who took care of everything else, while Carrie and I took care of the dead.

And finally, thanks to the muse for always being there, whether she wanted to or not.

About the Author

Chris Keefer was a newspaper columnist for twenty years, has numerous magazine articles to her credit, and currently writes creative non-fiction essays, local history articles, and the Carrie Lisbon historical mystery series. She lives in upstate New York, and enjoys birding, gardening, metal detecting, cycling, town historian duties, and a grandchild. Readers can visit with her online at authorchriskeefer.com.

SOCIAL MEDIA HANDLES:
  www.facebook.com/authorChrisKeefer
  www.instagram.com/authorchriskeefer

AUTHOR WEBSITE:
  www.authorchriskeefer.com

CPSIA information can be obtained
at www.ICGtesting.com
Printed in the USA
BVHW030857270223
659294BV00005B/240